Quarterdeck

By

David O'Neil

W & B Publishers
USA

Quarterdeck © 2014. All rights reserved by David O'Neil

\

W & B Publishers

For information:
W & B Publishers
Post Office Box 193
Colfax, NC 27235
www.a-argusbooks.com

ISBN: 978-0-6922803-8-6
ISBN: 0-6922803-8-3

Book Cover designed by Dubya

Printed in the United States of America

Chapter 1

Spymaster

London 1808

THE HOUSE WAS silent and for the moment time seemed to stand still. For Captain Sir Martin Forest-Bowers KB, a sad homecoming.

The maid took his hat and sword. "How is my lady?" He asked.

Rebecca, the maid, said sadly, "She lives, and we hope and pray, Sir."

Martin sighed and made his way up the stairs to Jennifer's bedroom in the room that overlooked the garden at the rear, away from the noises of the street.

There was still sunlight in the room which also carried the odour of sickness.

He hesitated before the doorway, preparing himself for facing his beloved wife, who had wasted away over the past weeks.

To his surprise Jane, his adoptive mother, and Jennifer's mother was there sitting beside the bed. He stepped over to the bedside. Jane was not looking well. She had spent her time and energy watching, and helping tend to, her sick daughter.

Now she turned to Martin. She looked puzzled then smiled. "Dear Martin," she said. "Come see." She turned back to the bed. Martin looked at his wife. Her eyes were open.

"She woke for the first time and the Doctor is on his way." The tears in Jane's eyes told the story. This was good news.

Martin hardly dared hope. When the doctor arrived he was cautious, but allowed a thin glimmer of hope.

Rear Admiral Lord Charles Bowers, Martin's adoptive father, came home later that day to receive the news, there had been a change. None of the family could bear to believe that it was possible that Jennifer would recover. After the months of her illness and the lack of any real hope the doctors were prepared to offer, it was safer not to expect anything.

After that day, when Jennifer opened her eyes for the first time in several days, the fever seemed to have lessened. The feeling of cautious optimism was beginning to creep into the house. Jennifer, Martin's wife, had been pregnant with their second child when things had started going wrong. She lost the baby, but had been ill ever since with blood poisoning. The fever that followed had apparently confused the doctors since they had tried all they could think of and still apparently had no real answer to her condition.

Martin had been recalled from the West Indies by Sir Anthony Watts, the mysterious 'plain Mr.. Smith', as he chose to known. His department in government was not widely advertised, its function being the gathering of intelligence and the protection of the secrets of the nation from enemies. From time to time, over the past years of Martin's service in the Royal Navy, he had been called upon to work with the agents and couriers working for Mr.. Smith. The demands of this secret service had irritated the Admiralty, not least because they could do nothing about it. When Mr.. Smith called, the Navy responded and, on this occasion at least, it enabled Martin to be with his wife at this most desperate of times.

He had been home for the past week but there had been no change until now. The next few days saw her rally, and while the family held their breath, she continued to make progress. The doctor agreed that it seemed she had finally turned the corner, and could expect to recover.

The weekend, four days later, found Jennifer sitting propped up on pillows and taking nourishment. The miracle had happened. Martin gradually allowed himself to believe that his beloved wife would survive now her fever had broken. She was going to live.

The doctor was clear. There would be no more children. The damage during the loss of her child had made that certain. But he was cautiously optimistic that in all other ways Jennifer should recover completely and be able to live a full life thereafter.

There was celebration in the household that weekend. Considerable weight was given to the fact that it was Martin's presence which had ensured Jennifer's recovery.

***

On Monday the following week Martin presented himself at 'plain Mr. Smith's' (Sir Anthony Watts's) residence as requested.

"I am delighted," said Smith, "To hear that you were returned in time to be with your wife at such a difficult time for you both. I do hear that she is responding to treatment and returning to health."

"You hear correctly, sir, and I thank you for making it possible to be here at this time."

Sir Anthony Watts waved his hand, in acknowledgement. "Perhaps we can discuss business now. I fear this is a matter that cannot wait..

Martin seated himself and gave Watts his attention.

"I will not bore you at present with too much detail, but it has been increasingly difficult to keep secrets from slipping through to the enemy. On two occasions recently we have had boats ambushed. On one of these occasions my agent was captured. His tortured body was found floating in the channel only two days ago.

"What I would like you to undertake is the organisation of a team of small craft, to collect and disburse information along the channel coast. At the same time, I think it vital to capture the traitor who is actually passing the information about my agents. He must be a member of my staff somewhere. To capture him would give me an advantage that I could use to keep one step ahead of the French.

"Is there anyone you suspect of your present staff?"

"That's the frustrating part. I cannot think of a single member who might betray me. As you must be aware, in this business security is paramount."

"Indeed, I see the problem. Perhaps I might be permitted to visit the offices you maintain for this purpose. I will need to know these people anyway, as they will need to know me."

Mr.. Smith stroked his chin thoughtfully. "I think a visit in plain clothes might be best in the first place. Your current celebrity could be an embarrassment at the moment, and it could invite interest where it would be better to maintain a low profile."

***

The following morning Martin attended the building used by the staff of Smith's organisation. The villa was located in Bayswater, the village to the west of London proper, next to Hyde Park. The area was being built-up more and more by the wealthy, as a suburb less noisy and smelly than the more business/commercial areas of the City of Westminster.

There were many more people involved in the work of espionage than he realised, Martin was intrigued to discover. He was able to recognise two of the people, who had been at times passengers on his ship. They made no sign of recognition, and he sensibly accepted their discretion, from his point of view.

His guide on this occasion was Mr.. Smith's personal assistant, a man named Hervey, whom he had met on several occasions when calling on Smith in the past. There were several men and three women here. In her-own office he found Alouette.

Over the past few years he had come to know Alouette in more ways than one. Their friendship had been established through shared dangers. Each had saved the life of the other on more than one occasion, shared hazards and shared beds. Now it was the bond of friendship that survived. Alouette, the émigré Comtesse de Chartres, was beautiful, dark-haired slender and intelligent. Widowed at eighteen, she had since thrown herself into the work of espionage, having been discovered and her talent for the work recognised, by Sir Anthony soon after her arrival in England.

She greeted Martin with a smile. Hervey left them together and went to deal with some other matters.

"What brings you to this hotbed of intrigue?" She asked once she had seen him seated beside the desk.

"A summons from your leader," he replied.

A knock at the door heralded a tray of tea and a plate of biscuits, and she paused while they were placed on the desk and the maid had left them alone once more.

Alouette poured the tea and offered the biscuits. "Tell me, Martin. How is your wife? I understand that she is recovering from her terrible illness?"

"As you say. Thank God she is recovering, showing signs now, according to the doctor, of complete, eventual recovery."

"I am so happy for you both. It must have been dreadful to have returned to discover that Jennifer was so ill."

"Of course it was a terrible shock, but her recovery, has made my fortuitous return a blessing." For some reason Martin did not feel it necessary to mention the fact that Mr.. Smith had organised his return.

Only then with a raised eyebrow, did Alouette invite a reply to her initial question.

"Alouette, I am delighted to find you here. For I have been charged by our master to locate the spy in our midst. As well as to establish a regular service, to deliver and collect our agents on the Channel shores."

"I see. So how can I be of help?"

"Now I have found you, I am reassured that I have a contact here which I can depend upon."

"Of course, I will help in any way I can."

"There is one matter I would ask your help with. I encountered three people in my work for the department, who had spent time in France, and had survived without harm." He passed Alouette a piece of paper with the names written down.

Once more he withheld the full facts. He had in his possession a scrap of paper. He was firmly convinced that the note implicated one of the three, but he would still give nothing away. He had been present when Alouette had been terribly mistreated in the hands of the French secret service. His suspicions were not directed at her. He mistrusted some of her contacts, and for the moment decided to keep what he knew to himself.

Alouette looked at the names. "I know all of these people. What does this mean?"

"I have met them all at one time or another, but I know nothing of their background or current circumstances. I was hoping I could ask you to let me know more about them, without the entire system finding out what I am expected to do."

Alouette leaned back in her chair. She smiled, the beautiful face showing the lines that were appearing around her eyes. The life she was leading was not allowing her to preserve her once smooth, innocent-looking, complexion. To Martin's eyes it enhanced her natural beauty, showing a little of the strength and character that were so much a part of her nature.

"Leave this with me and I will see what I can discreetly find out. Meanwhile, how do you plan to re-arrange the contact procedure with the French coast?"

"I am going south to speak to friends of friends next week. I hope Jennifer will be well on the way to recovery by then, so that I may leave her with her parents for a day or so without imposing upon them too much."

"Martin, what will I do with you? You surely know that the Admiral and Lady Jane do not feel imposed upon. She is after all their daughter. They have clearly demonstrated that they do not consider it an imposition to look after her in your absence on duty. Please accept that fact.

"I myself will be in the Mermaid Inn, in Rye, in 8 days' time. We can meet there and I will inform you of my findings on these people, and you may freely discuss your intentions regarding the network you have in mind. I presume your aim will be to recruit smugglers for the task."

"Something like that." Martin said. "I will be down on the South Coast by then and I will seek you out there. Until then, adieu." He bent over to kiss her hand but she stopped him placing her face in his path. "Still friends, surely, Martin?" She murmured.

"As ever." Martin said, kissing her gently on the lips.

***

With Jennifer getting better by the day, the house in London was now a more cheerful place. The shadows around Lady Jane's eyes disappeared as she was now able to sleep at night. Little Jane was enjoying the lighter atmosphere and she could be heard playing in the garden with her nurse, and now Jennifer was demanding to be allowed to sit in the garden when the sun was on that side of the house.

Martin was in attendance at the Admiralty to arrange for his temporary attachment to Mr.. Smith's control. The time factor of one year maximum had been imposed by their lordships. Smith smiled wryly at this but had accepted the arrangement regardless.

Martin made arrangements to meet certain people at the headquarters of the revenue department responsible for the prevention of smuggling on our coasts. It had occurred to him that they were probably the best source of information regarding the smugglers on the south coast.

At the headquarters near the Tower of London, Captain Albert Mainland, a former Naval Officer, had been seconded to command the preventative service. It had become evident that the war had allowing smugglers too much freedom for the illegal import of brandy and tobacco. From Mr.. Smith's point of view, the existence of the trade permitted the landing and recovery of agents, without advertising the fact. The loss of revenue from the taxes evaded seemed to be a matter of supreme indifference to him.

Captain Mainland was looking pleased with himself when Martin called. "What can I do for you, sir?" He asked. "T'aint often I get a call from the Royal Navy, not recently at all. So what will it be?" This was delivered in a West Country accent with great good humour.

"I am here, sir, to pick your brains, if I may? I am Captain Martin Forest-Bowers, at your service."

"I know who you are, Sir Martin. I get the Gazette. Why don't you sit yourself down and tell me what you're after and I'll see what I can do. Hey, Harold, bring in some o' that latest batch for us to try. Better bring glasses too. The Captain is a gentleman."

The manner and attitude of Captain Mainland, robbed the comment of any offence. Martin, who liked the look of his host, guessed they would get along.

Harold was a big Hampshire man, six foot at least, maybe forty years old. There was a streak of grey in his thick, dark hair. He had a peg replacing the foot and ankle below his right knee. Mainland introduced him, "This is Harold Watts. Lost his foot at Copenhagen, stormin' the forts."

Martin nodded. He had been told of the bloody landing and attack which had cost the lives of many of the men involved. He stood and shook the hand extended to him. "I'm proud to meet a survivor of that bloody event. How do you manage with the peg?"

"Proud to meet you too, sir. I manage fine now. The surgeon used his head instead of that bloody saw, and he managed to save most that he could. He did a good job with the stump too."

He placed a bottle and three glasses on the table. There were no marks on the bottle, but the golden colour of its contents suggested it was not water.

"I thought Harold should join us, because I have the notion that we might need his specialised knowledge." With this cryptic comment he picked up the bottle, which was not stoppered, and poured three generous measures of what turned out to be remarkably good brandy. "Now, sir. What can we help you with?"

Martin sampled the smooth liquid and nodded his appreciation. "I need to set up a system of boats to deliver and collect agents across the water. Obviously, I do not want them stopped or bothered by officers at either end. While I realise that smuggling, as such, is against the law, I really think that it is from the ranks of smugglers I will be able to recruit the people I need.

Mainland nodded seriously, and turning to Harold he said, "I guessed it might be something of the sort. Harold, you know pretty much who might be of help. What do you say?"

Harold scratched his head for a few moments. "You know what I'm going to say, sir. 'Tis Peter Vardy you would need for this, and—as you well know—he will be going away for a hangman's noose—if we allow it."

Albert Mainland looked at Harold. "Why did I know that would be what you would say?" He turned to Martin. "Do you have enough influence to get a man out of prison?"

"If it is the right man, I think I can. Who is this Peter Vardy?"

Harold said, "He's a cousin of mine. He was taken at Mudeford, in Hampshire, down by my old home. At the time, the dragoons who took him found his boat empty. They took him anyway because their officer's wife fancied Peter, and he fancied her. Major Moore was a local landowner. I understand Peter met them when he found the odd cargo lying about and brought it ashore. It was all well for a while until Peter met Mrs. Moore one day when the Major was out. Seems he caught them canoodling.

"Now he is in prison. They found nothing on his boat, so they put things there, including some documents addressed to people in France. He'll hang at the end of this week."

Martin looked at the two men in front of him. "Where is he?"

Mainland said, "Portsmouth!"

"Who is this Major Moore? Where can he be found?"

"Marsden Hall, just outside the village of Christchurch. The dragoons were raised as militia to begin with. The Major struts around the area as if he owns it all. No-one has managed to stand up to him for long." Harold said bitterly.

"Young bastard has been spoilt rotten, always talkin' about waiting for a call from Horse Guards to join Sir John Moore in the Mediterranean. Fat chance of that. I reckon he would piss his pants if that happened."

Martin made up his mind. He picked up his glass. "Your health, gentlemen. I will be in touch." He drank the brandy, and placed the glass on the table and left.

Chapter 2

The Recruit

PETER VARDY, SEATED in his cell in Portsmouth prison, contemplated his future. It extended to four days. In his present location it was not an inviting prospect. He thought it was not an inviting prospect in any location. He had begun to despair and considered ending it all. A rueful smile crossed his face. Not really much point when someone was going to do it for him, in four days. He sighed. He would miss Fay Moore. The thought of Major Michael Moore forcing himself upon his recently found love, made him angry and merely stressed the helplessness of his current situation.

The rattle of the key in the lock diverted his gloomy thoughts. Unusual at this time of day. Normally they only unlocked to allow the chaplain in, and he was not due for some hours yet.

The door opened and the chaplain entered, accompanied by Mrs. Fay Moore.

The chaplain spoke hurriedly. "Peter, Mrs. Moore has news for you that she insisted on bringing herself. I am very happy to…"

Mrs. Moore interrupted the Reverend in full flow. "Peter, you have been pardoned and will be released today."

Peter Vardy sat down, having risen at their entry. His legs felt a little shaky. He was processing what he had heard. "Pardoned?"

The chaplain went to speak again, but Fay Moore interrupted him once more. "It is true, Peter. And also Michael has been ordered to Gibraltar to join General Moore."

The murmur of voices as others approached broke the immediate impasse. The Governor of the prison appeared and a Naval Captain in full uniform followed. The small cell was becoming rather full.

The Governor ordered a warder to remove the shackles binding the arms and legs of the prisoner. Then he produced a document, and read the brief message out to the bemused Peter.

"In view of the fresh evidence which has come to my notice, *I have set aside the sentence imposed by the court on Peter James Vardy. He is hereby released from custody and set free without stain on his character.* It is signed, *Spencer,"* The signature was of Earl Spencer, the current Home Secretary.

He rolled up the page and shook the hand of the still unsure man before him.

The Captain spoke for the first time. "Peter Vardy, I would like you and Mrs. Moore to accompany me from here now, please. The sooner this business is completed with the minimum of fuss, the better." He turned and the small party left the scruffy cell. Peter decided that he would not miss the place, though he would never forget it.

They followed the Captain without question to the prison yard, where a coach awaited.

***

At the 'Crown' in Emsworth, they stopped. Their escort, who had already introduced himself as Martin Forest-Bowers, took them into a pre-booked room where there were clothes and a bath for Peter to use. Martin escorted Mrs. Moore to the lounge, to await while her friend shed the stink and the filth of the prison.

While they waited Fay Moore told Martin of the events from her point of view. "I realised that it is normal for marriages to be arranged, and I accepted the situation as one must. Michael was not a troublesome husband, nor was he attentive. I seriously felt that my presence was for show, as his interests were elsewhere. When I met Peter it was a shock. I did not anticipate my reaction, for I had never met someone I was really attracted to."

Martin interrupted the flow. "Madam, please, there is no need for you to disclose this to me. I will not judge you. From what I already know I congratulate you for escaping what must have been an empty existence."

"Captain, please indulge me. I have been forced to keep my own counsel thus far. It is such a relief to unburden myself. My husband had no idea, and there was in fact no reason for him to react, as we never really got together, if you take my meaning." The blush that accompanied this comment made Martin accept her statement without question.

She continued, "I have to tell someone about this. I am not sure if Peter feels that same as I do. We had no chance to speak of the matter. I did know that the

Adjutant of the Dragoons commanded by my husband was a local man who, it seems, was an old enemy of Peter. He was responsible for faking the evidence against him. He had him arrested and charged. Three of the troopers from my father's former employ, swore to him That the man had been falsely accused and the evidence fabricated. Captain Charles Hanson had arranged the whole business. It is he will assume command of the dragoons when my husband actually travels."

Martin listened and took note. In his pocket was what Sir Anthony Watts called insurance. It was an open warrant charging the recipient to give full cooperation and assistance to the bearer in the name of the King. It carried the Royal Seal. It meant in short that, on production, any British person was required to do whatever Martin asked. Unsure how this might help at the moment, he was sure his would think of something. The Captain would have to be neutralised in some way. It was merely a case of how?"

***

Peter Vardy appeared resplendent in clean clothing of quality, and smelling, as Martin indelicately put it, a little sweeter.

The two people were both unsure and awkward in meeting on the same level for the first time. Martin did not doubt the link between them. He swiftly had them seated to dine as his guests, and was pleased to see Harold, also looking well dressed for the occasion, stumping across to join them as arranged.

"Why, it's you, Sir Martin! What a pleasure to see you here. Peter?" He stopped and clapped Peter on his shoulder. "I just heard that Mrs. Moore had been successful." He swung to Fay who was seated beside the table. "I am so happy to see you here, madam. Your efforts to help my cousin were appreciated by the family. It's sad news to hear that the Major is leaving tonight for Gibraltar. All is confusion at the barracks I'm afraid. Young Lieutenant Marchmont is in a terrible tizzy re-organising things. Everything happening at once it seems."

"Please be seated and join us, Harold," Martin said, "But what is the reason for the tizzy, as you so aptly put it? I understood Captain Hanson would be putting things in order now the Major has left?"

"Of course, you would not be aware, sir. Captain Hanson's horse reared and bolted at the noise of a blunderbuss. The stupid guard on the Mail had an accident and dropped his weapon. It went off right behind the Captain's charger. It bucked him off and deposited the Captain on his head, in the yard of this very Inn at lunchtime today.

"The Major ordered the Lieutenant to assume command, and departed for Portsmouth to board his ship. He was unaware that the Captain was actually dead. The coach had departed before the condition of the Captain had been properly diagnosed."

Martin looked intently at Harold. The smooth untroubled face gave nothing away.

The news did not cast a pall over the party, rather the contrary. As the evening progressed the relations between Peter and Fay relaxed, until it was plain to Martin that both were now aware of the path their immediate future would follow. He suspected that the innocence of their relationship so far would not exist for much longer.

***

With the celebrations of the evening past, Peter Vardy, Harold and Martin departed for London. It had been established that the men would be delayed in London for several days, and it was no surprise to hear that Mrs. Moore would be staying at her London residence from the next day.

The three gentlemen were all invited to call upon her at the Chelsea residence.

***

Plain Mr. Smith was introduced to Peter Vardy simply because he was Harold's cousin. Martin, who had been given space in the headquarters house, sat and interviewed Peter Vardy.

It seemed that Harold had made a sensible choice in his man. Martin quickly established that Vardy was a loyal king's man. His arrest and conviction had clearly been contrived by his enemy. Blame was not therefore cast upon the magistrates.

It seemed that Peter Vardy had, like Martin, been educated to an advanced level for the day. He spoke French because he had crewed for smugglers from a young age, as did most of the young boys at the time and of the area. He had, until recently, been running his father's estate. The charge and conviction had created a scandal robbing him of the position which had gone to his younger brother. When the post of organiser and manager of Martin's cross-channel delivery service was offered, he considered carefully, and asked several questions before finally accepting it.

Martin, with the help of Harold, worked with Peter, and produced a list of people he would want to run the service. He also desired, and received, a new boat for his own use, pointing out that, to use the people he had selected, he would need to be present on a regular basis. 'Sharing the risks', was the way he put it.

It came as no surprise that Mrs. Moore was willing to participate in the operation. The boats would not always be required for the service. To establish the necessary cover they would be required to do moonlight runs, to keep the secret of the delivery operations. The French end was particularly difficult, since the coordination of the project was vital. Not all the loyalists on the French side were smugglers. Those who were kept things simple. The real dangers occurred when those who were not became involved. Empty boats were highly suspect on both sides of the channel.

Since there was little to be done about it, they just needed extra care when using the non-commercial rendezvous.

The grounds of Marsden Hall included a useful cove, which became the mooring place of the boat operated by Peter himself. A small cottage above the shore line was rented to him and he moved in, making a living from fishing and writing, copying documents for local businesses.

The smugglers, selected by Peter, lived a protected life. Whoever else along the coast encountered preventative men, this small part of Hampshire seldom suffered as badly as the coastlines both east and west.

The carefully arranged raids and captures were, as Harold observed, better rehearsed than the plays at Drury Lane.

***

Jennifer's health continued to improve and it became possible to bring her forth once more into the social scene.

She insisted on visiting Eynsham, where she managed to spend several days just relaxing in the house she had restored and extended. Coddled by Dorothea Applegate, the housekeeper at Walton Manor, her recovery was helped by the peace and quiet of the Oxfordshire countryside.

While Jennifer was at Walton Manor, Martin spent time with Harold and Peter at Mudeford. There were two trips to be made, and both passed off without a hitch. Alouette was delivered by Martin to the small village of Etretat, between Fecamp and Le Havre. The other delivery was to the east of St. Malo, an area Peter was well acquainted with. The re-established contact in the area, Etienne Labatt, was pleased to see him once more. They had not really met since 1802 during the temporary truce used by Napoleon to rebuild his fleet and construct the invasion barges he would never use.

The restored Jennifer joined Martin at Eastney, Lady Jane's home, where their daughter Jane had been staying during her mother's absence.

For the first time since her illness, Jennifer was able to enjoy the pleasure of lovemaking with her husband once more. The comfort of the house and the shared joy between them, the delight of having their daughter with them, and the avowed happiness of their hostess, Lady Jane, created an episode that they would long remember.

***

Back in London once more, Martin was aware of his restlessness. He missed the lift of a deck beneath his feet. His call at the 'House', as he now thought of it, was not productive as both Sir Anthony and Alouette were away, and he had kept himself apart from the other employees in the building. This he did for his own reasons, and oddly, at the suggestion of Alouette.

On a past occasion while in Ireland, Martin had encountered two men, escaped prisoners from a ship transporting them to Australia. Both were killers. Martin had delivered them to England at Sir Anthony's request. Now the two men, Carter and Allan, were waiting for him at the corner as he left the house.

Both properly attired in respectable clothes and neat and tidy in appearance, Martin hardly recognised them. They signalled that they wished to talk and crossed the street and entered the small park, on the other side.

Martin, ever wary of ambush, checked his pocket pistol and followed. Both men seated themselves at two of the benches there for the convenience of strollers. Martin took a seat near enough to converse but far enough to defend himself if needed.

Allan spoke for them both. "Captain, Sir. You may recall us from Ireland. I am Allan, and my friend is Carter. We reckon you did us a favour and saved us from transportation. We are both better fed and more comfortable than we've ever been. Working for his honour has been the making of us, but we are sometimes asked to work with some odd coves."

"Good, I am pleased that things are going well for you both. But what is this about?"

Carter took up the tale. "There are three people working in the house who are not what they seem. They all have a story to tell but they are all telling lies. I know we are not the ones to talk, but Allan here heard two of them at it in French. Not knowing too much of the lingo, he listened but only understood the odd word. He heard your name and the lady's, Alouette.

"He told me, and I have a fair bit of French. I er.. Have some small experience of the moonlight trade, if you knows what I mean?"

"Well, man. Speak on. Tell me what is it you are saying to me?"

"I started listening out, as it were, and I heard them say that, with Alouette in the bag, the next thing was to get you out of the way. I have the impression that they was something to do with the attempt on the Admiral by those two posh bastards we had a run in with in Ireland. One said that you were supposed to be croaked in a duel. But it all went wrong."

"What about Alouette? You know she has just gone to France. Is it a trap?"

"They are going to take her and her boat when they do the pick-up."

"Point these people out to me. We will arrange things here, then go to France to arrange things there. Are you ready to do that?"

The two men looked at each other. Allan grinned. "Fancy a bit of a holiday? How about it, Horace?"

Carter grinned back. "Too bloody right. There's a little maid in Boulogne who will remember me."

Martin stood up. "This will be strictly business. If you point out the people, I'll get things organised."

Carter stood. "The little French bit with the gap between her front teeth. The ugly, big bloke who said he came from La Rochelle but talks like a Marseillaise. The other one is the little Dutchman van Eyck.

The French woman he had noticed. The gap in her teeth and the shapely figure made her stand out in the offices, though she was always very shy. Of the others he was unsure, but he was certain of the girl.

In the absence of both Mr. Smith and Alouette he decided that the best way to act was to make his way to the French coast and prevent the capture of Alouette if he could. Certainly, stop the capture of the boat Peter Vardy was using for the pick-up. In the house Martin called the French girl into his room.

"You are Colette Blanch, French?"

"Oui, M'sieu."

"I understand you have been speaking with the man, Corot. Who is he? your lover?"

"Oh no, sir. He has had my parents arrested and imprisoned in Le Havre. He says he will have them killed if I do not do what he tells me.

"What of the Dutchman?" Martin asked.

"Van Eyck is an evil man. I will not talk with him. I see he wants my body. I am able to keep him away because of Corot.

"Corot thinks he will have me to himself eventually. So far I hold him off." She shrugged. "I may have to allow him for my parent's sake."

"Invite him round to meet you in the small park. Tell him you have some news after speaking with me."

She looked at Martin anxiously. "Do not worry. Friends will be there."

"Has he said anything about Madam Alouette?" Martin wondered.

"He had said that she will be captured before she sails from near Fecamp, the boat also."

Martin thought about that. "I will see that does not happen."

Colette asked, "What shall I say to Corot when we meet?"

"Tell him I am going to France tomorrow. Meet him tonight at perhaps seven o'clock, in the small park. If you can arrange it, sing a little song as I pass your desk when I walk through."

Chapter 3

Over the sea..

TO CARTER AND ALLEN, he said, "Be in the park to rescue the little French girl. Do not molest her. But I want Corot, the big ugly man captured. She should be there at seven."

Carter smiled. "Good."

"Bring him to the basement room. We will need to find out just what they plan for Alouette and Peter Vardy." Martin's voice was grim.

***

They brought Corot in at ten past seven. Martin waited for the men to appear. When he was brought struggling through the door and dumped into the chair, he was looking worried.

Corot was bound to the legs and arms of the chair. "You cannot do this to me. I am an agent like you. Why am I tied up like this?"

Martin said nothing. He sat and looked at the man seriously, unblinking. The longer he waited the more agitated the man became.

Eventually, Martin said, "Why were you in the park tonight?"

Without hesitation, Corot said, "I was invited by Colette, the girl in the office who works with us."

"Why?"

Corot shrugged. "You know how it is, a man and a pretty girl." His grin was sickly.

"And her parents? When were you going to tell her that they had been executed?"

Corot squirmed in the chair. "I do not know what you are talking about."

Martin looked at Carter, who bent forward and rapped Corot on the knee with a riding crop. Corot started in shock. "I would have told her tonight," he said hastily.

Martin sat back. He had not realised that Colette's parents were dead. Instinct had led him to put the question. It was an answer that told him much.

"Tell me where will they ambush Alouette?"

"How do I know? I was not aware that they will."

"Corot, I know you are working for France. I also know that you betrayed Alouette and the arrangements we have made for her retrieval."

Corot shrugged and looked sulky. "I cannot say. How would I know? I am not in France. They will decide there."

"And Peter Vardy, if they are going to take Peter at the same time then you must know where that will take place. I will let Carter ask you. I know he will enjoy watching you suffer. For me there is no pleasure in this." He rose from his chair as if to leave the room.

"Please! No. Don't go, sir. That man is a fiend."

"Yes. I cannot stay to watch. But you will be talking when I return, and we will speak again."

Corot was desperate, watching Carter as he drew out a long thin bladed knife. "I'll just skin him a little first, sir, to encourage him like."

Martin had his hand on the door handle when Corot broke. "Please, sir. I think it will be at Vattetot-sur-Mer. The pick-up place is a favourite for Peter Vardy and the rendezvous was mentioned when Alouette left. There is a message place in the Patisserie. She will call there and they will follow from there to the boat on the beach."

"When, and what time?" Martin asked.

"I do not know," Corot said.

Martin turned to leave once more

"No, I don't, I think, two days at between seven hours and eight hours," he said hastily.

Martin stared at him, thinking. Then he decided. "Lock him up!" He said to Carter, "Get Allen. We will go and see what we can do."

***

Up in the office once more, Martin went to Mr.. Hervey, Mr.. Smith's assistant. He explained about the prisoner Corot, and warned him about the Dutchman.

"I will take Carter and Allan and go to France to stop the capture of Alouette and Peter Vardy."

Mr.. Hervey, the rather severe man who ran the house, looked at him seriously. "Take the girl. She could be useful as a diversion."

"Colette?"

"Yes. I think it will be a good test of her story. In addition it will give you an idea about her future employment."

***

The little cutter swam into the silted, coastal waters off Fecamp, on the French coast. The dusk of evening was causing images to blur as the small party boarded the gig to make their way to the beach. Peters, Martin's servant, had, as always, accompanied him. He was at the tiller, while the four extra hands from the crew of the cutter took oars and rowed the party ashore. They landed in the shadow of a rocky outcrop, and Martin checked that all were ready, prepared for the operation they had planned. With Colette, Collins and Allen, Peters and the four hands from the cutter, the party of nine made their way up the beach to the point where the road through the village of Yport, wound its way to the town of Fecamp, half a mile away to the north.

The information they had was that Peter Vardy would be meeting Alouette in the small bar in the village this evening. Colette had volunteered to see what she could find out in the bar.

Martin looked at her, "When were you last in France?" He said.

"Three years ago!" She said puzzled.

"Things are a little different now I'm afraid. Any new face is suspect and in a small village like this, on the coast, you would be in front of the local magistrate before you could give your name. To arrive here in passing, you have to have transport, a reason to be there. I will take a look at things and report back. Collins, keep an eye on things."

"Will do, sir. This area seems quite good for the moment." He indicated the small paddock that was hidden from the road and the buildings of Yport, by a barn, and store. He led the party to shelter against the back wall of the barn.

Martin and Peters made their way to the bar. Without going in, they were able to see inside, through the open doors. Alouette was seated in the corner near the window. She was opposite someone Martin did not recognise. He did not think the man was a friend.

From the direction of Etretat to the south there came the sounds of someone coming.

Martin turned to Peters. "Fetch Collins and two of the men. Leave Allen with Colette and with one of the men, send the other to get the boat in the water and ready for us."

Peters thrust his pistol into Martin's hand. "I'll leave that with you, sir. I'll be back." He disappeared without a sound.

Martin took a closer look at the people in the bar. There were two other men there and there was no barman in sight. The sound of the approaching man was becoming more obvious, so Martin decided to move. Holding Peters's pistol behind him, he stepped up to the bar door and through into the lighted room. Alouette made no sign that she knew who he was. The man sitting opposite her stirred suspiciously but he had only started to lift his pistol when Martin brought his into view and pointed at his face. When the other two men started to move, he lifted Peters's weapon and pointed it at them. Alouette reached forward and removed her companion's pistol.

She covered him while Martin told the other two to sit beside their friend. He relieved them of two pistols and three knives. The sword carried by their leader, was added to the hoard.

Alouette said, "There is a store at the back."
Between them they herded the trio into the store room
and barred the door.

Peter Vardy entered on the run. "There are soldiers
on the road behind me. I heard them where I started to
run."

"Let's go then. We might find it difficult
otherwise."

As he spoke he realised it was too late. The soldiers
were almost at the door.

He snatched the pistol from Alouette. "Sit! Both of
you. You are my prisoners. Understand?"

He did not wait for them to acknowledge, He called
to the soldiers at the door. "Here, you, come and take
charge of these prisoners."

The first two soldiers came in and stood with
muskets poised, watching Alouette and Peter.

Martin went to the door. "Where is your officer?"
he called arrogantly.

"I am coming. I am here." The portly Sergeant/
Chef puffed his way to Martin who stood at the door of
the bar, attaching the sword taken from the secret agent,
currently locked in the store room.

"Have you no transport?" Martin said in an angry
voice. "I ordered a carriage to transport the prisoners to
Le Havre. Where is it?"

"I, I do not know, sir. Nobody told me."

Martin skewered the unhappy Sergeant with his
sternest look. He then said quietly, "Send for one, now!"

"Yes, sir. Immediately. Lebrun, run back to the
barracks and fetch the carriage."

The soldier detailed, ran off still clutching his
musket.

Martin then started on the soldiers standing panting outside the bar.

"Fall your men in, Sergeant!"

"Sir, yes, sir. Fall in. Fall in. "He shouted harrying the men into two lines." The eight men stood in line, while Martin brought the two prisoners outside, and instructed the two guards to fall in with the others.

Behind the line of soldiers, Peters, Collins, and two of the hands appeared. All were armed. They all eased back into the shadows without being seen by the soldiers.

"Sergeant! A moment, please."

The sergeant came over to Martin, who led him out of direct sight of the men. Once there he produced his knife which he used to stress his instructions. Putting the point to the tip of the man's nose, he said quietly. "I have four pistols pointed at you." He nodded at the place where Peters stood, pistol in hand. The others rose into view with their own pistols on show.

The sergeant gulped.

"Now you have no need to worry, as long as you do as I say. Nod, if you understand me."

The sergeant nodded.

Martin smiled, "Good man." He put his hand around the Sergeant's shoulder and as they walked he said "Tell the men to relax until the carriage arrives."

Alouette and Peter were now seated on a bench on front of the bar.

She spoke for the first time. "This is all a mistake. I am here to visit my daughter in Fecamp. I stopped for refreshment and my escort has gone. I do not know where?"

She looked helpless and appealing.

"Your escort, madam? The horses and carriage perhaps?" Martin's sarcastic comment made it quite clear that he did not believe her.

So Alouette wept, wringing her hands. She turned to the soldiers, "Please, help me. This man is mistaken."

The soldiers looked uncomfortable, most turned away from her. With most looking elsewhere, she and Vardy simply walked away from the assembly in front of the bar. They were joined by Peters and his party. The sergeant would have said something but the prick of the knife dissuaded him. Since their sergeant said nothing, the soldiers stirred, but said and did nothing, waiting for their leader to act.

Martin left the sergeant on his own, with a final warning that he was in the sights of the pistols and to say and do nothing.

He walked into the bar and made his way out of the back door. Then he ran for his life as the sergeant regained his nerve and called for his men to run to the beach.

"Stop them. They are English. It is a trick." Confused, but getting the message, the brightest of the soldiers snatched up their muskets and ran past the bar toward the beach beyond.

On the beach the boat was in the water. The two women were in, already aboard, as the others piled in. The oars were out holding the boat while Peters waited for Martin to arrive.

As Martin came near, Peters raised his pistol and fired at the nearest of the soldiers. He then used three other pistols to shoot, and slow down the soldiers even more.

As he boarded the boat after Martin, the pursuit was even more hampered by the soldiers' efforts to bring their muskets into action. Having run to the bar from the next village and then from the bar to the beach, most of the muskets had lost their loads. The first three to try a shot were misfires. The next musket fired, but the ball went elsewhere, certainly not into the boat.

Then the boat was out of effective range. The muskets, not being in the best order anyway, were generally regarded as a volley weapon, rather than a sharpshooter's gun. The detachment of soldiers involved were conscripts drawn from the local area.

On the cutter Peter Vardy asked to be taken to the village of Etretat, to collect his boat. He had left it with his crew, plus a load of contraband. "I will not be able to continue in this area for a while. I knew the sergeant and he knew me."

***

The result of the excursion to Yport and Fecamp was that Peter transferred his attention to an alternative contact point at Criel-sur-Mer between Dieppe and Le Treport.

It had become far too dangerous for Alouette to continue her visits to France. She had become too well known to the French, and there were notices posted for her whereabouts the length of the Channel coast.

She elected to train Colette to take over the courier activity which had been her task up to now. Colette, up to then had been not as committed as some of the others. When she discovered that her parents had been executed, that all changed. Her education was undertaken and Alouette found her an apt student.

Martin was becoming increasingly restless. When Mr.. Smith returned, Alouette went to see him on the subject.

"Captain Forest-Bowers has done what he came here for. Unless there is some other task he should undertake, would it not be better for him to renew his naval duties?"

Mr.. Smith sat back in his chair, regarding Alouette, who sat opposite him at the other side of his desk.

"Why? I do recall it was you suggested that we utilise the services of the Captain, a matter which I believe fortuitously coincided with the extreme illness of his wife."

The gentle sarcasm of his comment did not disturb the steady gaze of the Frenchwoman one bit. She replied briskly, "The task for which we required him, has been accomplished, with the dispatch and efficiency that Sir Martin applies to all the challenges that he has faced to my knowledge."

Plain Mr.. Smith held his hand up. "I have received the message. I will either find another task for him to perform, or, as you suggest return him to his beloved quarter-deck. Would that settle the matter for you?"

As Alouette rose to her feet she said, "I felt it was important to keep these matters current. I understand you are busy with many things on your mind at all times. It is important to see that the organisation continues to run smoothly. Mr.. Hervey does his best with the actual building and accommodation, but in fact, you direct the staff personally. I beg you consider delegating that task to another."

Smith waved her back to her seat. "Who would you suggest for such a position?"

Alouette looked at him sharply. "You are asking me for a suggestion?"

"I am." Smith replied.

"I think you are playing games with me. I am just an agent. What do I know?"

Mr.. Smith sat back in his chair, a small smile on his face. "You are, Mme Alouette, probably the most accomplished spy in my entire organisation. You know the work we do, and not only why, but how, also. You sum up peoples' characters better than anyone else I know. So tell me, Alouette. Who should I appoint to this position?"

Stunned, Alouette sat in her chair. "You cannot mean me?"

"Why not?"

"But I am a woman." She wished Smith would leave it alone. It was a man's job.

"What are you saying? You are less intelligent than a man?"

"The men will not accept orders from a woman." The suggestion was insane.

"Could you do the job?" Smith would not leave the matter.

"Probably, but…!"

"But what? Ask yourself. Is there anyone better than you here in the office?"

Alouette thought for what seemed ages. In fact it was two minutes. Then she nodded her head. "Very well. I will take the job. But, remember, I warned you."

Chapter 4

Deep waters

FOR MARTIN, APART from the short sharp events of the cross channel visit, life lacked the challenge of his real profession. His steps took him once more to the villa opposite the park, to enquire whether he might be released from Mr.. Smith's employ. The past two months had been employed with the finding and setting up of the cross-channel service. Now that aspect of operations was firmly in the charge of Peter Vardy, who was well able to manage without Martin's further input.

There had been a rumour of change in the air, but nobody had communicated any suggestion of the nature of the changes.

Today he had been called to confer. There had been no word of the subject of the meeting, just the simple date and time.

He was greeted as usual by the imperturbable Mr.. Hervey, who ushered him into the drawing room of the house. Inviting Martin to sit, he rang the bell to apparently signal for serving coffee. The appearance of the maid with the steaming pot and crockery was within seconds of the summons.

Martin seated himself, mystified. This was far removed from the normal, rather strict business manner, which he was accustomed to in this house.

The arrival of Alouette brought him to his feet. Having seen her seated, the departure of Mr. Hervey seemed to indicate there was purpose in the setting involving the two friends alone.

Alouette poured the coffee and passed him the cup before serving herself.

Martin realised that she was using the moment to prepare herself.

"You look well, my dear," he commented. "I detect there is a certain reticence in your manner which I associate with bad news?"

Alouette looked up at him sharply. "Has anyone been in touch with you from here?"

Martin recoiled. "Absolutely not! Why would you suggest such a thing? My only contact with this establishment is through Mr.. Smith, and yourself."

Alouette relaxed. "Oh, Martin. I am so sorry. This has been a difficult time for me. I am still finding my, how do you put it, 'my feet'!"

"What has happened? You know you can trust me. Tell me what are you so troubled about?"

"Mr.. Smith has passed over control of the organisation to me."

She sat back, lifted the coffee cup to her lips and emptied it.

Martin sat back and, smiled. "Oh, is that all?" he said with relief. "I was worried that some disaster may have occurred. It is long overdue. It was apparent that you were far better qualified for this operation than he."

"But, Martin, I did not know. I am a woman. The men…"

"Mr.. Smith created this group to protect our nation. Despite all, he knew someone had to do this. In the absence of any one else willing to undertake it, he stepped in and created the organisation.

"He has been searching for the right person to run it ever since. After you joined, it became apparent that you had the talent, and the will. Also you were able to oversee several operations at the same time. The only problem in his mind was the fact that you were a woman. It took him time to realise that you could control your staff better than he could. Fait accompli."

Martin sat back and drank his coffee. "So, Cherie, why am I here?"

Alouette sat for a moment and gathered her thoughts. Martin's comments had been re-assuring. It was with a more settled mind she undertook her self-appointed task.

"Martin, my dear, I believe you will be happy to hear that the department will no longer need your services at this time. I do not say that we may never ask you again, but I do assure you, you will never be ordered again. I would like to be able to call upon you for advice and assistance if it is convenient, but there will be no more official orders."

She offered the coffee pot to Martin, who shook his head, still absorbing her statement. She poured the remainder of the cooling coffee into her cup and drank it. She looked up at him enquiringly. He rose to his feet and stepped over to her side. He took her hand and raised her to face him. Then he drew her close and kissed her. As he stood back he said, "Alouette, we have shared dangers and been friends for some years. In fact I believe more than friends. I trust that will always be the case. I am happy for you in your new task. I am also happy to return to my own way of life. Please call upon me if you need me."

He stood back, releasing her, noting the glistening of a tear in her eye as he took his leave. Mr.. Hervey was waiting as he left the room. He took his hat, cloak, and sword. Hervey stepped over to open the door for him. As he did he said, "She is the right one. We will look after her."

Martin smiled at the normally unemotional face. "Mr.. Hervey, I never doubted it for an instant."

***

At the Admiralty later that day, he was seated with his adoptive father.

Charles Bowers was showing signs of age. His hair was now quite grey, but his stance was still erect when he stood. Though there was a slight thickening at his waist, he was not fat.

"Martin, now we have you back where you belong once more. There is a captured French frigate undergoing repair and refit in Portsmouth dockyard at this time. She is named Garonne, but will be re-named before long. I think it would be a good idea if you took an early interest in her before matters go too far.

Charles added, "Since you commanded HMS Fox successfully, perhaps HMS Vixen would be appropriate. It would look well in the List." He was referring to the Navy List which not only listed all officers, but also all ships.

"I will have the orders prepared for you. It will mean joining the Channel fleet, probably blockade duties to begin with. But it will put a deck beneath your feet once more.

He gave the news to Jennifer when he returned home. Her sadness was swiftly hidden as she recognised her husband's yearning to get back to sea. She had accepted that by marrying a sailor she was condemning herself with long lonely periods throughout her life. She loved her husband and was happy for him returning to the life he was made for.

Martin made all haste to see his new command. Taking Jennifer to Eastney, they joined Lady Jane and daughter, Jane, who had been helping her grandmother still recovering from the strain of nursing Jennifer through her lengthy illness.

From there, Martin made his way to the dockyard to see his new command.

***

The Garonne was a 40 gun ship, captured during an excursion by Lord Cochrane from Gibraltar. She had been recently built and, though damaged about the upper part of her hull, her lower hull was sound. Most of the major repairs had been undertaken and there was little that could be faulted with the work thus far. The repairs had been overseen by an appointed officer, Lieutenant Patrick Brooks, whose recovery from injury had been accomplished finally, just prior to the arrival of the ship for repair and refit.

Being on the beach without immediate prospect of a seagoing appointment, he had been delighted to stand by the ship during repair. It gave him, as he put it, food on the table and the odd drink, to keep body and soul together.

He was able to give Martin a detailed tour of his new command, and he impressed Martin with his general demeanour.

At Martin's invitation Brooks joined him for luncheon in the dockside inn. There Martin decided to learn a little more about Lieutenant Patrick Brooks.

"I was wounded during my service with Admiral Troubridge. We were rather battered during our voyage to India. On the stretch to the Cape I received a broken leg and a nasty splinter wound at the same time. The surgeon put me ashore at the Cape Colony, where I recovered. I was due to rejoin my ship on her return voyage, but, as you must be aware, the Blenheim was lost before it reached Africa. I did receive passage home in HMS Harrier, commanded by the admiral's son. Unfortunately, I was not yet fit enough to be considered by Captain Troubridge to remain in the ship."

"I see," Martin commented. "Where are you from, Mr.. Brooks?"

"My family lives in Ireland, where they have a small estate. My father was a soldier who served with Moore in Ireland suppressing the Republican rebellion in '98. He was wounded and retired from the army in the same year. I was at sea at the time. I have not been home since '04. I was considering a visit when I was released from Haslar Hospital. I was offered this position by the port admiral. I was fortunate enough to have served under him. He remembered me."

Martin was impressed by the young man, who at 24 years was at a critical stage in his career. The work, which had been done to ensure the ship was being properly restored, reflected the effort the young man had put into his task.

After some consideration Martin sat back from the table and called for a bottle of port. When it arrived and they had served themselves, he said, "Mr. Brooks, I may say that I have observed the way you have supervised the work on the ship. I would be happy to have you serve as one of my officers, if it would suit you?"

Patrick Brooks, flushed. "Sir, I am aware of your reputation. I would be most grateful for a place in your crew. I understand that the crew will be assembling during the next three weeks. You may be assured I will be making all preparation necessary to have them accommodated and settled in, ready for when you take command. When may I expect the first lieutenant to arrive"

"I am unsure at present. I have not yet located the man I requested. In the interim, I would expect you to assume the post, at least until the matter is decided."

"Of course, sir. Gladly!" Brooks could not believe his luck. The man before him was already a national hero. Though there were many jealous of his fortune, those who had served with him, were unstinting in their admiration. And that, decided Brooks, was the real test of a hero.

Martin's first choice for a first lieutenant was currently in the West Indies. The presence of the young man at this time and place was most convenient. Time would tell of course, but there was little doubt in his own mind that Mr.. Brooks would suit him well.

The Port Admiral was known to Martin. Apart from the recommendation of Lieutenant Brooks, he was able to suggest two midshipmen of experience and several men of the area, who had approached him at the news that Martin was to command the Vixen . His reputation did mean that there was a good chance of prize money he being a lucky Captain. The dockyard workshop carpenter had indicated that he was getting itchy feet, having served some years with Pellew before joining the shipyard to marry his sweetheart. Now with three children growing up around him he was ready to go back to sea, assured that his family would be secure.

Martin had no hesitation in engaging his services as ship's carpenter. James Hanson had been working on the re-fit and knew the ship from truck to keelson. In addition, though approaching forty years, he was fit and strong.

***

One month later, on a cold winter's day in January '07, HMS Vixen signalled her departure to the Port Admiral at Portsmouth harbour.

From her Quarterdeck, Captain Sir Martin Forest-Bowers was able to see the warmly-wrapped figure of his beloved Jennifer standing with Lady Jane beside their waiting carriage.

Through his telescope he caught the wave of her hand in farewell, before he closed it with a snap and turned to the business at hand.

His first lieutenant, Patrick Brooks, called to Midshipman, Neil Harmon, the son of the next door neighbour to the Eastney estate of the Admiral Lord Bowers, Martin's adoptive father. Young Harman had sailed his dinghy in the Solent from the age of seven. At thirteen, he had made a single voyage in a merchantman to Lisbon. He had elected for a naval career after experiencing the shortcomings of the ship's officers, which had nearly resulted in the loss of the ship. His agile figure raced up the shrouds to the masthead. From this precarious viewpoint he viewed the anchorage through his telescope. "Deck there! All clear to seaward, sir."

"Very good, Mr.. Harmon. Stay until we clear the Round Tower, if you please."

"Happy to feel the deck lift beneath you again, Mr.. Brooks?" Martin asked.

"Yes indeed sir," Brooks replied with a smile.

"No news of the first lieutenant, sir."

"I'm afraid not. So I suggest you move your gear into the first's cabin, and inform Lieutenant Cameron accordingly. In the circumstances, the senior Mid, Keats, should be made acting. After all, he is due to sit his exam for lieutenant this year, and he can stand watch with the Master temporarily.

"We are lucky to have a real doctor aboard. Doctor Mills was on the staff at Haslar, as I believe you are aware."

Brooks grinned. "You did mention that you would prefer a proper surgeon for the ship."

"I confess he appears to be better qualified than I anticipated." Martin admitted.

Brooks said nothing, aware that Doctor Mills had suffered a disagreement with some rather badly disposed gambling acquaintances over an overambitious bet on a horse which had fallen before the post. The Doctor pointed out that, in view of the fact that the horse had been shot within sight of the winning post, thus was unable to complete the course, all bets were off.

His creditors had disagreed. His hasty departure on HMS Vixen solved two problems, one for the Doctor, the other for the ship.

***

The battle to get the ship through the harbour entrance was won after three-quarters of an hour of sheer hard work, working sails and tacking against a wind which had turned almost contrary. Once outside, however, the ship took off on a long reach for nearly fifteen hours. As the wind filled from north to northeast the ship was able to point higher and higher. The run, down channel toward Ushant, required sail trimming only for the entire 250 mile voyage. They spoke to four ships before, in the morning of the third day, they encountered the sloop, HMS Bella from the Channel fleet, en-route to England with dispatches'.

Her Captain called across, "The weather drove the fleet to the south of Pointe du Raz. The winds were contrary. The fleet is gradually beating northward once more, but yesterday evening most were still south of the Goulet de Brest. I fear some enemy ships may have escaped the harbour."

They parted, allowing the sloop to continue her journey.

Martin spoke to Jared Watson, the Master. "Where would they go, d'you think, Mr.. Watson?"

"If they can weather the Pointe de St Mathieu, I would suggest up the coast, hugging the shore-line to make for Roscoff. Once there they can take their chances to go further up-channel or west into the Atlantic. I guess the escaping ships would not be of the line, perhaps frigates or corvettes."

"I agree, Mr.. Watson Let us pay a visit to Roscoff. It is not far off our course and at least we can advise the Admiral if any have made it that far. Alter course to fetch the coast at the Isle de Batz. We will take a look from there."

The Isle de Batz was just beyond the town to the west of Roscoff. The harbour was visible from the sea. Martin took advantage of the French lines of his command and sailed close to the harbour mouth to make sure of ships moored there.

Once more Mr.. Harmon was sent aloft with telescope to report on what he could see.

Almost immediately he reported four ships. "Three warships, two frigates," he paused "A corvette perhaps 22 guns, the frigates are both 38 guns.

"The other ship is a merchantman, a captured East Indiaman, from her looks. I will have her name in a moment as she swings at her mooring." He paused again, then. "Yes, I see her now. She is Harlech Castle 24-guns. She has the tricolour flying above the union flag."

"Very good, Mr. Harmon. You may come down now."

***

They joined the fleet the following evening, coming within sight of the flag, in the now calming waters of the aftermath of the storm which had driven the fleet off station.

Admiral Jervis was in England and unlikely to return immediately. His deputy, Admiral Hardy, received Martin in his cabin on the flagship. Having read his orders, he sat back, waving at the wine and inviting Martin to refill his glass. "Here you are, young Forest-Bowers; my nephew speaks very highly of you."

Seeing Martin's puzzled look, he smiled. "You were not aware that Commander Brown is my sister's boy? He was Middy under Captain Graham, when you assumed command after Graham died. Damn bad business that. You took him as lieutenant afterwards. He was grateful for your interest." He grunted and cleared his throat.

Martin said, "He was a willing learner and good with the men. I suggest he will go far. This war is by no means over, I believe."

"Quite right. That brings me to this report about the ships in Roscoff, two frigates, a corvette plus an Indiaman. What do you think?

"I think that the batteries at the harbour are badly sited. I also think that with two boats for each of the frigates, one for the corvette, and two for the Indiaman we have a good chance of scooping them all. The Indiaman is not alongside and I believe not yet unloaded. She was still down to her marks when she was observed. But how long for I cannot guess."

"If you continue on our present heading you should be at the east end of the Isle-de-Batz by tomorrow night. I will detach the sloop Pelican and the frigate Boscombe to accompany you for a cutting-out expedition. We will also give you the cutter we captured yesterday. She will be handy and we can fill her with men to tow your pulling boats, at least to the harbour itself. I'll draft the orders now and send them over. You can prepare the cutter. You can have someone to command her and get together with York and Hamilton from the Pelican and Boscombe."

Back on board, Martin called Brooks, "Signal Pelican and Boscombe, Captains to report on board." Martin was senior to both Lieutenant York and Captain Hamilton.

Lt Cameron prepared to receive the two officers whose boats were already in the water en route. Ship's Master, Watson, followed Martin into his cabin.

Martin grinned, "We will be cutting out the ships left in Roscoff!" He said, "The order is coming from the Admiral directly. The course will be to the east end of the Isle de Batz, where we will drop the men into boats and the cutter, Angelique, will tow them in. We need to be there in darkness. That is, we need to be within the harbour in darkness. Please work out the course and take into account the ships travelling with us, the Pelican, the Boscombe, and the Angelique. The lieutenant commanding the cutter will be Keats. He should be up to it. Send him in, would you?"

As Jared Watson left the cabin he smiled. Young Keats would be thrilled with his first command, of that there was no doubt.

The acting Lieutenant was on deck. Watson sent him to see the Captain without comment or hint of the reason.

"Ah, Keats. David, is it not?"

"Yes, sir." Keats stood at attention, swaying to the motion of the ship.

"Sit down, David. This will not take long. I will call you again with the others, but first I am putting you in command of a captured cutter. She will be used in the cutting out expedition that we are planning for Roscoff harbour. You will need to tow boats from the other ships to the harbour before detaching and cutting out the east

Indiaman, the Harlech Castle, which is hopefully within the harbour still. If it is not, then you will be called upon to assist the other parties as and where necessary. Do you understand?"

"Yes, sir."

"Off you go then and collect your command, Call upon the flagship to take on men."

"Yes, sir." The Acting Lieutenant stumbled from the cabin and ran to the gunroom to collect his sword and pistols, before reporting to the First Lieutenant to be given a boat to access his new command bobbing along beside the flagship. Once aboard, David Keats, with a twenty man crew at his disposal, set sail for the Isle de Batz, instructed to take the inside passage between the Isle and the mainland and reconnoitre the harbour, noting the position of the ships there, and any signs of activity, without revealing their presence. The fact that the cutter was recently captured from the French should prevent her raising the alarm. Her task was then to meet HMS Vixen, Boscombe and Pelican to the east of the Isle to take on an extra 40 men and take the boats in tow. The raiding party was commanded by Captain Hamilton of HMS Boscombe.

***

The planning session was of necessity short. Time was the main factor. Provided the ships were in place by midnight, the actual raid would commence with boarding the ships, by 2.00 am. If this could be accomplished quietly the chances were good for success. Lieutenant Brooks was in command of the attack on the second frigate, Lieutenant Keats the Indiaman.

The cutter could crowd sixty men on board. This would reduce the weight of the towed boats. Keat's 20 man party for the Indiaman, plus 10 men from each of the other boats, towed the balance of the raiders spread among the other boats. Inside the harbour the extra men in the cutter would be transferred to the towed craft to make their way to their target ships.

Chapter 5

The raiders

THE ANGELIQUE SAILED well. Her fore and aft rig enabled her to sail close to the wind and David Keats delighted in the feel of the lively craft. Having learned to sail a small boat from his home in St Mawes, Cornwall, sailing his present command was just like a bigger version of that 12 foot dinghy. The midshipman from Pelican, Michael Lewis, in charge of the extra men on board, stood with Keats as he watched the bo'sun's mate calling for the big mainsail to be tweaked to stop the leech fluttering. Keats smiled. "Well, Mr. Lewis. What do you say? She is a true sailor, is she not?"

"She certainly is, sir. We must be better than ten knots, I would think."

Keats shrugged, "Bo'sun, stream the log, let us see just what we are making."

"Aye, aye, sir."

The next few minutes passed as they waited for the call. Then the cry, "Eleven knots and a half, sir, twelve knots and holding." The west-country burr of the Bo 'sun's mate was loud and clear.

"Keep her as she goes, Mr. Harris."

The Master's Mate, Daniel, acknowledged with a quiet, "Aye, sir."

"Join me in a glass, Mr. Lewis. We will be some time on this course before we raise the Island."

"A pleasure, sir."

The two officers went below to the stern cabin, and Daniel breathed a sigh of relief, allowed at last to sail the boat unsupervised, for a while at least. He had no problem with Mr. Keats. He was learning his job well and seemed to be shaping into a good officer. It was just that like this he had time for his own thoughts, without waiting for orders that may or may not come at any time. Meanwhile the cutter flew through the grey Channel waters, toward the distant loom of the Isle de Batz.

The plan called for the cutter to be in sight of the harbour by the approach of night. Keats decided that they should sail past the entrance as evening approached, for a view during daylight. Then, to reverse course and sail back for a closer look with the approaching darkness behind them. Then having taken a good look, to make all speed to rendezvous with the HMS Vixen as early as possible, just in case they needed the extra time.

"Well, we need not have worried. It seems all is as it was. I swear they have not taken the cargo from the Indiaman. She is still as low in the water as ever. From the looks of the frigates most of the men must be ashore or at stand easy. Apart from the deck watch, there appears to be nobody about."

Harris approached.

"Yes, Mr. Harris?"

"Sir, we have two Frenchmen in the party here. What if we launched the dinghy and me and the two

Frenchies went to have a look around? We could meet you here when you come back with the raiders, sir?"

Keats thought for a few moments. "Damn good idea, Mr. Harris. You do realise that if you are caught, it could be the chop."

"Best not to get caught then, sir."

"Very well, get ready. We'll drop you when we turn."

Harris went and collected the two loyalist members of the crew, and called the bo'sun to launch the dinghy to take them ashore.

***

Daniel rowed the small boat easily into the harbour at Roscoff. His two passengers idly chatted in French as they passed under the stern of the frigate closest to their route. Harris glanced up and read the name picked out in battered gold letters across the stern. Guerriere. He knew that meant warrior. The other frigate was Justine. The name was just a name as far as Harris was concerned. He could not make out the name of the corvette. It had swung with the eddy and the name was not visible. There were only a few men on the Indiaman, armed with muskets. It seemed to Harris that it might mean the crew were still on board.

He drew the dinghy alongside the quay with an expert flourish, and seized the landing ladder to hold the boat steady allowing the two Frenchmen, to climb on to the quay.

There were groups of people standing around and talking on the quay, so the men separated and joined different groups. Both listened. Daniel seated in the boat was aware of the excitement from the noise coming from the many groups on the quay above him.

The two men returned to the boat fairly quickly. As Daniel rowed away across the harbour they told him the news. It seemed that the crews of the frigates had been arrested for mutiny. They had been ordered to escort the Indiaman and its cargo to Le Havre. Both crews had refused. They say the British fleet has returned. The second man said one of the group he was with mentioned the meeting between two British ships. "I think perhaps they saw Vixen meeting with the sloop from the fleet. Added to the voyage here from Brest in the terrible storm, their officers have little experience. The ships were damaged, and they have just managed to effect repairs."

"Did they say why they did not unload the Indiaman here?"

"Yes. It seems they have no lighterage here to handle bulk cargo. They had kept the crew on board to help sail her onward. Now there is confusion and trouble."

"Good. So now we go as fast as we can. As soon as we get beyond the harbour, we'll raise the mast and make all speed following the Angelique."

***

As they rounded the end of the breakwater both Frenchmen called out, "She is here. The Angelique is here."

Daniel redoubled his efforts with the oars as the cutter bore down on them.

Back on board he reported to Lieutenant Keats. "Sir, the two frigates have no crews aboard. The men have been taken ashore under arrest for mutiny. The crew of the Harlech Castle are being held aboard at present. She has not been unloaded as they have not the lighterage here."

"Well done, Harris. We will make all speed to meet with the Captain and let him know of this."

"Excuse me, sir. I was happy to see you here, but surprised."

Keats smiled. "Fortuitous, Harris. We lost the fore jib. Replacing it took enough time. Then the lookout spotted you returning across the harbour, so I decided to wait. It seems that was a wise decision."

The cutter was heeling to the wind, her keel cutting the water spurning the waves.

***

Because the Vixen and her consorts had made better time than anticipated, they were heading to close the gap with the returning cutter.

The news was passed when everyone met. Martin decided that they would sail into the harbour and board both frigates directly from Vixen and Boscombe, leaving the Indiaman to the Pelican and Angelique. The harbour batteries would be bombarded by both frigates on entry. While the cutting out was occurring. Martin guessed that the port was ill-prepared for an assault judging from the remarks made by the Master's Mate, Harris, and the opinions of the two French seamen who had accompanied him.

The Vixen led the ships into Roscoff flying a tricolour. The flag was replaced as soon as they were in the harbour itself and the port broadside guns were flaming at the rather crude embrasures mounting the battery protecting the harbour. Coming alongside the Guerriere the boarding party overran the deck watchmen and started setting the sails. A cable passed to the Vixen assured that the prize swung up to the wind promptly. Martin ordered the starboard broadside to prepare and brought the ship about, to leave harbour dragging the prize round behind her. The sails filled on both ships and the first gun fired from the battery on shore. It drew fire from the entire broadside in return.

Boscombe hauled Justine around in similar fashion, and all four ships started for the harbour mouth.

Pelican met opposition from the prize crew still on board. The intervention by Angelique whose people boarded from the other side of the ship, made the difference and the prize crew were overcome.

Lieutenant Keats fought his way through the remainder of the French seamen aboard, and made his way below to release the captive crew members. The crew swarmed into the rigging. While Pelican and Angelique added their guns to the bombardment the Harlech Castle got under way with the assistance of Midshipman Gibb and a reduced party from the boarders.

By now there was musket fire from the jetty, in addition to six pounder gunfire from a party of artillery men who arrived on the quay at that time. The stern chaser, long twelves from Boscombe scattered the horse drawn guns with her second shot. Vixen cleared the jetty of musket fire with a shattering salvo of grape shot. This not only cleared the jetty of living targets it smashed the walls of the buildings lining the jetty.

The British ships and their prizes left the ruined harbour to the sound of the cries of the wounded and the crackle of burning buildings. The guns of the town were silenced.

***

At the rendezvous with the fleet, the prize crews were sorted out. The three prizes sent off to Portsmouth. The members of the expedition were well pleased with their night's work. All would benefit from the sale of the prizes. The Indiaman was a special bonus. She was loaded with a valuable cargo, which would fetch more than the combined value of all three warships.

For the blockading fleet, the excitement of the incident soon faded into the background of boredom entailed in the continuous cruising back and forth blocking the access to and from the Port of Brest. The only craft to gain relief from the daily grind was the cutter Angelique, and HMS Bella, the smaller of the two sloops attached to the fleet. Both were dispatched with mail and orders to and from the fleet to one of the south coast ports, normally Portsmouth. Martin was kept in regular touch with Jennifer through their regular letters.

It was because of the regular communication, that the eventual relief for HMS Vixen came about.

The flag for Vixen's Captain to repair on board broke at the masthead of the flagship as the two ships came close. Martin was called by Lieutenant Brooks, who advised him of the summons. As he came on deck struggling into his better jacket, Brooks told him. "The Angelique came alongside the flag and passed up mails, scarce half an hour ago. The panic began soon afterwards. I think it was only then, they noticed that we were here."

***

The jolly-boat bobbed over the waves under the charge of Midshipman Harman. Martin sat huddled in his boat cloak, trying to ignore the bitter wind that seemed to seek every gap in his attire, sending an icy spear to remind him that he was vulnerable no matter how well he wrapped the cloak about him.

He was piped aboard the flagship with the usual, if a little hurried ceremony, and happily ushered swiftly below to join the Admiral in the great cabin. The only other person present was Hardy's flag Captain, Lord John Burke. Hardy waved Martin to a chair and Burke poured a glass of cognac, which he passed to a grateful Martin.

Martin took a sip of the brandy, feeling it slip down through him like fire, the warmth spreading through him. He reinforced the effect with another sip before concentrating on the Admiral who put his empty glass down, and began to speak.

"I understand you speak French, and you have some experience with dealing on a personal basis with the French in their own country?"

"Well, sir. I do speak the language. When I was in the Mediterranean I took part in several excursions ashore collecting and dropping agents for our Government."

"Good. Yes. Good. I see." Hardy was reading a paper in front of him.

"Tell me. Do you know the Comtesse de Chartres? She seems to be some sort of agent for our people?" He looked up at Martin with raised eyebrow.

Martin thought about it, then said, "I am not aware of the name, sir."

"Uses a pseudonym 'Alouette.' Does that ring a bell?"

Martin relaxed. "That is a familiar name. I have delivered and recovered the lady on several occasions in the past, though I understood she was no longer visiting France."

"Seems she went back for a specific reason, and is in some trouble at the moment. A school, operated by nuns, had up until recently been left alone. Apparently one of the more notorious of the hoi polloi, a man called Portet, discovered there was a girl's school full of children of the former nobility still unravished, and set out to put things right. This Alouette woman discovered the plot and got there first, got the girls away, but now is stuck in a place called Parthenay, fifty miles inland from La Rochelle. I have been told to do what I can to get the lady out. They have only mentioned the schoolgirls in passing, as it were. The lady is the important one."

He looked up at Martin who was looking surprised at the mention of the name Portet.

"That is a name I did not expect to hear."

"Seems to be known in London also. He was on his way to Dartmoor Prison. He escaped on the way. This is the first they heard of him since."

Looking at the map that Burke had produced, Martin said, "Then this is even more urgent, than ever. Where is he coming from? Do we know?"

"The Convent school was just outside Dijon. That is all I know. The nuns were not told where the girls were going. But it would not be difficult to guess, the general direction at least. After all it's a big party. "

Martin looked at the area. "Knowing the lady, sir, I think it unlikely that she will move without the girls. Do we know how many there are?"

"Thirty two, between 13 and 16 years I understand."

They will need some sort of carriages in that case. Can I ask for any volunteers who can speak French, especially Frenchmen if we have any?"

Burke spoke. "We have dispatched the cutter around the fleet, with orders to collect any Frenchmen from the crews. I believe we have several among us."

"Good! That is most helpful, sir. I myself have three on board, and at least another three men who were poachers but never caught." He smiled. "They seem able to find things wherever they happen to be, if you take my meaning, sir. If we can gather sufficient men, we have a chance, with a forced march, to get to the girls before the Portet does."

***

Martin found 24 men from the other ships in the fleet to add to his own three, plus two poachers and Peters. Dressed in an assortment of clothing they were a motley-looking crew but Martin had plans to do something about that. Just outside La Rochelle at Lagord there was an artillery unit with horse-drawn guns. The security was, as Peters put it. 'Bloody disgusting.' The platoon of gunners was billeted in a barn, the horses held in a second barn and paddock. The guns were all pushed into the open wagon shed. Only the commissary wagon was outside. The canvas tilt laced tightly at both ends, where the officer slept with a companion of his choice from the local area.

Martin spoke to the men when Peters and MacLean, one of the poachers returned. They left Godden, the other poacher on watch.

"There are 24 men in the barn, plus the officer in the wagon. We need all the uniforms. We also need to be quiet. Try to avoid bloodstains!"

I'll deal with the officer along with you, Peters. The lady may need attention."

The grins among the others quickly disappeared when Martin reminded them, "Time is against us. We must succeed and we do not want people after us, for a while at least."

He signalled the approach by tapping Peters and then strolling across the yard to the parked wagon. The sentry was asleep, McLean lifted the musket from him, and with the man's bayonet signalled him to be quiet and start undressing.

Martin and Peters went to each end of the wagon. Martin cut the tie that closed his end of the cover. He then climbed onto the wagon and stepped inside. Pistol in hand, he nudged the man laying alongside a semi-nude girl. Peters entered the other end of the wagon as the man stirred and started to speak. Martin said in French. "Say nothing. Get up and leave the wagon."

The girl stirred and woke. Peters grinned at her as she grabbed the bedcover to cover her exposed breasts. Peters grabbed her dress and thrust it at her, then gestured for her to leave the wagon with her companion. Outside in the yard the place was filling with semi-clothed sleepy artillerymen.

Martin's men dressed in the soldiers uniforms. All the soldiers were bundled back in the barn. Godden and McLean with the help of three of the Frenchmen were busy saddling horses. Another pair brought round two horses and harnessed them to the wagon. All the spare horses were put on lead reins, made from cut-down gun harness.

Leaving four men to keep the prisoners quiet, Martin and his party mounted horses and, with the other horses led, they set off followed by the wagon for the fifty-mile journey to Parthenay. By morning they had made over fifteen miles. They stopped at a river to water the horses and swap saddles. The wagon arrived as Martin decided to leave with an advance party. Leaving six men to follow on in company with the wagon. He took the other twenty men onward, switching horses twice before stopping to rest early the next morning for three hours. The party rode into Parthenay at midday, the horses tired but not finished. The switching of saddles as they had progressed had given them enough rest to keep them going.

At the Abbey, Martin rode into the yard where he was greeted by the Abbot.

"Ah, it is good you have arrived. The lady is impatient, and the girls restive."

"You were expecting us then, Abbe?" Martin asked curiously.

"But, of course. You are Monsieur Portet?" The man sounded uncertain, noting Martin's uniform.

"No, I am a soldier. Monsieur Portet is on his way. May I see the lady, please?"

"Of course. Have your men water their horses and they will find feed in the stables behind the church."

Martin handed the reins to MacLean and followed the Abbot, followed in turn, by Peters.

Alouette did not turn a hair at the sight of Martin. She curtseyed to him and said, "Can we continue our journey now you have arrived?"

"Of course, Madam, We must rest the horses but we will leave this evening."

Tell me, Abbe (Priest), have you wagons to transport the girls?" He used the expression priest deliberately, as abbot he should have been addressed as Pere (Father), but Martin wanted it to be clear that he was in charge.

"The wagons the girls came in have been attended-to. They are ready be used." The abbot was sounding a little cooler by now, at the lack of respect being shown.

McLean appeared and looked at Martin. Martin stepped away to hear his report. "The lads found the wagons the girls came in. They're being harnessed now. There are plenty of horses in the stables here, so I took the liberty of swapping saddles from ours to theirs, and the leaders to their fresh horses as well. The monks there did not like the idea, but we convinced them."

"Well done, McLean. I'll bring the girls."

Turning back to Alouette, he said, "Would it be possible for the girls to be ready to travel now?"

Alouette smiled. "Why, sir. Of course. I will fetch them." She bobbed a curtsey and went, leaving the abbot, grim faced.

"What is this, sir? You are not waiting for M Portet?"

"Tell me, Abbe. Have you ever met Portet?" Martin asked

"Why, no But he is an important man."

"And he did ask you to keep the girls here until he arrived?"

"Yes, he did."

"And the horses were they also gathered for M Portet and his party?"

"I received a message by Semaphore with instructions."

"Abbe, M Portet you would have discovered had you asked Madam Alouette, is a gross pig, who wished you to keep the girls here so that he could select which ones he would rape personally, and which others he would allocate to his murdering bunch of brigands. Your own fate if you remain here will be execution. The crime will be for harbouring escaping émigrés. Your older monks will probably share your fate, and young ones will probably suffer the same fate of any women to be found here. Am I clear? Do you understand, Abbe? M Portet, I repeat, is a disgrace to France and the world. I suggest you clear this place of all humanity until he has been and gone. Use the horses you have and leave, as far away as possible. You can return later when they have gone.

"If he gets within range, I will kill him. So, Abbe, I hear the girls coming. I will wish you farewell and good luck. Be warned. For the sake of your monks, if not for yourself."

Martin turned and joined Alouette as she swept the group of chattering girls through the hallway and out into the yard. The horses were standing waiting, as were two large wagons. The men were happily assisting the girls into the wagons.

Martin signalled the men to mount-up, and helped Alouette onto the lead-wagon seat. He said, "Portet should catch-up, if we allow him to."

Alouette smiled, "I will take a musket, I think, when that happens." She took his hand in hers and kissed it. "Dear Martin, I should have guessed it would be you."

Martin smiled. "Who else would it be?" Then he turned to the two poachers who stood awaiting instructions. "Godden! Keep your two horses. When Portet arrives let us know how many men he has and how far he is behind us. I think we will arrange a surprise for him. Do you understand?"

Godden grinned. "Sir, I understand. It will be a pleasure. From what I hear it is time this man was sent on his way like! You may depend on me, sir." He nudged his horse and disappeared into the cover of the trees.

Turning to MacLean, Martin said, "Lead out and scout the road ahead. I do not want any nasty surprises with our present cargo!"

"I understand!" MacLean said. Wheeling his horse he rode over to Peters and passed over the rein of his lead horse to him. Then with a wave he also disappeared into the trees where the road entered the huge woodland area that lay between Parthenay and the coast.

Chapter 6

Ambush

THE TWO WAGONS, escorted by the mounted men of Martin's command, made their way through the woods following the road back to La Rochelle. The people they met stood aside warily as they saw the uniforms of the party.

The excited chatter of the girls gradually died down as the sheer boredom of their slow progress over the rutted surface of the road began to make itself felt. Even the flirtatious looks between the older girls and some of the younger men lost interest as the boredom and discomfort set in. Three hours after they had set out the party stopped for a break, and the riders swapped saddles, and the wagon horses were changed.

While this was happening the artillery wagon arrived with its escort.

The girls stretched their legs and made giggling excursions into the trees to carry out calls of nature. They were then shared between the three wagons which gave them more room to stretch out. The party moved onwards after an hour. By late afternoon they were at Allonne, where they took over the premises of the Marie to accommodate the girls overnight.

Godden appeared when they had been moving for an hour the following day.

He re-joined the column and reported on the situation to Martin. "The party under Portet is about an hour behind me. There are twenty men with him. They look like brigands to me."

Martin asked about the Abbey.

Godden shook his head. "The abbot was there on his own. They shot him!"

Martin looked grimly at Godden. "He had no chance. The leader, Portet, I suppose, shot him before he finished speaking."

After looking around the area thinking, Godden coughed and said, "If I might suggest it, sir. There is a spot. I passed it about ten minutes ago. Looked about perfect to me."

MacLean returned from his place ahead, realising the wagons had halted. Martin sent him off ahead with the wagons and six of the French sailors.

Alouette insisted on joining the ambush party as they returned to the spot suggested by Godden. "You need as many muskets as you can find. I'm a good shot as you know, so there's an end to it." She took her musket and mounted one of the spare horses.

Between Godden and Martin they sorted out positions for the ambush of the followers. Peters took charge of the back-up group of four who were stationed to stop anyone who got through the main ambush.

Ensuring everyone had ammunition and some cover, they settled down to wait.

The noise of the closing column gave advance warning of their approach. "I'll fire first. Then choose your target and don't let any escape."

Martin settled down behind the log he had selected and lined his sights on the bend in the road ahead. Next to him lay another loaded musket. His sword lay unsheathed by his hand.

The leader of the column clattered around the bend and Martin fired. Not waiting to see the man fall he picked up the other musket and fired once more.

Then he was on his feet sword in hand, running to intercept the staggering figure he recognised as Portet, who was unwounded but his horse had been killed. He had been unseated and tumbled to the ground. Seeing Martin, he drew his own sword and struck out at his attacker. Martin parried his blade and lunged. The sword missed his body but ripped Portet's coat. Martin was just able to recover in time to evade his opponent's blade, but he tripped and fell back on the ground. Portet raised his own blade to deliver the coup-de-gras to the hated British Captain.

Martin waited helpless to stop him.

The voice was cold and hard, and it stopped Portet in his tracks. Shocked, he looked up at someone behind Martin. "Remember me?" Alouette said and watched as Portet recognised her. Only then did she pull the trigger.

The roar of the musket from behind him shocked Martin. Then he watched the red blot appear on the breast of Portet's blue coat. The man staggered back trying to complete the sword strike, his arm dropping, without success. He collapsed to the ground, and Alouette spoke from behind Martin. "Bastard, burn in hell."

***

The ambush was a success. None of the riders had escaped. Three of Martin's men had received injuries, none serious. All were treated by Alouette. It seemed to

Martin that she had more to do with their eventual recovery than the treatment they received. The bodies were buried under an overhanging section of the slope. The horses were collected. The one dead horse, having been dragged off the road into the woods, was partially butchered by Godden, the remainder of the carcass left for the scavengers of the forest.

They caught up with the column later that day and the three wounded were transferred to one of the wagons where they were pampered by the girls, much to the envy of those who had escaped injury.

When they arrived in the vicinity of the Artillery base two days later, Martin called a halt while MacLean and Godden scouted the farm. They found their own men still in command of the prisoners, having fed well on produce from the farm and the local market, cooked by one of the prisoners. Because the unit were strangers in the area, nobody ever questioned the men in uniform who shopped in the market.

Martin sent MacLean to contact the cutter, at the agreed rendezvous. Meanwhile he and Alouette went to work on the Lieutenant in command of the artillery platoon.

***

Lieutenant Maurice Dumas was an amiable young man who found life in the army in his current position agreeable. He could feed reasonably well and never seemed to have trouble finding company to warm his bed. His section of the battery was unused up to now and he was beginning to believe that the army had forgotten him. Having posted his platoon here, he had been ignored.

Sitting with the delightful lady and the English Captain could have been awkward, but they were both pleasant company and they had actually made their position clear. They had rescued the girls from their convent and were removing them from possible harm here in France to England. He had no problem with that. After all he did not think the thirty-odd girls were going to alter the political structure of the current government. It was what was suggested thereafter that intrigued him.

"Alouette has mentioned to me that your position could be difficult if it were discovered that your platoon had been captured and made prisoner, while men in your uniforms went to rescue these girls, and killed Portet and his brigands whilst they were at it. As we know Portet was a disgrace to France, but the people who used him are powerful. They have long memories, and they do not like mistakes or what they might decide is dereliction of duty."

As he thought about this Maurice felt the truth of this suggestion and his heart sank at the outcome of this episode. After all he had been in charge when they were captured. "But we are prisoners. You will take us to England?"

Martin shook his head sadly. "We will not have room in our boats I am afraid. We will have to leave you here."

Maurice's world suddenly stopped. Only too well did he know the attitudes of his superior officers. They, like him, were not professional soldiers. They were grocers and fishmongers, and they worried more about avoiding blame than protecting their juniors. The future suddenly appeared bleak and possibly terminal. "But what? why....?"

Alouette raised her hand. "Lieutenant, I may have a solution to your problem." She turned to Martin. "If I may?"

Martin shrugged and nodded.

Alouette turned back to Maurice. "Lieutenant, if the Captain returns the uniforms, and the horses, and leaves the extra wagons and horses that he has acquired, your men could possibly share the benefits of the sale of the extra items and, in so doing, forget we were ever here." She gazed at the Lieutenant with the full intensity of her beautiful eyes.

Martin watched as the young man added up the sum of what Alouette was saying.

"I would not need to report anything about this incident!" Maurice murmured.

"Exactly!" Alouette answered. She sat back and waited while Maurice Dumas examined the options.

"Perhaps the Lieutenant is worried about the young lady he was entertaining when we arrived?" Martin suggested.

"No!" That is not a problem. As you may have noticed there has been no enquiry from the village since you came. The lady concerned would rather her association with me was not broadcast. There are those who would inform her father and fiancé. She will continue to say nothing and I will inform her that it was an exercise carried out with another platoon."

"I presume that you approve of Madam Alouette's suggestion then, Lieutenant?"

Maurice rose to his feet. "I will speak to the men. I am confident they will agree with the solution you have proposed, Madam." He saluted Martin and turned and left the room.

MacLean returned and reported that the cutter would be ready that night and Martin, Alouette, the girls and rescue party settled down to wait the day out.

Meanwhile Lieutenant Dumas paraded his men, and selected the horses for the guns, now recovered from the barn. Settling on the horses that they would be keeping was a matter that took time, but, having been selected, the platoon was mounted and paraded through the village of Lagord, for the benefit of the local population, and to allow the reunion between the lieutenant and his lady friend to be arranged.

At the farm there was some unease at the possibility of betrayal. But as Peters reminded the men. "The soldiers had more to lose than we have. There has to be a lot of money involved in the sale of the wagons and horses, and the army is not going to forgive them all being captured so easily."

When the platoon returned the French cook prepared the evening meal, for soldiers, sailors and girls alike.

At the rendezvous at midnight, the crew of the cutter were astonished to see the party return escorted by French soldiers, who lifted the girls into the boats so that they should not get wet, and then stood on the shore and waved the raiding party off.

***

In the cabin on HMS Vixen once more, Martin indicated that there would be no mention in his report of the 'entente cordiale' which had prevailed when they departed the French coast.

The Admiral had decreed that Martin should deliver his cargo of young ladies direct to Portsmouth where a reception committee would meet them and re-unite them with families and/or relatives.

The relationship between Martin and Alouette was now a friendship akin to brother and sister, rather than as lovers. Both recognised this and in many ways it simplified matters between them. As Comtesse de Chartres she was at a social level which permitted them to meet on equal terms. Alouette had also decided that now she would no longer be making excursions to France. Future operations now being delegated to Colette, she would probably marry.

The return to the fleet from Portsmouth was an anti-climax after the chatter and presence of the girls for the trip home. The turnaround in Portsmouth had not been lengthy, a matter of topping up stores and water, with the chance for a brief meeting for Martin, with Jennifer and Lady Jane, before they were back at sea, returning to the boredom of the blockade once more. The bundle of documents and letters they carried for the fleet, the only obvious sign that they had ever left.

Chapter 7

Silver

"ANGEL'S CATCHING US from astern sir."

They had been back with the fleet for several weeks, currently at the most westerly point of their beat, the weary beating back and forth was a depressing business for everyone Martin thought, wondering what errand had brought the cutter out to catch them.

Martin turned and saw the fore and aft sails of the cutter Angelique sailing incredibly close to the wind, catching up, obviously with some urgent orders. He looked ahead, then astern once more. Lieutenant David Keats had remained in command of the cutter after playing his part in the action at Roscoff. Admiral Hardy had confirmed his appointment, and his rank as lieutenant. Now in command of his own ship he was called upon as messenger and liaison between the ships of the blockade fleet.

As he drew alongside Martin had the Vixen brought up to the wind to give Keats a chance to pass his messages. Keats called across, "The French have entered Spain. They promised the King he can have Portugal. The troops are sent to support the King and help with the annexation of Portugal. So war had been declared, and we are supporting the Portuguese."

Martin sent over a bag of letters and returns, and watched the Angelique drop astern and spin about to commence her long trip back to the fleet.

The long Atlantic swell lifted HMS Vixen high as she made her way west. In general the crew were pleased to get away from the boring grind of the blockade, charged with meeting the Santo António e São José, a Portuguese warship carrying a silver cargo from the Brazilian mines. They were approaching their rendezvous point to the north of the Azores.

"Sailing up and down in all sorts of weather, waiting for something to happen, can be extremely boring." Midshipman Neil Harmon said to his fellow Middy Athol Gibb.

Athol Gibb, from Arisaig in the west of Scotland, smiled grimly. "For a half-grown man, you have a strange idea of what life is all about. You have food enough, and a bed for the night, aye and good strong clothes to wear in the bad weather. There's little left for you to complain about, so you're bored. Perhaps if you spent a little more time on your books, you would not have time for boredom."

"Mr. Harman! Foremast top, if you please. Take the large telescope and don't fall asleep. Dropping off from that height could be painful." The voice of Lieutenant Cameron interrupted the discussion and galvanized Mr. Harmon into action. "Mr. Gibb, since you seem to have nothing to do at the moment perhaps you would join me in some calculations to establish our current position on the patrol line."

With a resigned sigh Athol Gibbs acknowledged the order, and went to check the log to begin the dead reckoning details for the approximate position of the ship. The noon sightings should confirm or condemn his reckoning. It did make it clear to him that it was not wise to hang about where the officer of the watch might notice him.

He bent to begin his calculations when a cry from the masthead announced that there was a sail in sight.

"Where away?" Cameron called.

"Off the Starboard bow, to the west, sir. Topsails of a big ship."

"Mr. Gibb! Inform the Captain. There is a sail in sight…"

"I am here Mr. Cameron. Is that Mr. Harmon aloft?"

"It is, sir."

"Mr. Harmon, can you see if it is a war ship?" Martin called.

They waited as Harmon watched. Waiting to catch the moment when both Vixen and the stranger were lifted up by the sea at the same time, allowing Harmon to gain a brief glimpse of the hull of the other vessel.

"She is a ship of the line, sir." He called, and there is another, no, two more sail showing now, and smoke over the water."

Martin turned to Lieutenant Brooks who had joined them on deck. "All hands, Mr. Brooks. Let us take a closer look. It sounds as if we may have made our rendezvous already."

"Aye, sir. All hands on deck to make sail."

There was a rush of feet across the deck as the hands leapt to their places, the rigging now alive with men removing the reefs allowing the sails to spread. The ship seemed to lift in response to the extra drive from the wind before heeling under the pressure of the wind.

Martin looked up and turned to the Master, Jared Watson, "Studding sails, perhaps?"

Jared Watson smiled, showing his several teeth. "Worth a try, sir. Worth a try!"

"Mr. Brooks?"

"Let them fly, bo'sun. Rig the studding sails."

"Aye, aye, sir."

"Send up the studding sails." He called and they felt the ship respond as every piece of canvas she could carry took her crashing through the Atlantic swell. The broadening wash spreading a great white smear on the steel blue waters tracing her progress.

The deck party hung on to the nearest handhold and the ship raced through the water toward whatever was happening between the ships on the horizon.

The lead ship was hull up now and it was clear she was involved in a running battle with the other two sails visible.

***

Santo António e São José was a sixty-four gun ship of the Portuguese Navy. She had been entrusted with the output of the gold and silver mines from the South American colonies. The two French frigates had attacked without warning, and it was only the quick thinking of the Captain Antonio Ramos which had allowed then to elude the French for so long. Now the battle had been opened, they were doing all they could to keep the dogs at bay.

The appearance of the frigate ahead had made the Admiral Campos seek his cabin where he thought he might pray for guidance. Captain Ramos smiled cynically. Rather he was there than on deck spreading panic among the men.

The guns all around the stern of his ship were firing at regular intervals, with little effect it seemed.

From forward there came a shout, "The frigate approaching is British."

Antonio Ramos was not an aristocrat. He was captain because he was good at what he did. He commanded the ship because there was no other in Rio capable. The former captain had visited the bordello once too often. He was found in the gutter stripped and robbed of everything, with his throat cut, and patterns drawn with a blade on his chest and stomach. Locals said he must have taken an native girl against her will."

Now Antonio Ramos commanded the ship. But they could not allow it to sail thus, so they appointed an aristocrat Admiral to sail with him to command the expedition.

He looked at the two Frenchmen still hanging back, nibbling at his stern, he wondered why they had not attempted to out sail him. Their ships were better sailors.

With his mind made up he decided. "Both broadsides load and prepare to run out on my order."

The men ran to do his bidding.

The querulous voice of the Admiral sounded in his ear, "What is this? I gave no order."

Ramos turned on the man. From his height five foot ten he looked up at Admiral Campos who loomed over him from his six foot, going-to-fat bulk.

"As captain I command this ship. And I fight it."

The Admiral looked spiteful. "Then I relieve you of command, Captain."

One of the French ships fired a random shot and it passed close to the two men on the deck.

The Admiral dropped to the deck. "Surrender!" He screamed. "Captain, surrender now!"

Ramos turned to his first Lieutenant. "Throw the coward into his cabin and lock the door."

Turning forward once more, he called, "Guns ready? Standby."

He turned to the sailing master. "Stop her as she lies."

The master called to the bo'sun. "Back the mainsail and cross the spanker boom."

The ship slowed swiftly and the two French frigates overtook her rapidly.

"All guns run out."

On both sided the gun-ports opened and the guns were run out. Both frigates were abreast of the Santo António.

"As you bear. Fire!" Ramos's voice was drowned in the roar of the broadsides. The ship shuddered with the shock of sixty nineteen pounder guns being fired at the same time. The effect on the two French ships was catastrophic, both ships had fired their own broadsides, but their lighter shot and their intent to intimidate the Portuguese ship and capture her went sadly awry. On both frigates, masts toppled. The Boniface to port lost her mainmast and also her mizzen, and suffered serious damage to her starboards guns. The men crowding the decks were strewn in a bloody mess beneath the raffle of sail and rope that fell with the masts. She stopped and dropped astern. The Caprice to starboard fared almost as badly. Her foremast teetered cut half through by a shot from the Santo Antonio. Like her compatriot her decks were a bloody mess, and she also lost way with several of her port broadside guns dismounted.

Santo António sailed on, having suffered damage from the French frigates without losing her rigging. The guns had survived but there several new gaps in the bulwarks, and she also had many casualties.

Captain Ramos had survived, as had the others in the small group around the wheel.

First Lieutenant Marco Santos had a splinter in his arm, but he ignored it as her came to report to his captain. "Sir, the Admiral stood in the path of a round shot, while on his way to his cabin. His body fell overboard with several others, and a large section of the starboard bulwarks."

"Get that wound seen to, Mr. Santos." Antonio Ramos shrugged over the fate of the Admiral but was more concerned with his men. "Also, Mr. Santos. Well done!"

The crew were still clearing the decks when HMS Vixen arrived. Martin ordered the doctor and the bo'sun's mate, plus a dozen men, to take the jollyboat and assist the damaged Portuguese ship. Then continued to the two French frigates. Both were afloat, the damage had been entirely to their gun-decks masts and rigging.

Martin ordered a gun across the bows of Boniface. The French colours were still flying on the stump of the mizzen mast. Her captain fired one gun then the flag dropped to the deck as she surrendered. The Portuguese ship had come about and took station keeping the Frenchman under her guns, while Vixen set off after the Caprice limping off toward the distant east. As Vixen caught her she swung round to defend herself, showing her un-smashed port side to the British frigate.

"Standby guns, port side broadside. Run out!" Brooks called. With her greater manoeuvrability, Vixen spun and crossed the stern of the French frigate.

Without her foremast the Frenchman was slow and she suffered the onslaught of the entire broadside from the British ship, the guns fired in turn as they crossed the stern of the Caprice. The ornate giltwork still surviving from her past role under the King of France was shattered and the windows smashed as the cannon shot ploughed their way the length of the ship.

The Tricolour was hauled down as the Vixen came about to repeat her attack with the other broadside.

The two ships made their way back to the other prize and the Santo António.

Martin was piped aboard the Portuguese ship as the two prizes were secured and prize crews allocated between the ships.

The losses for the French had been huge.

The two ships had both prepared to board their quarry, convinced that the plans they had agreed with the Admiral guaranteed the surrender of the Santo António. They had not anticipated the arrival of the British ship, but when they saw her they hoped to secured their prize before the Vixen closed the range.

The captain of the Boniface was bitter at the betrayal of the Portuguese Admiral. The silver was the real prize. He was quite open about the plan. The Admiral had requested that on capture of the silver ship they were to dispose of the crew, and destroy the ship. He had stressed the complete destruction of the Santo António and her crew, leaving no embarrassing witnesses. The Caprice was under the command of her First Lieutenant, the Captain having died in the engagement with the Vixen. Out of seven hundred men in the two French ships over two hundred had perished, and over one hundred injured, between the broadsides of the Portuguese and the second fight with the Vixen, Caprice alone had lost one hundred and sixty men, including her Captain.

The four ships made their way to Oporto. In his cabin on their arrival in the port, Martin read his instructions again. 'You are directed to escort the Santo António and the silver to the central treasury in Lisbon. Under no circumstances should this silver be allowed to fall into the hands of the French.'

The Captain, Antonio Ramos, was on his way over to the Vixen to confer with Martin, so he put the orders away in his desk and reluctantly donned his dress coat to greet his guest. They were seated in Martin's cabin when there was scurry of feet on the deck above. Then the alarm sounded from the Forte de São João Baptista da Foz, the fort guarding the harbour entrance.

Mr. Brooks knocked and reported that a French man-of-war had appeared off the harbour. It was making no effort to enter. The Fort at the north side of the harbour entrance had signalled that they had brought their guns to readiness.

Martin said, "What ship?"

"She is Redoutable, 70guns. I believe she was one of the ships that came from the America's with the two French frigates."

"Thank you, Mr. Brooks. Perhaps you should join us. Have a watch kept on the Frenchman. I have the feeling he will try to keep us here, waiting for reinforcements."

"Aye, aye, sir." Brooks was gone for a few moments then returned and took a place in the cabin with the other officers.

Captain Ramos raised an eyebrow. "This could be awkward!" He declared. "In effect, it shuts the door on us. How do we transport the cargo to Lisbon?"

Martin smiled. "Captain, at present we have a ship of the line outside the harbour. If we transferred the cargo to a frigate under the guns of the fort, she could wait her time and slip out of the harbour and outrun the Frenchman. However, I cannot escape the feeling that there will be a reception waiting in ambush at the mouth of the Tagus, ships that sailed to Lisbon direct. I fear we may need to carry the cargo overland."

"But that will require wagons and troops to escort them." Ramos suggested.

"True, but, though we may not find sufficient troops here, we could reinforce them with our own men." He turned to Lieutenant Andrew Charles who commanded the Marine detachment on Vixen. "Well, Andrew. Can it be done?"

The Marine scratched his chin, thinking. "Yes, of course, sir. But it would take most of our men. I was informed that the French General Junot has already sent an advance party of skirmishers into Spain, in support of the ultimatum to bar British ships from Portuguese ports. I think we risk losing Vixen if the reports can be trusted."

Martin listened to this news with some concern. Then to Captain Ramos, "Antonio, we must decide now if the silver is to go into the treasury in Lisbon, to be possibly lost to a French invasion force. Or if we should try to get it out of the area to await the time the people of Portugal can make use of it."

"Captain Forest-Bowers…Martin. I am only a Captain. My superior, the Admiral, was a traitor. This sort of decision should be for a senior member of Government. Sadly, I cannot even trust the Governor here. He was a friend of the Admiral. For all I know there are troops gathering at this time to steal the silver from my ship. This is why I am anchored out here in the open harbour, rather than alongside."

"Right, in that case we will get the Caprice repaired. We can replace any damaged guns from Boniface.. Can you find extra seamen to add to the prize crew to fight the ship?"

Brooks broke in at this point. "Sir, there are British seamen here in Oporto. There was a shipwreck just to the north, of the sloop HMS Raven Most of the crew made it to the shore. They were waiting passage back to England, perhaps……"

Martin interrupted him. "Right, Mr. Brooks. I want the prisoners transferred to the Boniface and the British seamen shipped on the Caprice and put to work getting her ready for sea. Off you go!"

"Yes, Sir!" Brooks left the cabin in a rush. He could be heard calling for the bo'sun as he clattered up the stair to the main deck.

***

The foremast of the Caprice was being replaced under the supervision of the carpenter, French prisoners straining on the ropes controlling the mast as it was raised and then lowered gradually controlled by large strops wrapped around the lower half of the spar.

The two French ships were anchored side by side to allow the transfer of equipment from one to the other with minimum effort. Three guns had been replaced and ammunition and powder transferred. It was three days after the meeting in the cabin. The Santo António was also busy, her crew repairing damage from her encounter with the frigates; the numbers increased by recruits from ashore. This had caused trouble with the Provincial Governor.

He was demanding that the silver cargo be placed in the hands of the authorities in Oporto. So far Ramos had fended him off. But the Governor of the fort, who was an ally, was worried that he might be replaced by a collaborator friend of the dead Admiral Campos. Also he was not too sure of the loyalty of his troops, who were all from the local area.

The morning of the seventh day in port there was still only the Redoutable offshore and as she beat upwind against the northerly wind, at a range of two miles, Vixen, Caprice and Santo António passed the fort at the harbour entrance. The French ship went about to cover the way south towards Lisbon.

The three ships turned north-west to take as much northing as they could.

The Frenchman went about once more to correct his error of judgement. His manoeuvering had lost him ground and against the frigates he would have had no chance of catching them. The Santo António however was an old ship. Not really built for speed, she was a compromise between a carrier and a warrior. Unfortunately, she was not that good at either function, and she struggled to keep up with the frigates.

As evening fell the Frenchman was getting close and Martin realised that it was time to do something about it.

He had placed Brooks in command of the prize. He signalled Caprice to close on the Vixen and, as the ships ran parallel, he called across to Brooks. "Go to port. Cross the bow of Redoutable and give her your broadside. Try to smash her bowsprit. I will cross the other way and try also. Load with chain. If you miss the bow, aim at her rigging and masts."

Brooks acknowledged and the Caprice put her helm up and ran down on the French ship.

The noise of the guns shattered the evening peace stopping for an instant the cry of the gulls.

The bow of the French ship splattered splinters across the fore deck area of the ship some of the rigging was destroyed though the bowsprit stood.

As Vixen started her run Martin heard the guns of Caprice as she fired on the big Frenchman. Guns on the French ship fired in response, but Martin was too preoccupied to give too much thought to the matter as he had his own battle to attend to. As he crossed the Frenchman's bows the guns of the port broadside fired as they bore. The bowsprit went in a smother of canvas from the jib-sails, to drop into the water tangling with anchor on the way. The ship slowed and swung, bringing her head round and guns round to bear on Vixen. Luckily, they were slow to react and the first of the reloaded guns of Vixen's broadside were already in action. The gunner, realising what had happened, had called his gunners to knock out the quoins which elevated the guns to fire into the rigging. The barrels dropped. The chain shot and langrage they had loaded smashed into the open gun-ports of the enemy ship with devastating results, and though several of the enemy guns fired and smashed into the British ship, many passed across the deck without hitting anything. The scrap metal and chain shot, ripped and tore at the hull of the French ship, causing damage injury to ship, but horrific injuries to the crew members it reached.

The frigate drew away from the dangerous zone under the enemy guns and, with guns reloaded, crossed the exposed stern, and despite the action of the chase guns, poured the entire broadside into her. The Caprice added her weight of shot to the task. Martin was not surprised that the effect of the thirty six 12 pounders and the two 24 pound carronades was to cause the ship to lose steering, when the rudder post was destroyed in the bombardment.

***

Martin's decision to abandon the action was a pragmatic one. Regardless of the steering problems the Redoutable suffered, she was still bristling with guns, and her crew outnumbered the combined crews of both frigates. In other circumstances this would not have stopped him, but there were other French ships about and the Santo António was vulnerable to attack. Despite the martial attitude of Captain Ramos, many of the crew were politically pro-Spain. As such they were not trustworthy. The presence of the frigates made the matter of trust academic.

He signalled Caprice to discontinue the action, and the two frigates left the French ship, helpless for the moment at least, to her own devices, while they returned to join their Portuguese compatriot still making progress northward to England and safety.

Chapter Eight

The Mission

THEY MET WITH the Brest blockade four days later. Some delay had occurred when the spanker boom on the Santo António broke during heavy weather on the way north. Captain Ramos said ruefully, "Sadly, when a ship is as old as this, things happen." The comment accompanied by a shrug said it all.

Admiral Hardy was surprised and concerned at the news Martin brought from Portugal.

"You say the French are over the border and are marching on Lisbon, under General Junot?"

Martin nodded. "The latest news we had was that the Spanish, with the co-operation of Prince John of Braganza, Regent of Portugal, were entering the country virtually unopposed.

"According to those I spoke to, including Captain Ramos, the people in general are very angry. The suggestion of Spanish rule is not acceptable. In the opinion of the Captain the people will rise against the invaders."

Hardy sat back in his chair. "I will add your report to mine and ask you to convey it to the Admiralty. You will continue to escort Captain Ramos, and the prize of course, to Portsmouth. There you can leave the prize, and recover your crew members. Though I believe it better you carry on with the silver ship to London. I would be happier to know the overland journey was a short as possible with that much silver."

Martin called on the Santo António and spoke with Ramos, before returning to Vixen. He explained the Admiral's feelings in the matter of the silver. Since it was destined to be lodged in the Bank of England, situated in London, the decision made sense.

So the three ships resumed their voyage, sailing onward from Ushant to Portsmouth where they left Caprice. With a full crew once more, HMS Vixen and Santo António completed their journey to the Thames.

The arrival and securing of the Santo António in St Katherine's dock was greeted by the Portuguese Ambassador and a company of Grenadier Guards with two huge wagons.

HMS Vixen was anchored in the tideway, while Martin was rowed ashore with Peters, his servant.

With Captain Ramos in tow, Martin had a carriage take them to the Admiralty, where he handed over the documents from Admiral Hardy along with his own reports.

The arrival of the two captains caused a stir in the reception area. It was not so surprising Martin thought. He was an Admiral's son. He remembered how he had been made to wait on his first visit as a lieutenant, until Nelson had walked in, that was.

The captains were ushered directly into the conference room and wine was produced while they waited the arrival of Admiral Bowers.

"My first visit here was a little different." Martin commented. He told Ramos of that occasion.

Antonio Ramos was beginning to understand who this man really was. *Friend of Admiral Nelson, adoptive son of Admiral Bowers, Baronet, and Post Captain and, perhaps thirty years old.* His musings were interrupted by the arrival of Admirals Bowers, and Cornwallis.

Charles Bowers, his still abundant but now grey, hair was tied back. Cornwallis wore a wig. Charles greeted Martin with great affection and Ramos noted that the reputedly impassive Cornwallis seemed more than polite, showing friendliness that seemed genuine.

The four men seated themselves around the table and discussed the reports sent by Hardy.

At the end of the discussion Cornwallis drew Captain Ramos to one side. "Captain, a word, please!" Bowers and Martin were gazing through the window discussing their family, now the official part of the meeting was over.

Admiral Cornwallis had been a friend of Nelson and was well respected by the men under his command who named him Billy Blue. He regarded Antonio Ramos keenly. "

"Sir, I have to inform you that your action in bringing the silver to this country has upset many influential people." He held his hand up to stop the Captain speaking. "I have no problem with your action which I regard as correct assessment of the situation and the right thing to do. We are all aware that the silver would have been lost to Portugal if it had been placed in the treasury in Lisbon. The Ambassador here has removed you from your command, and your ship had been detained until further notice." He stopped, noting the dismay on the Captains face.

"I understand you will be staying with Sir Martin. Please do not worry too much. Your crew will be accommodated. I expect to be in touch over the next few days, possibly with news and a suggestion." He patted the Portuguese Captain on the shoulder and turned to call the others to join him for lunch.

***

HMS Vixen moved down river to moor at Chatham. On the face of it the rigging was being checked and refurbished. All the small maintenance jobs that needed doing, were done, and a certain amount of shore time was managed for officers and crew alike. The business of the prize money for the frigate Caprice was speculated upon and, when it was established that the ship would benefit from it, a celebration was organised.

For Martin, the time spent with Jennifer and little Jane was a relief after the extended period of absence. Lady Isabella, wife of Lady Jane's brother, Giles, had now given birth to their first child, and seeing young Jane mothering the one-year-old William was a delight all the family shared.

Antonio Ramos thought he would feel out of things at Martin's home, but his worries were soon allayed by the reception he received from both Jennifer, and Lady Jane, who was a regular visitor. His bachelor status established, the ladies immediately set about finding suitable partners to make up the company, and keep the Captain entertained.

The Portuguese Ambassador was recalled to Lisbon, and the Charge d'affaires placed temporarily in charge. His first action was to release the Santo António from her place in the dock and allow her to be surveyed at Chatham. The alliance between Britain and Portugal had already been formalised by Parliament.

Unfortunately the ship was condemned by the dockyard though a considerable allowance was offered against her scrap value. In a gesture of goodwill the repaired and refitted prize Caprice was offered to replace the Santo António, suitably renamed Sao Paulo. The, now refitted, forty gun frigate was formally handed over to Captain Ramos, as the flagship of the Free-Portuguese Navy. His formal promotion to Commodore was almost an anti-climax. The ladies of the Forest-Bowers family would not let it go unremarked and a reception in his honour was given.

Captain Giles Masters, brother to Lady Jane, and close friend of Martin returned, looking ill, from his West Indies posting. He was placed firmly in the hands of the ladies. Their avowed purpose was to return him to full health in the shortest possible time. This process was interrupted by the party but threatened to be resumed as soon as it was over.

The entire garden in the square opposite the two houses of the Admiral and Martin was taken over with a marquee, for the occasion, and invitations, to what appeared to Martin to be the entire population of London and included the Royal family, were issued.

The orchestra from the Opera House was to provide the music, and an army of servants recruited to attend to the guests.

Thankfully the weather co-operated. The new Commodore was launched in style and to the delight of the female element the meeting between the new Commodore and the Comtesse de Chartres struck sparks immediately. Jennifer, seeing the two together, nodded thoughtfully. Martin was disappointed at the attitude of both Alouette and Antonio having hoped there could be an agreeable outcome from the meeting between his two friends.

He mentioned it to Jennifer, who smiled and said "Wait and see."

He wondered if he had missed something. Then shrugged in exasperation.

Martin was long past any embarrassment about his former association with Alouette. She had always been completely open with him about the convenience of the friendship that had grown between them. Neither regretted their intimacy. Both were happy with the deep firm friendship that now existed between them. If Jennifer ever suspected anything, it was never voiced. She was confident enough of Martin's love and had accepted the friendship, based on shared danger, without question.

Admiral Cornwallis was unmarried, and happily so. Hostesses made a point of arranging suitable ladies to partner him at soirees and events. Sadly for the ladies, he did he did not form an association with any of them. At the reception for the new Commodore he took Ramos to one side. "I will be ready with orders in three days' time. Sir Martin has been advised and will be joining us at the Admiralty. I suggest you make no plans for social events beyond the end of this month. So, sir, you have three weeks to make whatever arrangements you have to make. Congratulations on your promotion, Commodore." He shook Ramos by the hand and moved on to speak with some of the other guests.

Ramos sought out Martin and mentioned the Admiral's comments.

Martin smiled. "It's typical of the man. He does employ the personal touch rather than issuing orders. We meet to discuss our orders in three days. Enjoy yourself, Antonio, and, concerning the Comtesse, she will come round when she gets to know you better I am sure." He tapped the side of his nose reflectively his eyes searching the crowd. "Come, Antonio. There is the lady now. Let us see if we can smooth things a little." Without waiting he ploughed through the throng to the lady in question. She turned to the two men, relieved to get away from the man who was pestering her.

"Martin, how timely. And you, Antonio, what a coincidence. I was just thinking of you."

Startled, Antonio reacted. "And I was thinking of you," he said, as he bowed over Alouette's extended hand, kissing it, rather than brushing past it as many did.

Martin said, "We were looking for you to let you know what was happening." He lifted his arm and she slipped hers through his, before seeking and finding Antonio's on her other side. Together the three people slipped out of the crowd and into Martin's house, where they found a few moments peace in his study.

Alouette, as always, knew when to be direct. "Right, gentlemen. What is this all about?"

Martin said, "Excuse me, my dear. Antonio, I'll have to leave it to Antonio to tell you the news." Ignoring the dismayed look on Antonio's face, he slipped out of the room leaving them on their own.

Uncomfortably, Antonio sought for words to explain why he should be attempting to explain his future movements to someone who had displayed a complete lack of interest in him.

Alouette let him suffer for a few moments before rescuing him. "I have known Martin for many years. He has on several occasions saved my life, and I have saved his on at least two. I have the utmost confidence in his judgement, so I would suggest it would be in both our interests to be seated and forget, how can I put it, the frisson of friction we created upon our first meeting."

Astonished, Antonio studied the beautiful woman before him. Then he said quietly, "Comtesse, I apologi...."

Her fingers touched his lips. "Please, it is past. We meet now, this instant, for the first time. Do we not?" The small smile that accompanied these words took his breath away.

When the door finally opened Antonio ushered Alouette through the door, and, meeting Martin's eye, nodded slightly.

As they returned to the main party outside, Alouette whispered to Martin, "We are now friends. Do you feel better?"

Martin looked innocent, aggrieved, and happy in turn. "I'll tell Jennifer."

"I will tell her myself, if you don't mind!" She was smiling broadly at the time. It took the sting from her words, so he knew he was forgiven. He looked at Antonio. The man looked wary but there was a small smile on his face.

Alouette spotted Jennifer and made off to see her . Martin, smiling, said to Antonio, "What happened to you?"

Antonio shook himself. "I was struck dumb. When you left the room, I could not think of any words. I blurted out, 'I have to go away at the end of the month'.

She said, 'What are you trying to say to me?'

He went silent, thinking for a moment, "I believe that lady just proposed to me?"

"What did you say?" Martin was confused and intrigued.

Antonio continued, "I believe I said 'yes'. Because when I could not think of the words, she said 'Are you saying that we only have three weeks to make any arrangements between us?' I must have nodded.

She then said. 'Are we talking about betrothal and eventual marriage?' I do not know what made me say it, but I said 'yes'!"

Martin said with a smile, "That sounds about right. Tomorrow we must search for and find a ring to seal the betrothal. What do you say?"

His bemused colleague nodded, then grinned. He seemed to have snapped out of his trance. "Definitely, tomorrow we will go shopping."

When Martin got together with Jennifer later, she took his arm and held him close. Whispering, she said, "You rogue, you! You planned the whole thing."

Martin laughed briefly. "I started matters. But it was Alouette that finished them. Are you pleased?"

"You know I'm delighted. They are both such nice people. They deserve each other. Mother is happy too. She plans to announce matters officially in the Gazette this week."

The events following the party developed in a relaxed manner for the period of Martin's sojourn in England.

The Comtesse was becoming a regular guest in the Knightsbridge house. It had been where Antonio and Alouette first met, and the acceptance of their friendship had been greeted with pleasure by their friends. When they finally announced their future plans, it was already an open secret."

***

Three days after the party Martin and Antonio had presented themselves at the Admiralty and were quickly ushered into the presence of Admirals Cornwallis and Bowers.

Greetings over, Charles Bowers had then turned to Commodore Ramos. "What do you know about the gold shipment from Brazil?"

Antonio looked up in surprise. "Why do you ask sir?"

Cornwallis interceded. "Your Ambassador mentioned the possibility that the French might attempt to intercept the annual shipment. He did say that you would know from where it would be shipped. I understand they change the port of origin every year and that you are aware of the port for this year. Admiral Campos was the only other person who knew?"

Antonio nodded. "That is true, and the Admiral had no way to tell anyone else. He died the day I informed him. The arrangement was made at the time I collected the silver shipment. The Admiral was busy with a lady at the time and actually had to rush to catch the ship when I departed Salvador with the silver. His place on my ship was not anticipated.

"If you consider collecting the gold we would have to depart by the end of the....month." He grinned, "I did not think. Of course you wish me to collect the gold shipment. But my new ship will not be big enough?"

Charles Bowers said, "We thought perhaps two frigates might manage?"

Ramos considered for a few moments. Then, nodding slowly, "If we replaced the ballast, I think it is possible." He said slowly, "The silver is already here. In the past the treasure fleet was loaded with gold, silver and precious stones, and depended on a war fleet to protect it. In recent years the treasure has been split among different ships, protected by secrecy rather than brute force. The problem is that the value is still so huge, temptation drives people to betrayal."

Martin joined the conversation. "With the current French invasion, although it takes time for the news to travel, should we not worry about the gold actually getting to the port of departure wherever it may be? This is a time for the opportunist to step in, and with such a prize at stake?" He left the question in the air. All present realised the inference.

Cornwallis spoke. "We can only try! Commodore, I suggest the ships sail under the command of Sir Martin, and when you arrive at your destination, decide the action to take between you on the spot. We are not in a position to do more than guess at what you may encounter, therefore we have to depend on you to make the proper decisions at the time.

"We will trust you to act as you see fit. If that is agreeable, I suggest we make no reference outside these walls to anyone, including the Ambassador. We have no reason to doubt the acting gentleman, unfortunately that may not apply to any replacement the Portuguese government may appoint." He looked keenly at the two captains. "Are we agreed?"

Both responded immediately. "Yes, sir."

***

As they left the Admiralty Martin said to Antonio, "I wish to go to Chatham and have the ballast cleared and restowed on Vixen. It will allow the carpenter to examine the hull and it can be installed in such a manner so as to make it easier to be replaced, if and when needed."

"My crew from Santo António are travelling to Portsmouth in two days. My first lieutenant Santos is already there. I will go and arrange for the ballast in the Sao Paulo to be removed and stowed as you suggest."

"We can go and join Lady Jane at Eastney while you make your arrangements, perhaps the Comtesse can join us for a few days. But first, my friend, have you done the shopping we planned at the party?"

The puzzled look on Antonio's face made Martin laugh. "Do you forget? You asked a lady to marry you three days ago, is your memory so short?"

Antonio smiled and shook his head. "How could I forget such a thing? But I am afraid you are behind me my friend."

From the pocket of his uniform jacket, he produced a ring box, not new but old the velvet cover worn.

Antonio passed it to Martin, gesturing for him to open it.

Curiously, Martin lifted the lid. He gasped. The ring was an emerald surrounded by rubies. Not huge, but beautifully designed in a gold setting, It was obviously old.

Antonio said, "Great Grandmother passed it down to Grandmother. She left it in turn to my mother, who left it me. I decided that it was the right thing for this occasion. If Alouette would rather have a different style ring, I will of course obtain one. Do you think she will like it?"

Martin smiled having recovered from his surprise at the sight of the ring. Placing his hand on Antonio's shoulder, he said with feeling, "I am certain Alouette will be delighted with such a beautiful personal ring."

"Then let us go and find out if what you say is true." Antonio laughed and boarded the carriage that waited them.

***

The activities over the next two days covered the visit to Chatham by Martin and arrangements for Jennifer and Alouette to visit Eastney. This was made simpler by the presence of Jane in London. The message dispatched to Eastney by mail coach ensured that the house was ready for the reception of the family, and guests.

At the house while the ladies settled themselves, Martin and Antonio went to the docks to check on the Sao Paulo.

Now repaired completely, and having been surveyed whilst being repaired, the ballast was still stacked on the dock. The final touches to the new copper sheathing still being applied. The arrangements for the parcelling of the ballast when it was reloaded were agreed with the dock master, and confirmed with Lieutenant Santos, who was arranging for the accommodation of the crew until the ship was returned to the water.

During the next few days Martin was able to spend some time with Alouette alone. She confided that Mr.

Smith had offered to defer handing over completely until the departure of Antonio on his next voyage. The matter of the wedding had of necessity been put off until the conclusion of the cruise which would commence at the end of the month. Martin noticed that the emerald ring was happily worn, and exhibited, attesting to the betrothal.

***

Sadly, the time passed all too quickly. The re-launch of the Sao Paulo with her parcelled ballast signalled the approach of the day of departure.

HMS Vixen sailed round to Portsmouth for final victualing, and to join with Sao Paulo for their joint departure.

Admiral Charles Bowers saw them off standing with the three ladies. His final action was to place a package on Martin's hands. "From Cornwallis!" He said quietly. "In the event of conflict, this is a written order."

The small group stood on the quay watching the two boats being pulled out to the two frigates flying the ensigns of Britain and Portugal. Both ships were under way while the small boats were still rising from the water.

The small party ashore stood there until the frigates cleared the harbour, only then mounting their carriage to return to Eastney.

Chapter eight

South

THE FRIGATES MADE way down channel. Without anything being said, Martin noticed that the sailing masters of both ships were competing to get the utmost out of what were two swift ships. The result was felt in slight adjustments to the ballast, and improved familiarity with the sails, including the fine tuning so important in the handling of warships.

Having called upon the Brest blockade off Ushant with the latest news and orders, the two frigates embarked on the long haul south and west to the mainland of South America.

At this stage Antonio Ramos, handed Martin a chart with their destination marked.

"The gold caravan should be in Caravelas, by the time we arrive.

The two captains sat down together and marked rendezvous points on the chart in the event that they were separated during the long voyage south. They expected to take up to five weeks to reach their destination.

Antonio mentioned, "Delays could be encountered in the doldrums, or not! The winds in the southern part of the Atlantic range from strong and contrary, to nothing in the doldrums. The current winds are fair and we could expect help from the trade winds further south. Once past the doldrums, its pot luck I'm afraid."

"How about pirates?" Martin asked.

Antonio laughed. "Your guess is as good as mine. The worst I have ever encountered was in a barque. Luckily he had the legs of my ship, otherwise it would have been the yardarm for him. He did not lack courage. He just decided discretion was his best option and sailed out of trouble."

***

The two ships made good time until they reached the doldrums. There the winds dropped and became fitful, before finally, disappearing completely.

By agreement the first two days were spent checking and renewing worn ropes and repairing sails. The third day was given to allowing the boats to be launched and races rowed between the two ships. The make-and-mend period ended. The fourth day both ships went back to work. The longboats started to pull the ships to the south, toward the area where they could expect a renewal of the winds. It was on the third day that the Manaus hove into view.

The call from the masthead warned Martin that there was an object on the horizon. As the day progressed it became evident that it was a wrecked ship. Both frigates sent a boat party to investigate.

The boat under the command of Lieutenant Brooks came alongside the wrecked ship as Lieutenant Santos with the boat from the Sao Paulo reached the other side.

Santos called out to Brooks. "It is the Manaus, she was to carry the silver that we carried. She did not arrive and we were instructed to bring the silver instead."

Brooks climbed aboard. The starboard bulwark was four feet clear of the water, not difficult to climb, but the wood was slimy to touch as the wreck had been adrift for a long time. The stump of the foremast was festooned with weed and there was the smell of rotting seaweed in the air. From the visible damage it was evident that the ship had been involved in a gun battle. Lieutenant Santos joined him. "She has been in the Sargasso sea, I think, after the battle."

"I agree." Brooks said, "Let us see if there is anything inside." He stepped carefully over to the stair down to the door in the low sterncastle. The door was jammed shut, but it gave way to the assault of musket butts. The Captain's cabin was a mess. The contents largely covered in green mould. The skeleton in the chair, indicated that someone had survived the battle, though he also had died. In the drawer of the desk that had been anchored to the deck, was the ship's log, It was damp and discoloured, but the drawer had prevented it from falling to bits, like most of the other paper in the room. Santos opened the book carefully. The last entry was a year ago. The writing—scrawled and blotted—was a farewell to family.

Santos looked no further, and he turned to Brooks, "This I must give to my captain. The captain of the Manaus was his friend. It seems that she was left to sink by whoever attacked her. I would guess that she drifted into the Sargasso, and that is one of the reasons she is still afloat."

Brooks looked at Santos curiously. He had heard of the Sargasso Sea, but not too much. "Why should that help keep the ship afloat?" He asked.

Santos smiled. "The Sargasso is weed. Masses of floating weed spread over a large area of the ocean. It has the effect of calming the rough sea. When a storm lifts the water into high-breaking waves that causes trouble for ships elsewhere, in the Sargasso, the weed has a calming effect. It gets broken up into patches surely, but the overall effect is to stop the waves breaking over a large area of water. It has been observed, and it has given rise to the stories of a pirate haven in the centre where ships have drifted and are now gathered into a township of survivors, who prey on passing ships." Once more he smiled. "The story belongs I fear with those other stories of ghosts, and ghouls, and sea monsters that eat ships." He tapped the side of his head. "Where a story is told there will always be believers!"

***

Two more days of slow progress was followed by the first flirt of wind. After discussing the matter with Antonio, both decided that the boat crews towing the ships be worked during daylight hours only and the pulling be shared throughout the crew, limited to two hours only.

***

Antonio turned back to the log book. "This will probably tell us of the fate that befell the Manaus, and of Captain Carlos Diaz."

Reading the log book, he and Martin realised that the fate of the Manaus had been decided by an attack that took the crew by surprise. It had come after nightfall with the crew exhausted from towing the two-deck ship throughout the day. Attacked by four small craft each armed with 3 x 18pound carronade guns. All were propelled by sweeps and were highly manoeuvrable. They attacked without warning, and the guns of the Manaus could not depress enough to cause the attackers damage. All the attacking craft were loaded with men and they swept through the ship killing everyone they found. The survivor had been Lieutenant Pietro Diego, second officer who had been knocked unconscious and tumbled over the stern rail. He fell onto the stern gallery and lay there for several hours before he awoke to find himself the sole survivor of the crew. Though wounded, he managed to crawl into the captain's cabin through the stern window. He was able to get some food from the steward's store, missed by the pirates. Finding the ship's log on the floor of the cabin, he wrote entries into the log detailing his own experience and the story of the attack as he saw it. He also mentioned that the attackers must have come from a base well out to sea, perhaps a bigger ship of some sort. The boats were all man-powered. He had the impression they were of shallow draught.

The weed was gathering around the shattered hull and this apparently triggered the conjecture that the raid could have been made by people from the legendary colony of lost ships, supposedly in the depths of the Sargasso Sea.

***

The discovery of the wrecked ship caused both Captains to launch guard boats. For the period of the dark of the night, the guard boats lay off, and listened for the sound of oars, or anything else that may be a threat.

It was a relief when the wind returned.

In the log book of the Manaus it was clear that she was expected to be carrying silver. Apparently the change of plan had not been anticipated. The Santo Antonio had been given the cargo instead. The French attempt to annex the cargo had been a private enterprise agreement between the Admiral and the French, and this was one of the reasons for the Admiral's belated appearance on the quay to join the ship for the voyage.

Following directions from Antonio, the secret section of deck in the Captain's cabin of Manaus was located and the ship's strongbox recovered.

Despite the fact that the ship was Portuguese, Antonio invited Martin to be with him when the box was opened.

Having no idea what may have been placed in the box, Martin was intrigued and curious as the carpenter chiselled the lock open. When the carpenter left them Antonio raised the lid, exposing the contents to view.

The first thing Martin noticed was an ingot of gold. It was just there, the stamp of the Portuguese Royal Treasury was evident through the accumulated dust that still clung to the otherwise dried-out contents.

Antonio lifted the heavy metal brick from the box to reveal an ornamental box made of what looked like ebony, black wood at least. There was a lump in the middle of the lid. When Antonio lifted the box out, his thumb rubbed the lump to reveal a facet that flashed green in the sunlight that lit the cabin. He wiped the box with a piece of cloth and the stone set in the box lid took fire. The box itself was beautifully decorated with inlays of nacre and other gemstones. Opened, it revealed an array of jewellery that sparkled in the sunlight. Martin gasped! It was obviously an extremely valuable collection.

The oilskin-bound package at the bottom of the box showed the imprint of the box, indicating that it had been kept in that state for a long time.

As Antonio took the package of papers from the box he nodded at the jewel box and commented. "That, I believe, is a relic of Carlos's time in Macau, China.

Antonio looked thoughtful and scratched his chin. He lifted the oilskin wrapped packet, and carried it over to his desk.

Seated, he carefully opened the seal on the packet and exposed the papers within. On top was an envelope which contained Carlos's Will. Antonio put it to one side and checked through the rest of the documents. Martin, sitting on the other side of the desk, waited patiently, passing the time drinking his wine and relaxing.

Eventually Antonio opened the envelope and examined the Will document. Having read it he placed the document on the desk and leaned back.

Martin poured a fresh glass of wine for his friend. Antonio picked it up and absently drank it. Placing the glass back on the desk he said, "Martin, do you think I am a trustworthy person?"

Martin smiled. "Probably! Why do you ask?"

"This is a Will created by my friend Carlos Diaz. He has left his entire estate to me, entrusting me to look after his sister who is currently in Salvador. It is where Carlos had his home. I have stayed many times there when I have been in Brazil."

"Do you know the lady in question?"

"No, not really. I met her when she was a small girl. She was bright and lively, fun to be with. I think it will be four years since I saw her last. Would you believe I was known as Uncle Antonio when I visited his home? Maria is more like a daughter than a sister. She is, was, twenty-five years younger than Carlos. She must be fifteen years old now. I believe in Carlos's absence she stays with her grandparents.

"Senor Diaz, his father, had married a second time to Mariette Borgas, an old colonial family. That was after Carlos's mother was killed in an Indian raid on their plantation. Maria's mother and their father died thereafter, during the war against Paraguay in '02.

Martin thought for a moment. "Will you bring her to England?"

"I do not know. I will think about it on the way south. I have the idea that my friend expected me to take her into my home, until she has reached the age to inherit. I will then pass her father's legacy to her. By naming me, he saved his fortune falling into the hands of the Borgas family, as Maria is too young to inherit.

For some reason Carlos did not entirely trust the family." He shrugged, "Onwards to Brazil, I suppose. There, all will be resolved."

***

With the return of the breeze the ships hauled in their boats, and with all sail set they headed south to the coast of Brazil and the port/city of Salvador. Both captains had agreed that the sooner that Antonio's ward was retrieved from her grandparents the better.

The trade winds kept the crews busy handling sails. They were able to make good progress on the stretch down the coastline of Brazil.

Five days later the two frigates anchored in Baia de Todos os Santos (All Saints Bay). Salvador had once been the capital of Brazil though it was no longer the city it once was. The past 55 years had seen a slump in growth since the capital was removed to Rio de Janairo in 1763 and the once rich city had settled into its role as a backwater. The officials greeting the ships reflected this in their casual attitude.

At the request of the Commodore, Martin accompanied him in the carriage to a secluded quarter of the city, where the home of the Borgas family was to be found.

The carriage drew up in front of the cream coloured, colonial style house, the covered porch framed by a shower of bougainvillea, in red and blue.

Their arrival was greeted by whirlwind of lilac and white that rushed out and embraced Martin, who had descended first while Antonio collected the assortment of things he had brought with him.

The astonished Martin laughed as he felt the soft arms round his neck and the breath of the pretty girl on his face.

"Pardon me?" He said in halting Portuguese.

The young woman fell back in confusion. "Oh my! Senor! My apologies, I believed that you were my Uncle Antonio." She stood back and Martin, smiling, said, "No apologies needed, Maria. The pleasure was all mine." He swept a deep bow. "Captain Sir Martin Forest-Bowers, British Royal Navy, at your service."

The young woman curtseyed in response. "Maria Diaz." Her voice was controlled and musical. The giggle was nearly concealed.

Antonio had meanwhile descended from the carriage bedecked with parcels and his voice interrupted the dialogue between the two. "You cannot be little Maria?"

She turned to her adoptive uncle, and spun around before him. "I have, as you may observe, Uncle Antonio, grown up!" Then she flung her arms around him disregarding the packages flying in all directions as he lifted and swung her round with a joyful shout of greeting. "Where is little 'Mophead'? She has gone. Who is this woman who has taken her place?"

"She has apparently forgotten her manners!" The icy voice from the doorway had the effect of a bucket of cold water on the happy reunion between the two.

Martin turned and looked at the figure in the shadow of the portico. Tall and slender, the woman, he knew, had to be quite old, but her back was ramrod straight; her features retained the beauty of her younger years. Senora Gabrielle Borgas was an imposing figure. Her manner expected acknowledgement in kind and it was a chastened party who entered the house at her invitation.

The tone of the greeting was the tone of the meeting.

Antonio explained about the circumstances of the death of Carlos and produced the will which in effect transferred the guardianship of Maria to Antonio, provided Maria agreed, and the disposition of the properties owned by Carlos which would eventually revert to Maria.

The Senora looked at the two men with her icy blue eyes. "This is impossible! Maria will remain here under my care. I have arranged a betrothal with a suitable young man. Her life is here and here she will stay.

Martin saw that Antonio was rather stunned at the attitude of the Senora. He said diplomatically, "Perhaps we should hear what Maria has to say on the matter?"

"Rubbish! She is a child. I speak for her as her grandmother."

Martin turned to Maria. "Do you wish to accept the guardianship of the Commodore?"

Maria looked at Martin, then at Antonio, and finally at her grandmother. "Betrothal? When were you going to inform me?"

For the first time the Senora looked uncomfortable. "I was going to tell you at the right time. These things are best dealt with over time and with careful selection and due respect to dowry and suitability."

"And who is selected for me, may I ask?" Maria's voice had become as icy as her grandmother's.

Gabrielle Borgas lifted her head defiantly. "Count Arturo de Campo. A suitable wealthy man who's….."

Maria did not allow her to finish. "That stupid posturing idiot! His whoring and gambling have made him the talk of Salvador. What title he holds is worthless. As is his inheritance that he has dissipated. He had the charm of slug. How dare you consider that I would ever agree to marry such an excuse for a man!"

"As my ward you will do as I say. You have no say in the matter. Go to your room, child. I will deal with you later."

Antonio stood up at that point. "Maria, have the maid pack your things. I will send for them. Your brother's house has been prepared for me and I have the services of a suitable duenna to look after you, until the legal aspects of this are settled." He turned to Senora Borgas. "Madam, I am disappointed in you. While I could understand a grandmother's wish to keep grandchildren close, your manner and attitude have convinced me that there is a mercenary aspect to this situation that I find distasteful. I suggest you contact the Count and advise him that any contracts entered into between you and him, are hereby cancelled. In the terms of the Will of the legal guardian of Maria, I have been the guardian of the young lady for the past fourteen months. Please submit your account for the care and accommodation of my ward to my lawyers. They will see that it is attended to. If Maria wishes to contact you she may. But it would be in your interest to allow her to contact you, rather than the other way round."

Martin listened to Antonio with respect. He had not been confident in the face of Senora Borgas. He rose to his feet. "Miss Diaz?"

She took his arm, then turned to her grandmother. "I had no idea,." she said. She tugged Martin's arm, to leave the room. Martin saw she was on the verge of tears, and made haste to get her out of the house while she was still in control.

The maid who gave her the hat and parasol, whispered, "Good luck, miss."

Antonio joined them in the carriage. "Thank you, Martin. Are you all right, Maria? I did not expect that to happen."

"Oh, Uncle Antonio. Nor did I. She has always been distant, but I have never been spoken to like that before."

"Who is this Count fellow?" Martin asked.

"He is all I said about him and more," Maria answered. "He is whispered to be a member of the raiders who always seem to know which ships are carrying the best cargoes. That may be just his enemies' talk. We have never actually met, though at a ball I saw him. He was disgusting!" She said no more.

Antonio said, "I presume you have no objection to becoming my ward. Mind you, I have not been able to discuss this with my fiancée?"

Martin smiled. "I am sure Alouette will be happy for you both.

Maria looked at both men wide-eyed. The banter between them, their ease in each other's company and in her presence, was refreshing after the stilted formality of the Borgas house and elsewhere in the community. "Uncle Antonio, please. What does all this mean?"

Antonio looked at her sadly. "It means, my dear. that your brother was killed by pirates when his ship was ambushed in the doldrums a week north of here. In his will he asked me to become your guardian and left all his property to me, I presume, to pass on to you when you come of age. It seemed he did not trust the Borgas family to ensure that you received your due from his estate. How do you feel about all this?"

Maria looked at the man who had been her brother's friend, a man known only from short visits in the past. Her recollection of him was of a smiling person who played with her, however, and always brought her a present when he visited. She did not hesitate. "We accepted that my father was dead, when he did not return when he was expected.

I am happy to accept your guardianship, Uncle Antonio. I would leave this unhappy place without regret. Please let us visit the lawyers and make my parting from this stifling city as soon as possible."

Chapter nine

Eldorado?

THE TWO FRIGATES sailed in company south, to the small port town of Caravelas within the estuary of the Rio Caravelas.

The arrival allowed Maria and her duenna to spend time ashore, a situation welcomed by the duenna who was slow to acquire her sea legs. Once ensconced in the hotel, Maria was taken in by the daughter of the Viceroy who was visiting relatives in the area.

The Commodore and Martin were able to concentrate on the task at hand. The treasury agent, Senor Alfredo Lopez, was helpful and hopeful, "Gentlemen, it is not in my power to give you what has not yet arrived. The gold shipments are en-route but there will be delays. Possibly long delays if the rains come while they are passing through the forest. I have received the message that the gold from Minas Pardos and Patios have passed Nanuque and reached Minas Novas. That was still 200 kilometres away. They set out from there seven days ago. They are still a week maybe ten days away." He shrugged, "This is Brazil, gentlemen. It is not an easy country."

"Are there any troops here that can assist the convoy to get here sooner? I am troubled by the thought that the pirates that sank the Manaus will attempt to raid the convoy before it reaches the coast. Has any raid like this been attempted before?"

The agent's smile vanished. In a dull voice he said, "Every year we lose gold. I decide what we ship from here, only me. I had to tell Admiral Campos, and of course yourself and Captain Diaz. No others, I swear."

Martin looked at the man keenly. "No others, Senor Lopez? Is that what you are saying?"

Lopez nodded uneasily. "No others!" He confirmed.

"Does your wife know?" Martin persisted.

"Of course she does. I trust her implicitly."

"With your life, Senor?" Martin refused to let it go.

Antonio looked at him curiously, wondering at his interrogation of the agent. He said nothing, waiting to see what the agent would say.

"How about your wife's friends? Her hairdresser, the ladies she socialises with, are they trustworthy too?"

The agent was worried now, confirming Martin's suspicions that the knowledge of important events would maintain a social status in this small town at the top level.

To Martin's eye, the agent was not as confident as he had first maintained. "Maps!" He snapped.

The Agent jerked as if struck. Then he hurried to a cabinet and produced maps of the area.

On the big map of the area Martin jabbed a finger at the town of Mucuri 50 kilometres south on the coast from their current location. "This river, can it be navigated by boat?"

Lopez looked. "Yes, it can. It is used by fishermen, and canoes come down from the very head of the Rio Mucuri."

Martin looked at Antonio. "Very good, Senor Lopez. I see that you have done all you can to ensure the security of the gold. I will send a party to meet the convoy." Antonio bowed briefly and turned to leave.

The agent saw them to the door. "About a week, Commodore, maybe ten days."

As they walked down the street to the hotel where Maria and her maid awaited them, Martin said, "I will take my ship to Mucuri and we will make all speed upriver to intercept the convoy. If you send a party to meet the convoy from here, we can possibly scotch any plan to steal the gold, and even perhaps catch the men who killed your friend."

Antonio agreed. "Lieutenant Santos is trustworthy and he can lead my men by the road. There are horses in the barracks, though I fear your party will reach them by river first."

The party was selected to take to the boats and intercept the gold convoy, using the longboat, and the jollyboat.

***

As was reported, the river Mucuri was navigable. At first there was breeze which allowed them to sail for four days up the winding waters. But from there on it was hard work, as the trees closed in stifling what wind there was. They came upon the boats six days from the river mouth. Warned by a musket shot, they approached a bend in the river cautiously, Martin sent his scouts ashore to locate the source of the shot.

They reported back two hours later. The tall Scotsman, MacLean, led the scouts. His clipped accents when he reported reminded Martin of his excursion in

France, just a few months back, another time, another world.

"Ten boats, three men all armed, but they have doxies with them, 'Tis a picnic they are having. Laughing and shouting and spending money they don't have. I heard one, an Irisher I think, saying the gold was on its way. Most of the boats are there for cargo, but I guess there will be about eighteen men after the gold with a bunch of muleteers to drive the mules carrying it. This sort of thing seems to be a regular game they play in places like this. Mostly its 'turn a blind eye'. But this lot are plain greedy, there are enough bottoms for three tons at least to my way of thinking."

Martin scratched absently at an insect bite as he pondered the matter. "What do you think, MacLean?"

Without hesitation MacLean said, "Take them away, along with the girls. With a bit of luck the men with the gold will think the lads lost their nerve and buggered off with their women."

"Mr. Gibb, take a party, and capture the three men and their women. Bring them here as quietly as possible."

Gibb, already growing out of his uniform, sweaty and dishevelled from the journey upriver, was taller now, more assured, popular with the men and learning fast.

Turning to Maclean he said, "Gather a party together and we'll go hunting."

"Aye, aye, sir." Maclean walked off, signalling to selected men.

Martin sat back against the transom, uncomfortable unwashed, but pleased that they were not faced with wading through the jungle.

The dash down to Mucuri had been assisted by the Brazil current that paralleling the coast southward. The sail upriver had been difficult because of the shoals they encountered and the dangers from the underwater life in the river. The caimans, floating like logs in the warmed top layer of the water, were huge. They had seen one on their travels take a calf from the bank of the river. There were snakes, and he had seen what he thought to be the anaconda. It was big and seen only in parts, the visible sections rising out of the water in a series of semi-loops. He sometimes thought, as he slapped another mosquito to oblivion, this place was selected to get rid of every sort of nasty, poisoning, biting, tearing sort of creature on God's earth. Every year more and more people were coming to this country. As they spread out the animals would leave or be hunted.

He began to think he did not really care.

The six prisoners were placed under guard.

***

The party lay in wait for a further two days before the scouts reported the approach of the mule train. With his men Martin set up an ambush placing the men where their musket fire would not kill the wrong people. The small cannon normally mounted on the deck rail was set up on a mount produced by the carpenter, and loaded with pistol balls for the best effect.

When the ambush was sprung, the muleteers froze on the spot. The armed men fired at the escorts and on three occasions tackled them with their cutlasses. The hectic fight lasted ten minutes and felt to Martin like ten hours.

Finally, they gathered the survivors of the raiders and the muleteers and downloaded the gold from the mules, placing the packs into the boats. This was not the entire shipment. It seemed this was the annual skim, which was normally spirited away every other year.

With the surviving raiders added to the other six prisoners under guard, they set off down the river. The muleteers were told to return home with their mules.

The descent of the river was faster than the ascent. Just two days after the ambush the triumphant party returned to their ship. The prisoners went to the local jail, though Martin doubted whether they would remain locked up for long. As soon as the ship was out of sight, he guessed, they would be released.

For Antonio's men there was a rather more difficult task. His men had to traverse the terrible road to the interior. While it was not the rainy season, the dust and ruts made the road a challenge to those seamen who still suffered from seasickness. The wagon and mules could make progress through the dust and ruts but there was little comfort to be felt in these conditions.

The warning given of the approach of the main convoy was sufficient to allow for an ambush to be set.

The ensuing firefight was won before the pirates realised that there was anyone capable of opposing them. The soldiers of the original escort had been ruthlessly slaughtered, despite the agreement reached in advance between the officer in charge, and the pirate captain who had just used it to discover the details of departure and route. The pirate ambush had been devastating and effective.

Lieutenant Santos and his men had managed to lay their ambush before the track divided between the road north to Alcobaca and Caravelas.

The survivors of the ambush had been dumped in the wagon and transported with the gold to the treasury in Caravelas.

Their return was greeted with mixed reaction in the port. Martin had already returned. The gold his party had recovered been loaded aboard HMS Vixen. He discharged the ballast overboard during the night and replaced it with the gold shipment. He had no illusions about the honesty of the local population. During the voyage north the ballast was trimmed to balance the ship properly once more.

In Caravelas, the prisoners taken by Lieutenant Santos were placed aboard the Sao Paulo, in view of Antonio's own misgivings about the local population.

Martin arrived the day Santos returned so he and Antonio conducted their investigations together, interviewing the prisoners individually, and transferring them to Martin's ship when they had extracted as much as they could from each of them.

The pirate leader, Captain Maranz had been wounded in the ambush. He had maintained a close mouth for the entire journey back to Caravelas. Antonio noted his dismay when the prisoners were placed on the ship, rather than in the town jail. When the time came to interrogate him he was transferred to the British frigate, where it was made clear to him that he would be subject to British justice. Despite his protests and several applications from the civil authorities, he was held on the ship.

His arrogant attitude had been based on the expectation of help from friends on shore. before he realised that they would not be dealing with him, he had been heard to boast of the taking of the Manaus. When questioned he did not deny it. "I thought the strategy was good, I knew that if any escaped, the raid would be blamed on the people of the Sargasso Sea."

Antonio said quietly, "Do you know these people you speak of?"

"Of course not. That's an old wives' tale. There are no such people!" Captain Maranz spat the words out contemptuously.

On the Vixen was a carpenter's mate named Furby. Jacob Furby was somewhere between fifty and ninety, perhaps some stop between, a little knurled, gnome-like man with hands that could carve wood into shapes of beauty. Having had a chat with his Captain before the arrival of Maranz in Vixen, he was ready to do his bit in the interrogation.

The second interview with Maranz was on the subject of local officials in his pay. The lack of co-operation on this subject was disappointing, until Furby walked into the room and spied the pirate. "I know him, Captain. We picked up several of the people who escaped after he had attacked their ships. They drifted into the weed and we picked 'em up. Some have joined the colony. Other took their chances with their boats. This one will be welcome in Dorado." He turned to Martin. "We calls it that, because it were the treasure we found when we were shipwrecked and adrift in '90. There were women aboard, going to Jamaica in bondage. We brought the place to life when we arrived. The one thing we are always short of was meat. This one is quite well fed." He pinched Marantz on the arm. "I reckon they'll harvest him. We have a good surgeon. We can probably make him last a month at least!"

"He seems to think the stories about the colony in the Sargasso weed is rubbish, an old wives' tale no less. I suppose he'll think again when he gets there."

Maranz was getting agitated. Could it be true that there was a collection of wrecks in the weed? 'Dorado' that meant gold. Ships carried gold. There could be treasure there. He thought the horrible little man sounded convincing and he looked odd enough. He looked at the grimacing face and shuddered. He was talking of cannibalism.

"I can help you find the people who informed us about the gold," he suggested. "But only if you promise not to send me to the Sargasso with this gargoyle." He said spitefully.

Furby smacked Maranz on the cheek. "We'll enjoy a bit of fresh meat." He said and walked out of the cabin.

Watching, Martin studied Maranz as Furby walked out. He looked terrified!

He looked at Antonio and nodded then turned to Maranz and said, "It's now up to the Portuguese. I am here as a guest. There is little I can do." He walked out after Furby. He left Antonio with the sweating Maranz.

It was not surprising to Martin that Maranz elected to take Antonio's proposition, rather than chance the hazards of being handed to Furby for an uncertain future as a prospective main course in the Sargasso.

There was little they could do about the enemy in the Brazilian treasury. The name of Don Carlos Reza was duly noted and entered in the log of the Sao Paulo.

When they arrived in England his infamy would be recorded and a warrant issued.

Maria was discovering the joy of freedom from the oppressive control of the Borgas family. She accepted the constraints of life aboard ship and insisted on learning the routine and tasks undertaken by the crew. All the officers and midshipmen on both frigates were enchanted by her ready wit and her acceptance of the rigours of life at sea.

Chapter ten

Homeward bound

HER ADOPTION OF Martin as ex-officio uncle meant that there was a place for her on Vixen whenever she felt like a change. It gave her a chance to practice her English and gave Neil Harmon and Percy Gibb a chance to join the list of admiring escorts. Weather permitting, she happily passed from ship to ship, and in the doldrums she signalled the start of the races rowed between the two ships.

As they left the doldrums and picked up the NE trade winds, the weather became changeable and the ships now made serious progress homeward. Maria was forced to stay on the Sao Paulo. The need for speed and the wind that drove them conspired to separate the two ships, though they did not lose contact.

As the days past they neared the channel. The weather was blustery with patches of sunshine between the ragged clouds. The frantic pace slowed a little, but the urgency to complete their mission allowed for no hesitation now. The enforced hiatus of the doldrums were a memory. The relentless progression of sail trimming and changing, the hammering of the waves, sometimes storm driven, and the clank of the pumps heard more often as well as the working of the ship's timbers.

The first sighting of a ship was as they were passing between the Canary Islands and Madeira. Fishing boats from Funchal were hailed and were happy to sell their catch to the two ships that approached them. The islands had not been troubled by the French and there was little real news. The trade between Lisbon and Madeira had been haphazard since the war in Europe, though there was news that the British had landed an army in Portugal in August, and achieved two victories over the French. Wellesley was named as the commander of the army. There was little other real information of what was happening.

The race home was resumed after a short conference between Martin and Antonio. They agreed that if the information was correct, the Sao Paulo would stand off while Vixen called in at Lisbon to check on what was happening. Given contacts by the Commodore, Martin would check on the status of the rule in the capital city, and if possible he would confer with the British commander.

***

Rear-Admiral Porter was a small sandy-haired man who seemed to be always busy, but he was pleased to see Martin when he reported his arrival in Lisbon. Seated at his desk, he still exuded the energy and bustle that was his trademark.

"So, Captain. I have heard good things about you. What brings you to this backwater of the world?" The voice had the distinct flavour of the Northumbrian area, the smile friendly.

"I am on passage from Brazil with part of the Portuguese gold shipment. I am under orders from the

Portuguese Ambassador in London to deliver the shipment there in the current situation."

Porter stroked his chin, thinking. Then, making up his mind. he grinned and said, "Just between us, say nothing about your cargo. I will give you my latest dispatches for London and they will include my instruction to continue your voyage. There are still several French sympathisers here and the gold would be a prize worth having."

He signalled Martin to sit and called, "Stewart, here man. Bring th….." He stopped when Stewart, his servant, appeared with a tray of drinks and an included plate of substantial bread and meats.

He placed the tray and food on the desk and said, "Will there be anything else, sir?" The polite words had a hint of a smile about them which caused Martin to conceal his own amusement at the mixed feelings on the face of the Admiral.

"That will do nicely, Stewart I am not to be disturbed until I ring!"

"Very good, sir." He inclined his head and silently departed.

"One day I'll catch him out." The Admiral muttered quietly.

Martin said nothing and helped himself to the bread and meat, while the Admiral wrote a personal note to accompany the satchel of dispatches lying beside his desk.

When he completed the letter he sanded it and, satisfied that the ink was dry, he folded it and sealed it with his personal seal. He placed it in the dispatch satchel and closed and sealed it. "Always have a dispatch bag ready in case of a homeward ship calling," he explained. "It pays and saves lengthy delays, missed tides and weather on occasion." He poured himself and his guest a second glass of the local wine. "This is a compensation for the turgid social life of this place at present. Families sent all their good-looking daughters away so that the French could not defile them. We are left with the starchy older generation, and Fado recitals, for entertainment. The wine and this brandy," he lifted his glass and took an appreciative sip. "Was a gift from friends with an estate, north of here. The brandy is exclusively retained for the people of the estate; made, I am told, from the dregs of the pressing. However produced, it rewards the drinking." He tossed the remainder in his glass back and returned to business.

Tossing the satchel of documents onto the desk he said, "If you are in London when I eventually return, I'll buy you a proper dinner, but time is important now. Stewart has placed some of the brandy in your carriage by now, I wager." Holding out his hand, he shook Martin's and sent him on his way.

As he had mentioned there was a case of the brandy in the carriage to accompany his journey home.

***

HMS Vixen rejoined Sao Paulo off Portugal. Antonio and Maria joined Martin while the two ships ran together northward for the Channel and their destination.

Martin explained to Antonio about the situation in Lisbon, and the recommendation of the Admiral. "I believe that with the Royal family in Brazil, he did not trust the authorities to deal with the gold as it should be. So I was sent onward with dispatch," he said with a grin, lifting the bag of documents he had been entrusted with."

Maria elected to remain with Martin until they entered the channel, a decision thoroughly approved by the officers and men of the Vixen, where she was now regarded as a favoured member of the crew.

The progress of the two ships was interrupted once more when they encountered the blockade fleet off Brest, where they collected more dispatches.

Vixen lost her young passenger for the final dash to England. They sailed into the port of London to report their successful retrieval of the gold.

The Ambassador was delighted to see them with the gold shipment. His instruction to Antonio was to continue his co-operation with the Royal Navy, certainly whilst Portugal was under threat from the French.

Martin's appointment at the Admiralty was almost an anti-climax after the journey back with a huge value of gold.

His adoptive father was pleased to see him. Admiral Bowers was showing his age, Martin thought, but Charles sounded his usual robust self.

As he stood to greet Martin, he was not as erect as before. His shoulders were not as square. His back not quite so straight. But his eyes were alive and as bright as ever.

"Sit down, my boy. We have matters to discuss." He called out."Cameron, bring coffee for three." He turned to Martin, "We are being joined by your friend Sir Anthony Watts."

He sat down and said "You will be crossing the Atlantic on your next assignment. If it is acceptable, you will be in company with Commodore Ramos and his ship, though you will be in command of the expedition. Sir Anthony will explain the background to the task. Because of the distances and the presence of known elements of the French fleet you will have extra crew and officers, and there will be five ships in the flotilla, two sloops and a schooner, in addition to the two frigates."

"Who commands?" Martin asked.

"You will. You will raise your flag as Commodore for the cruise. Commodore Ramos has indicated that his place in co-operation with the Royal Navy is as Captain of his ship. There is no place for him as Commodore as there are no other Portuguese ships for him to control. He has no objection to sailing under your command. By the way I am commanded to inform you that both of you are to attend a reception hosted by Jane and the Comtesse de Chartres, They are introducing Maria Diaz to society. Jennifer is involved and I believe, has already informed you of a social event arranged for tonight."

"Well, I was not told of the reason, merely of the occasion. I will make a point of finding something suitable as a gift. After all, I am her adoptive uncle."

***

When the party assembled, the centre of attention was produced, arrayed in an ice-blue gown setting off her dark-haired beauty, her bare shoulders pale against the glow of her cheek and the colour of her eyes.

Her neck was bare of ornament, until Antonio stepped forward, and with a smile said, "May I?" He produced from his pocket a necklace that glittered and flashed in the lights of the room. "The occasion deserves a fitting gift. He stepped behind Maria and clipped the necklace in place, a row of diamonds and sapphires around her neck with the pendant star of a diamond surrounded by small sapphires.

Then, in his turn, Martin produced a bracelet of filigree silver, set with diamonds and sapphires. "For our adopted niece, Maria! Welcome to the family."

Jennifer cried, "Perfect!" She swung round to Martin. "You dear, thoughtful man." And hugged him.

Martin reddened uncomfortable in the glow of approval his gesture had produced.

Maria having surveyed herself in the large mirror on the wall rushed over and hugged the two men. The little girl suddenly became the adult once more. In a serious warm voice she said quietly, "My parents would be happy to know how my adopted father and uncle have cared for their daughter."

The party attended the ball, greeting the guests as they arrived. The great and the famous of society were entertained at one of *the* events of the season.

As Martin remarked to Antonio during the evening, observing the antics of some of the guests, "Despite the apparent wealth of these people, they arrive at these events prepared to eat and drink in a manner that suggests starvation for a week at least."

"My bo'sun would take delight in knocking some of the young men into shape," Antonio said drily.

Martin grinned, "And some of the women too, I suggest!" He indicated a lady whose bosom was overflowing her bodice, and in danger at each step of the dance she was engaged in.

Antonio took one look and had to turn away to cover the irrepressible laugh it produced with a coughing fit.

Jennifer noted the presence of Acting Lieutenant Neil Harmon in the presence of Maria who was surrounded by a group of young people, including two ensigns in scarlet uniform.

Alouette commented, "I notice that Maria has her protector close."

Jane and Jennifer both looked over at the group of young people. Jennifer smiled, "Why, so she has." Jane said, "He appears to be sidelined by the others." She frowned.

Alouette said, "Oh, no. See how Maria looks at him every now and then. Making sure he is still with her. He also is aware. Aha!" As she spoke Neil lifted his arm, and suddenly Maria was at his side and they were strolling quietly through the open doors to the garden.

Jane looked at the other two ladies. "How did you know?"

"There is no real mystery. Maria has been anxious about the guests for the ball ever since arrangements were begun. Mr. Harmon's name was mentioned on several occasions. When he appeared at the reception Maria became suddenly quiet." Jennifer shrugged. "That confirmed what we had surmised. Mr. Harmon's demeanour was the final factor. It indicated that if no formal arrangement had been made, there soon will be."

Jane said, "But surely she is only fifteen......." She stopped.

Jennifer giggled, and Jane smiled, remembering.

Chapter eleven

Atlantic Squadron

THE SPRAY BLEW back across the deck as the wind lifted from just abaft the port beam, Martin tasted the salt on his lips as he paced the quarter-deck of the frigate. Placed, as tradition dictated, astern of the mainmast, the mizzen or after-mast rose from the centre of deck. The raised poop deck at the after-end extended to the aft rail. The steering was on the quarter-deck and the view forward, allowing the officer on watch to see the length of the main deck.

The sun appeared and disappeared as the clouds scudded across the sky. There were large areas of blue to be seen and the sailing master, Jared Watson, observed to the doctor who had joined him on deck, "The weather is set fair. This south-westerly wind is mild as you can see. These conditions normally mean dry rather than wet weather."

"Now tell me, Mr. Watson. Why are you so sure?" Doctor Mills was no fool!

"The birds, Doctor, and the smell of the wind, plus instinct. It's a great thing, instinct."

He strolled forward to call out to the bo'sun.

The doctor scratched his head still not really convinced.

Martin glanced at him. "Not everything can be reduced to scientific formula, Doctor. It is quite well established that, when the weather changes, the feel of the breeze can signal the change. My own instinct is that the master is correct. For the next few days we should have little in the way of bad weather." He smiled. "How are you settling in at sea?"

Roger Mills, the doctor, looked surprised at this question, having been with the ship for several months now he was thinking himself part of the crew. "I am well suited sir, and happily pleased to be away from Haslar hospital, and the dubious attractions of Portsmouth."

His departure from Portsmouth, and his position as surgeon at Haslar Hospital, had been precipitous. As a result of over-indulgence, he had gambling debts exceeding his income to a degree that meant penury and disgrace. His arrival on board had been in the nature of a pier-head jump, one step ahead of the men sent to enforce payment, one way or another. The first voyage had produced enough in prize money to clear his debts. He had remained with the ship because he found that here he was among friends, and he was accepted without question for what he was, as a doctor. He was called upon to treat everything from boils to pox, though most of all, battle wounds. Oddly, working flat-out to a chorus of gunfire was not as frightening as he at first feared. He had found that whilst thus involved he could ignore the sounds about him and concentrate on the task before him.

Martin looked keenly at the man beside him. "I'm well pleased with your appointment to this ship. You have done well since you joined us."

He nodded and strolled off along the deck.

As Doctor Mills went below to finish sorting the stores they had brought, he thought that the opinion held by the crew about their young captain was quite understandable. His concern for the people in his ship was genuine, a rare quality in the Navy of the day. Word of early trials endured by Martin Forest as a boy had come to him from various sources. On reflection, it was not so surprising that, as he had made his way in the world, he had not forgotten how hard life could be.

On deck Martin viewed the other ships of his command. To port, the schooner HMS Hera commanded by Lieutenant John Harris, was leading the way two miles off, followed by HMS Spartan, one of the Sloops-of-war. Her commander was Colin Marlow, the most experienced of the Lieutenants in command.

Away almost on the horizon was the Sao Paulo, accompanied by HMS Lively, the sloop commanded by Lieutenant Keats promoted out of the cutter used in the cutting out operation at Rochefort.

The rank of Commodore sat lightly on Martin's shoulders. He was well aware of the temporary nature of the title, and thus hardly thought of himself as other than the senior Captain in command of the small squadron.

The task before them was not likely to be an easy one. Sir Anthony, the enigmatic Mr. Smith, had explained that there was real concern over the growing strength of the American Navy. The emergence of increasing numbers of armed, so-called trading ships under the American flag had coincided with the disappearance of several merchantmen on passage to and from the West Indies. The launch of the first of the new frigates, according to Sir Anthony's spies, was accomplished with little publicity, and apparently the matter could be of concern to British warships. The design of the new frigates included hull structure akin to a seventy four, with increased length permitting a broadside of 22 heavy guns, eighteen or twenty-four pounders, at a guess. The lofty attitude of the politicians of the day by creating the arbitrary trading embargo on goods consigned to France had caused increased friction with American ships. In addition there was conflict over the stop and search operations conducted by British ships. More and more cases of seizure of so-called deserters found in crews of American ships had raised the level of tension in diplomatic relations between the two nations.

To Martin's amusement, Sir Anthony, having carefully explained the situation, then proceeded to instruct Martin to ignore these matters and avoid contact if possible with the Americans. "Your task is to seek, and intercept—if possible—a group of ships currently in the north-Caribbean area inciting revolt among the slaves, and pirating ships wherever they are found. The Jamaica squadron is reduced by losses of men to fever, and day to day operations. With the demands of the blockades in European waters there are few reinforcements available, so their resources are stretched to the limit.

"Following the Louisiana Purchase by America from France in 1803, the ships are believed to be part of the renegade forces of mixed French and Americans who are seeking to acquire the Bahamas as a base for control of the northern Caribbean. As far as we know this is not sanctioned by the Washington Government. However we cannot really be sure."

Martin listened to the explanation with interest and when Sir Anthony stopped he commented, "So, what you are sending me to do, is to stop the raiding, protect the Bahamas, and avoid conflict with the American government. Have I got it right?"

Sir Anthony looked at Martin sharply, seeking the slightest hint of sarcasm. Noting none, he nodded. "That would be about right." His dry humourless voice invited no further comment.

Now, here on deck, Martin saw the humour of the occasion. His burst of laughter surprised the crew men nearby. Without comment, Martin resumed his interrupted walk with measured strides.

***

The cross-ocean voyage continued without sighting anything more threatening than the seabirds trailing the ships.

On the eighth day HMS Hera signalled 'Enemy in sight' followed by a number 3. Martin interpreted it as three ships, and signalled the rest of his ships to close up.

Hera reported she had sighted three ships, one square-rigged, the other two, schooners. The description given by Sir Anthony was not specific enough to specify the type of ships used by the renegades, but, since there were no friendly ships reported to be in the area, it was reasonable to suspect any ship that came into view.

Martin was waiting for his captains to join him, when a hail from the schooner Hera's masthead lookout drew the attention of all the people within hearing distance.

"Man in the water!"

The Hera spun round with a display of agility that no square-rigged ship could match. She flew away downwind in the direction indicated by her lookout.

The three strange ships were now over the horizon beyond sight of the British ships. Martin was concerned for the Hera, though her course took her to the south of the direction the strangers were taking.

The sight of the man in the water was a tribute to the sharp eye of the lookout and the bright red shirt worn by the man in the water.

He had been clinging to a spar which still had canvas wrapped partially around it. When the Hera returned with the man, it was evident he had been in the water for some time. His wrinkled skin testified to that, but the fire in his eyes told Martin why he had survived since the attack on his ship nearly 24 hours earlier.

Unusually for a sailor, he could swim. He had come across the piece of wreckage when he was ready to give up.

He was relieved when he saw the schooner drop a boat, realising that it was not one of the pirates who had sunk his ship. They had been taking shots at the other survivors in the water, laughing at each hit they made.

Jacob Carling had swum under water as far as he could before coming up for air. Though the odd shot came his way, the marksmen concentrated on the easier targets near the ship.

Though he knew his escape was probably an empty gesture, he could not just give-up. The dinghy from Hera brought the survivor to Vixen and the doctor directly.

Martin sent the boat back with instructions to Lieutenant Harris, her Captain, to standby for orders.

Martin listened to the survivor's story with interest. Carling was an American, mate on the Joshua Harkness out of Boston, trading between Savannah and the French Leeward Islands mainly in sugar.

"Who attacked you?" Martin asked.

"They was flying the American flag, but they could have been anyone. They spoke like Americans and, by god, they shot like them too. My father taught me to shoot a rifle, and those men had rifles, and could shoot. I guess they were Americans." He lay back with a sigh. The bunk where he was placed would have normally have accommodated the Third Lieutenant. Since the third, Neil Harmon, was in fact acting, and he had remained in the gunroom as senior, it had been placed at the disposal of the Doctor.

Jacob Carling lay in the bunk speaking slowly but clearly. Martin was seated on the chair beside the bunk in the cramped confines of the small cabin. The doctor stood disapprovingly in the doorway.

"She were a square-rigged ship, sixteen guns in her broadside. Sailed up to us without any sign of trouble. When she got into range the guns were run out and they gave us the entire broadside. She was so close the wads from the nearest guns flew out and set fire to the port rigging. There was a lot of crashing and banging as the cargo shifted, and both masts fell. I decided that was not a good place to be and pushed the dinghy overboard. Didn't do me no good as they sank it as soon as they saw it. I escaped in the shelter of the sinking ship. I guess I just swam and swam until I found that spar and sail in the water. It gave me a chance to rest and sheltered me from the sun." He lay back head beginning to nod.

"Do you have any idea who it was that attacked you?"

The doctor interrupted at this point. "Captain, I think Mr. Carling has had enough for just now he needs rest."

Reluctantly Martin rose to his feet to leave the little cabin, before he stepped through the door, Jacob spoke again. Martin turned.

"I knew. I recognised him. He were in uniform like your'n. It were Captain Newton, Roger bloody Newton, formerly of His Majesty's ship....." He collapsed back on the berth and was asleep in an instant.

On deck once more Martin spoke to Jared Watson, "Have you heard the name Newton, Roger Newton?"

The Master scratched his chin, "Only one I knew was Captain of the Hasty 32, under Cochrane. In the Mediterranean, when you were there I believe. Do you not recall he was to be charged for attacking an innocent village, C something, I think. Cefalu! Yes, that was it, on the north coast of Sicily. Landed and killed all the men, then held an orgy in the village square. Ravished all the women then slaughtered them and slung the bodies into the mass grave with their men. Only one got away!"

"Ah, I remember. Yes. He made a run for it with his ship and got wrecked on the island, Marettimo, as I recall. Cochrane was furious. Lost with all hands, they just found some wreckage after a stormy night. Never found any survivors, though several bodies were washed ashore, identified as members of Newton's crew."

"That's what I thought," Jared added. I always wondered why more were not found I am now suspecting why."

Martin looked at him, eyebrow raised. "Now we know, don't we?"

"I suppose the men in the water were men who did not want to sail with the pirates, cynically used to cover up their crime."

"I get the impression that you might be right, which illustrates why they were shooting people in the water. Definitely no witnesses to remain, by why smash an American ship?"

After a moment, Jared said, "Perhaps they did not want any report of their presence in the area at a significant time. They are on a secret mission and wish to remain anonymous."

Martin nodded slowly in agreement, "Please set course for the Bahamas, Long Key, I think. I seem to recall there is sheltered anchorage where we can base ourselves without creating too much fuss." He turned to Antonio, Keats and Morton of the HMS Spartan, "Well, gentlemen. It seems that the chase has begun." He turned to Lieutenant Brooks. "Mr. Brooks, make signal to Hera. 'Shadow the strangers and rendezvous at Long Key in seven days. Avoid contact at all costs!'"

Quarterdeck

Chapter Thirteen

Away the boats

LIEUTENANT JOHN HARRIS found the detachment from the small squadron exhilarating. The schooner was a true flyer, now released from the need to hold back and to keep station on the other ships.

He set sail after the three suspect ships, depending on the sharp eyes of his lookout to warn him when the tops of his quarry appeared on the horizon.

It was a tribute to the state of the hulls, the set of the sails, and the skill of the crews of the suspect ships that the task of catching them was harder than he anticipated. It was not until mid-afternoon that the chase came in sight.

As soon as the chase was confirmed, he dropped back and took a parallel course to come abreast of the three ships to be in a position to close up to them during the night, on their beam rather than astern where it would be natural to watch for a pursuing ship.

John Harris was excited, though he made sure he did not let his crew know about it. He made great effort to appear calm and unruffled in front of the men. An admirer of the Commodore, and also of his hero, Admiral Nelson—whom he had served under as a midshipman on Victory—he had observed their composure when the bullets were flying, and desperately prayed that he could emulate them when the time came.

Meantime, drills! He called to his first lieutenant to exercise the guns both port and starboard in turn. Actually firing was better, but the sound travels too well over water.

They kept in touch with the strangers with short excursions into visual range, before dropping back out of sight.

The cat and mouse game carried on for three days with the weather worsening gradually. On the fourth day the schooner was battling a full gale and, from their observation of the other ships, they were suffering rather more. The biggest ship, now recognised as a frigate, had lost her topmast slowing the trio of ships to the extent that the Hera was ahead of the ships she was pursuing. Harris decided that this was the opportunity he needed to get to the north of the strangers, and gave orders to let the ship run free north-west across the course of the battered trio. When the Hera hove-to she was positioned on the other beam ahead of her quarry.

The stratagem worked, and by the time the three ships passed her, the storm was reducing, though the waves were still high. The lookout on Hera reported a glimpse of the ships as the schooner topped one of the bigger waves.

Harris ordered the helm up five degrees north, to clear the horizon properly, then resumed the mean course, guessing that the other ships would maintain their mean course.

In his cabin he once again extended the course on the chart and decided that the destination would be, possibly Governor's Island.

***

At the Long Key anchorage Martin was beginning to worry about the situation he was encountering. They had spoken to fishermen and there had been rumours of landings at night by small boats with boxes and bags of what was believed to be weapons. The sightings had been on New Providence, the location of the city of Nassau, both West bay and East bay were mentioned when Martin tried to narrow them down. He could do no better. Though he spoke French, the patios of the local men was almost incomprehensible. Marlow was off New Providence with Spartan at present with men laying in ambush for any smugglers coming ashore, at West beach.

As he strode the deck he watched the men on the HMS Lively replacing worn rigging after the ravages of the recent storm. On the Sao Paulo the men were occupied with similar work, though since her refit had been recent there was less need for replacements.

Antonio crossed the deck of the Vixen joining Martin at the fife rail. There were few obvious signs of the recent storm. The calm blue/green waters of the anchorage, the white beach and the fringe of palm trees nodding in the light breeze, made a picture of tropical paradise.

Turning to his companion, Martin remarked, "This is how we recall these places. In England they have a different picture. They see the lists of dead from disease, the sick men and women returning after staying in the area for a year or so."

"Don't forget the pirates, treasure and the slaves working on the sugar cane and coffee." Antonio suggested.

Changing the subject Martin said, "How are the repairs going?"

"There was little seriously to be done. Most of what is now being completed is minor and could have been completed in passage." Antonio looked at Martin, curious. "You are concerned about something, my friend?"

"I'm uneasy. I am still wondering about the origin of this so-called American invasion. As far as I can see the country is still absorbing and settling the affairs of the people of the Louisiana area. I cannot reconcile this suggestion that the American Government are actually considering a takeover of these islands when they have already got problems with Mexico in the south and the west. Their army is committed to try and resolve these situations, and are not—as far as I'm aware—in a situation to undertake an invasion here. There are, however, signs that someone is preparing to do just that, but who?"

Antonio shrugged, "My father used to say, 'In this sort of situation follow the money!', and he always swore by that. If it is not the government, look for the money-trail that will take you to the source, and probably the answer to your question. My guess would be business, the source of money in the islands themselves. How about current trade with Britain? Could it be more lucrative with other countries? It's the sort of thing that can generate unrest and rebellion. After all, consider the independence of America itself. The disturbance in Boston where the tea was flung into the harbour, that incident was the spark that set the country afire.

"Taxes! Finance! Insurgence!" He smiled. "The stuff of revolution, I fear. Here it would not be supported by nationalism as such. This would be painted as politics, but actually be power and wealth. And so, my friend, with your permission I will go and write my thoughts to my beautiful Alouette."

"Of course, Antonio. I should be writing to Jennifer. Thank you for your company and advice."

As Antonio returned to his ship Martin went below to write his letters, still a little troubled, though not quite as deeply as before.

***

It was a long night for Lieutenant Harris. As darkness was falling he decided that he would take a chance and run hard for Governor's Island and be there when the other ships arrived. They had been delayed by the repairs they had to make and he thought he would have time to conceal the schooner in the small islands to the north or perhaps behind the island itself.

***

In Nassau the Governor, Sir Anthony Warren, said goodnight to his daughter, Catherine and watched the blond-haired young lady climb the stairway to her room. The swish, as the skirts of her dress brushed the marble stairs in time with the pace of her graceful walk, accompanied her. The lingering scent of her perfume remained, seeming to accentuate the loneliness he felt since the loss of his beloved Elizabeth a year earlier. Losing his wife had been unexpected and devastating. His daughter, Catherine, had done all she could to share his loss, but it was still his loss!

He sighed and turned back into the room he had now adopted as his official office. He was at his desk when the visitor arrived.

Sir Adrian Maxwell had requested the meeting at this hour to prevent speculation and gossip. As possibly the richest man in the islands, he was tall and aggressively handsome with dark hair and flashing brown eyes. His continued avoidance of the traps laid by the mothers of the island had been a matter of extensive speculation among the upper classes. His attraction and adventures among both married and unmarried women was quietly known about, and publicly ignored. He was still the catch of the season, nay the decade, if he would allow himself to be trapped.

Sir Anthony neither liked nor trusted him, without publicising the fact he was aware that Maxwell was attempting to persuade Catherine to marry him, with complete lack of success.

He suspected that this was the reason for the present meeting and prepared to rebuff any such suggestion, since Catherine had made it quite clear that she had no interest in marrying him. She despised him and rejected him on every occasion that they met.

The man entered by the open French window, having come through the garden. Without a coat and no stock, the dark hair was visible through the opened front of his white shirt. There was a sword at his side and a pistol in his hand.

Sir Anthony looked at his guest calmly. "I presume there is a reason for you arrival armed to the teeth?"

"Indeed there is, the moment has arrived. I am taking over the rule of the Bahamas in the name of the States of America."

Still irritatingly calm, Sir Anthony enquired, "Am I to presume there is a horde of rebels outside poised to sack Nassau?"

Maxwell grinned. "Not entirely. I have my followers in place, re-assuring the army and the business community that your illness has caused you to step down and appoint me as temporary Governor until you recover."

"Is there some date you have in mind for my 'recovery'."

"Ah. That will be in the gift of your daughter, when our wedding has been arranged. It would be I think appropriate for you to give the bride away, do you not think?"

"That long? I do suggest you shoot me now. It would be far too wearying for me to wait until hell freezes over." These last words were said with a ferocity that shocked Maxwell.

"We must work on that. Perhaps your screams of pain will alter her mind. I'll see what we can arrange, because arrange I will. You may depend on it. I will have her, whatever you and she may say."

He gestured with the pistol. "Up and out into the garden, your escort awaits."

Sit Anthony rose to his feet and stepped through the open door to the garden beyond.

Maxwell called out, "Rowland, take our guest to the summer house. Make sure he is comfortable."

A voice answered, "What about the girl?"

"I told you, Barrat. The girl will be my responsibility. Go with Rowlands and go quietly."

The entire conversation was heard by Catherine from her room above. The open window had allowed her to hear the arrival of Maxwell and his men. Realising that she could do nothing for her father at the moment, she slipped into the breeches of a midshipman, part of fancy dress worn when she was a little younger. It was more of a struggle than she remembered from that time but, having managed, she pulled on a blouse and a short blue jacket, and crammed her hair under the midshipman's hat. She took her jewellery box and another bag with a simple dress and small clothes. The dirk was real, as was the pistol thrust into her belt. The conversation below was still going on when she descended the stairs and left the house through the front door. There was no sign of movement as she made her way on foot out of the gates and turned down the road to the town of Nassau. A movement beside the road caught her attention. Reaching for the pistol she said quietly, "Come out. I know you are there."

The coloured boy came into view. Catherine sighed with relief. She had known him since they were both children. They had grown up together. She would trust him with her life. "Oh, Mathew, it's you. Thank goodness."

"I was worried, Miss Catherine. Those men with your father are bad men." He saw her attire in the reflected light from one of the houses. "Why are you here dressed like that?"

"The bad men are trying to catch me for Maxwell!" She was still speaking quietly.

The man considered for a few moments then, "Come, miss. I think it's time we go fishing. No one will search for you at Hog Island."

The pair made their way down to the harbour where they climbed into the fishing boat used by Mathew. It was owned by friends of the Warren family who were currently in England. The 30-foot yawl had a cabin and an open cockpit for half its length. It had been used for line fishing by the family. Mathew, now fifteen years old, had been allowed to use the boat to supply both families with fish, and, therefore, also to look after it. It was, as always, immaculate. The paint and varnish work was maintained, clean and in good condition. The fishing lines that Catherine had often cast from the boat ran over protective canvas that preserved the wood from abrasion. Mathew bought food from the open harbour stalls and carried two small kegs of water into the boat before leaving the quay. Catherine stayed out of sight until they were out of the harbour and in the open sea.

Between them they sailed the boat to the seaward side of Hog Island, fishing on the way.

Having landed on the beach, they made a fire where others had before and cooked fish, and ate some of the fruit Mathew had brought.

It was then Catherine told Mathew everything she had heard between Maxwell and her father.

***

Mathew had been with the Warren family since he was born. Catherine had played with him and shared her sweets with him, and insisted that he shared her lessons with her private teacher.

More like her younger brother than servant, the bond of trust between them was enhanced when the slave trade was officially abolished and Sir Anthony gave Mathew his freedom, employing him on a regular wage thereafter.

Mathew heard what she said and then made his comment. "The problem is that Maxwell has a case. All the business men complain about the tax they pay on all trade with England. Their profits from selling to America are much higher and the shipping is cheaper. He would get support from many of the other traders and plantation owners. The slave trade has been abolished by Britain, but not by America." He shrugged.

"How about you, Mathew? What do you think?"

Mathew smiled. "You have always been direct. Catherine, I do not trust Maxwell. Nor do I trust those Americans I have met here. I will stay as I am, Bahamian British."

***

HMS Hera arrived at Long Key to find HMS Lively waiting. The sloop was underway as the schooner sailed into the anchorage.

The signals were simple and direct. "Commodore sailed for New Providence this morning. We are to follow and wait in the lee of Hog Island. Sao Paulo is patrolling offshore just in case. What have you found?"

Hera sailed close alongside Lively. Lieutenant Harris used his speaking trumpet to call across between the ships. "All three anchored at Governor's Island, they were doing repairs. I suspect they are here for a reason, otherwise why not go straight to Nassau."

Lieutenant Keats was no fool and he realised that the Commodore could be putting his head in a noose. He cracked on all sail and called back to Harris, "We must warn the Commodore as soon as possible, Will you find Sao Paulo and pass on the news to Captain Ramos?"

The schooner was already turning when the acknowledgement flag swooped up on the halliard. The schooner heeled to set course to the rendezvous with the Portuguese frigate.

The approach to the harbour at Nassau was busy when HMS Vixen made her appearance. Martin had not made a serious attempt to rush to the Bahamian capital. He had never met Sir Anthony Warren and was preoccupied with the problem of warning him without causing a panic reaction. As they approached Hog Island, a small boat put off from the shore and someone dressed in Midshipman's uniform was waving.

"Mr. Brooks, if you will!"

Patrick Brooks saw the boat indicated by the captain and called the master to slow the ship to allow the small boat to come alongside.

"Hand the mainsail, a touch on the lee side, bo'sun." Jared Watson called.

The boat came alongside in froth of foam and the midshipman hooked onto the boarding stair with a boathook, while the other crewman threw a bag up to the frigate's deck. Then taking the boathook he held the two craft together while the midshipman climbed aboard. He then released the ladder and the boat sheared off and turned back to the island.

On the deck of the Vixen Lieutenant Cameron looked at the midshipman in astonishment. As he had climbed onto the deck, the hat Catherine, the Governor's daughter, was wearing, came off releasing her long blond hair to flow in the wind.

"Who are you?" Cameron stuttered, overcome by the vision before him.

Catherine grinned, "I am Lady Catherine Warren, daughter of the Governor of the Bahamas. Take me to your captain, please."

The tall figure of Martin appeared the hint of a smile on his face. "Can I help you, Milady."

"If you are the captain, then 'yes' you can. My father has been taken and replaced by Sir Adrian Maxwell in the name of the American government."

Martin held up his hand. "Perhaps you would be more comfortable, more formally dressed. I presume the bag contains clothing?"

At Catherine's nod he continued, "My cabin is at your disposal. I will join you in a few minutes. Mr. Brooks, let us have a tangle in the rigging. Shall we say fifteen minutes before we resume progress?"

Brooks acknowledged the order and called the master once more.

***

Properly dressed again, Catherine sat demurely in Martin's cabin and told him everything that had occurred over the past two days. Martin listened without interruption.

Then he spoke, "I am most grateful for your information. What you have told me accords with what we have already suspected. I will call upon the Governor and, if you explain the location of the summer house, my people will arrange for the release of your father. Are you certain of the names Rowlands and Barrat?"

"I heard the names quite clearly. I certainly have no doubts."

Martin stroked his chin thoughtfully, "The reason I mention it, is that I was involved in transporting two men, named Rowlands and Barrat, to the Indies."

"Well, it is clear to me that the men have been employed by Maxwell, wherever they came from." Catherine was quite definite.

Chapter fourteen

Questions and Answers

MARTIN SENT FOR Lieutenant Brooks, and Lieutenant Cameron. To Brooks he gave his orders. "You will have the ship stripped for action and the guns run out to cover the town. There has been a coup here by American sympathisers. I will go and see the Acting Governor, the Marines will accompany me." To Cameron he said, "You will take a plain-clothes party to the address this lady will give you. There you are to rescue the Governor of the Bahamas who is being held prisoner. The men holding him are criminals, and extremely dangerous. Take no risks, shoot without hesitation, but ensure the Governor's safety."

Brooks and Cameron both acknowledged their orders. Catherine accompanied Cameron to the gunroom where she drew a map with the location of the summer house.

"There is an easier access to the place but I would need to show you." She said.

"That cannot be. It would be far too dangerous." Cameron sounded quite firm on the subject.

Catherine looked at him directly, turning on her full power of persuasion. "I would not be spotted if I dressed in boy's clothes. Getting in by the back way means we can enter the building unobserved. Not only would it give us an advantage, it could save lives. No one else will need to know."

In the Captain's cabin she slipped out of her dress. Retaining her drawers, she climbed into the breeches she had donned for her escape. She donned the grubby shirt. Looking in the mirror, apart from the hair and the curve of her breasts she could pass for a rather nice-looking boy. She giggled at the thought and dragged her hair back and stuffed it under her hat. Adding the belt, she slid the pistol into the loop provided and checked her dirk was secure. With the addition of the cloak found for her by Cameron, who could recognise her? She spared a thought for William Cameron. He would get in trouble if her part in this rescue was discovered. The thought made her feel guilty at the way she had exploited her assets to gain his cooperation. She shrugged. That was a problem she would face when the time came. Meanwhile!

***

The jollyboat slipped away from the seaward side of the anchored frigate mingling with the other harbour traffic. Carrying the twelve-man group it pulled to the shore and tied up at a pier beside an empty warehouse. With weapons concealed, the group scattered and reformed several streets back from the waterfront, where the town ended abruptly and the plantation land began.

The summerhouse was a house that had been built some fifty years before for a plantation owner, who had it designed for his beloved wife. She sadly died before it was ever used. It had lain idle ever since. Catherine, like most of the youngsters of the town, had played in the grounds of the summer house as a child. As they approached she lifted her hand and directed the party into the overgrown road behind the building. The storm drain under the road was clear. The rainy season had delivered a final flush-through two weeks ago. Catherine led Cameron, followed by the entire party, in the crawl through the pipe. The drain ended at a metal grid, where the pipe ran under the corner of the house. At the grid Catherine indicated one of the vertical bars of the grid and pantomimed levering it out. "Here!" Cameron looked puzzled still, so she drew the dirk she carried and inserted it between the bar and the metal plate behind it. Yanking back with the dirk, the grid moved and swung back Cameron grabbed it before it could hit the side of the pipe. The party followed her, crawling through to a point where a hatch was visible in the top of the pipe. Once more the dirk did its duty, the hatch squeaked on clogged hinges, but opened and allowed the party through.

When the group were all assembled in the cellar of the house, Catherine explained where they were, using the rough drawing of the house she had prepared. Cameron gave his orders and the men spread out to search the building. Catherine and Cameron waited listening for any sign that they had been discovered.

The men returned one by one, bare feet quiet on the wooden floors. The pair checking the ground floor spotted two men at the door watching. The last pair returned with the news that there was a prisoner on the top floor being held in what they guessed was a back bedroom. He appeared to be tied to the bed. There were two men playing cards, apparently on watch over him.

Cameron divided the men, the Bo'sun and three men were left to deal with the men at the front door, while Cameron led the others up to the top floor.

Catherine went with Cameron's party, to identify her father, as she put it.

They crept along the edge of the landing close to the wall, so that the boards did not creak. At the corner Cameron peered round at ground level.

"Damn!" He whispered.

"What?" Catherine asked.

"One is sitting in the passage the other must be in the room with your father."

"Let me see." She said laying on the floor, and lining her head to see round the corner.. As she looked the second man came out of the room and joined the other man. "I'll distract them." Catherine said, and rose to her feet. She pushed her pistol in the back of her waistband and removed her hat, shaking her blond hair loose. Before Cameron could protest she stepped around the corner and walked toward the two men.

"Is one of you named Rowlands, The seated man stood, "I'm Rowlands!" He said.

"Maxwell, sent me to speak to my father. We have come to an agreement so he will be released soon. She reached behind her, pushing her breasts out before them. Both looked instinctively at her shapely figure. Then she produced the pistol. "Cameron!" She called.

There was a clatter of feet and Cameron and three others appeared.

Rowlands flung himself backward and reached for his own pistol. Barrat stood shocked as Catherine shot Rowlands. Barrat reacted, reaching for the slight figure in front of him. The marlin spike flew past Catherine's head and hit Barrat between the eyes with a thud that could be heard throughout the entire top floor. Barrat dropped where he stood, Rowlands wounded, cried out when he saw Barrat fall, "You killed him, bitch!" He said, "He was my friend."

Catherine scooped-up Barrat's pistol, checked the load, and shot Rowlands in the head.

"Now you've both paid for kidnapping my father. She turned and went to the figure on the bed. Taking the gag from his mouth, she kissed him and said, "Time to go home, Daddy," and cut the bindings attaching him to the bed and rubbed life back into wrist and ankles.

As he stood the Governor spoke to his daughter, "Thank you for the rescue, my dear. We will address the matter of the boys clothes when we return home. Now get that hat back on before anyone sees you."

***

Martin and his escort of marines made their way through the streets to Government House. The twelve marines marched between the lines of houses with few witnesses. None of the population seemed to be taking much interest in the so-called revolution.

At the gates of the mansion the soldiers on duty stood to attention, unsurprised at the arrival of the armed party. They were completely unaware of the events that were supposed to have resounded throughout the colony.

Martin informed them he was visiting the Governor. They stood aside as Martin approached the Mansion with his Marine escort.

Sir Adrian Maxwell was seated at the desk in the Governor's office when Martin entered unannounced. He looked up at the interruption. "Who the devil are you? He demanded.

"I am Commodore Forest-Bowers RN of His Majesty's Ship Vixen, and who, sir, are you?

"I am Sir Adrian Maxwell, acting Governor of the Bahamas. I should have been informed of a naval presence in the Islands."

Martin smiled grimly. "I have just informed you, sir. Now where is the Governor?"

"He is ill at present and I have been placed in temporary charge as acting-Governor."

Martin smiled grimly. "By whose authority pray?"

"Why by order of the Governor himself." Replied Maxwell.

"You have the order to hand, I expect?" Martin allowed a touch of impatience to enter his voice.

Maxwell shuffled papers on his desk, "I have it here somewhere." His hand rose lifting a pistol that had lain beneath the documents. The rising pistol stopped suddenly as the sound of the click of a hammer being cocked sounded from the room window.

The pistol was laid onto the desk carefully.

"Good. That is better." Martin stepped forward and took the pistol himself. "Now sit down and tell me when were the ships due to appear?"

"Soon enough, you'll see." Maxwell sneered. "Your puny ship will not stand a chance."

"If you are talking about the recently built American frigate, I'm afraid you will be disappointed. The former naval frigate Hasty 32 plus two schooners seems to be the total size of the invasion fleet currently lying at Governors Island. To reassure you my ships are keeping them under observation in the meantime."

Maxwell was beginning to lose his cocky attitude, as he began to realise that things were not going the way he had planned.

There was a disturbance at the door and voices approached along the hallway. The door opened and the Governor Sir Anthony Warren walked in.

"Arrest that man." He indicated Maxwell. "The charge is treason."

The man with him stepped forward and gripped Maxwell's wrist, clamping a metal band to it, he took Maxwell's other hand and locked it into a second.

Martin nodded at two of the marines. "Go with them," he ordered.

When the four men had gone Martin turned to Sir Anthony, "Sorry it took so long. Your daughter, Catherine, warned us as we passed Hog Island. It took a little time to arrange matters."

The Governor smiled, "I was relieved to know that my daughter was safe. That fool thought he was going to marry her, despite the wishes of us both. The man is probably the richest in the Islands He had long complained about the taxes charged by the Crown, justifiably. I have been working to equalise matters regarding taxes, but these things take time. It will happen. Of that I am certain. For all his wealth Adrian Maxwell is a stubborn fool, and now it has cost him everything, possibly even his life."

As Martin looked at the determined man before him he was impressed. He guessed that this man would make happen, given the chance, whatever was needed."

"Very good, sir. Shall I leave the marines with you when I return to my ship?"

"I do not think that will be necessary, Commodore." He looked up as Catherine swept in accompanied by Lieutenant Cameron. Properly dressed now, she made a stunning sight to Martin's eye.

Martin was unaware of the part Catherine had played in the rescue of her father. Though he realised something was amiss when he saw Cameron's face.

"Father, before you do or say something you will regret, I have to explain something." Turning to Martin, "I'm pleased you are here, sir, as I feel that you also deserve an explanation, since I believe Mr. Cameron is intending saying nothing on the subject in his own defence."

The two men addressed stood slightly shocked at the approach. Martin was the first to react. "Perhaps we should all sit down and you can explain."

He raised his hand to stop Cameron from speaking. "Ladies first," he said, gallantly.

They all seated themselves and Catherine started.

"The summerhouse was not an easy place to attack, certainly if it is important to take the occupants by surprise. The area all about the house is open and visible from the upper windows. When I drew the plans for William," she coughed, "Lieutenant Cameron, I realised that it would be impossible to approach without giving warning. It was only then that I remembered where as children we used to play, and the culvert came to mind.

"We used it several times and we found ways to bypass the locks of the metal grills in the culvert. It is not an easy thing to convey to someone who does not know the place. I then realised I would need to accompany the raiding party to see them through the culvert and into the building.

"I knew that lives would be at stake if we tried any other way." She looked at Cameron. "We were both concerned that, without surprise on our side, my father could be killed."

Cameron nodded in agreement.

"I used the clothes that I had used to escape the house here, when you were taken by Maxwell. As a boy I passed unnoticed then, and on this occasion also. I was able to guide the group through the culvert, and open the gates silently to allow us through, and into the Summer House. I stayed with the party for protection. When we reached the floor where you were being held, I saw the men and realised that a woman would not be threatening to them, so I pulled off my hat and strolled down to the men calling one by name and telling them that Maxwell had sent me. The man, Barrat, suspected. The other man Rowlands, was only interested in my body. So I shot Rowland, and wounded him. He was pulling out his pistol. Someone threw a marlin spike at Barrat who dropped on the spot. I grabbed the gun from Barrat's dead hand as the wounded Rowlands shouted and started to aim his own pistol. I shot him with Barrat's gun. Everything happened in a flash, and Mr. Cameron, despite his protests, stood at my side to defend me all the way from start to finish. Without his sensible acceptance of the situation and actions thereafter, our people could have been killed, including you, father."

She stopped and, overcome by the release of the tension she had been under, turned to Cameron seated at her side, and collapsed in tears into his ready arms.

For a few moments the room was silenced except for the sound of Catherine's sobs. Martin was not surprised, guessing it was probably reaction to the events of the past several hours.

Sir Anthony broke the silence. "Please, Lieutenant, would you take my daughter up to her room. The maid should be there to look after her." He looked at Martin, "Do you need the Lieutenant further?"

When Martin shook his head, he added, "Off you go, and thank you for your part in my deliverance."

Cameron drew Catherine to her feet and supported her out of the room to the foot of the stairs. Catherine looked up at the stairs rising upward and started to say "I don't thi...."

Without further ado, Cameron swept her up into his arms and mounted the stairs. She snuggled against him making him aware of her presence so close in his embrace, he could feel her breath against his cheek, and the brush of her lips as she whispered, "Dear William," so quietly that he only just heard her.

She indicated her room, and without missing a step he carried her through the door and laid her on the bed. Kissing her on the forehead whilst he was still bent over her. She smiled and hung on, not allowing him to straighten up until she placed a gentle kiss on his lips. "Thank you, William, for everything."

He heard the rustle of skirts behind him and straightened up as Catherine's maid came over to her mistress. Now awkward and embarrassed, he withdrew from the room, closing the door quietly.

Marie, Catherine's maid, looked at her mistresses face, "He the one?" She asked in the island lilt.

Catherine smiled dreamily, "He the one!"

"Do he know yet?"

"Not yet. I'll tell him soon." She allowed Marie to help her out of the dress, and the breeches that were still in place when she hastily donned the dress to confront her father.

In the office below Sir Anthony asked Martin about young Cameron.

"He is young but has great promise. His father is the local squire in a Devon parish as I recall. No other attachments to my knowledge." He paused puzzled, "Is there some reason for your .....? Ah, I see what you mean." The attitude of the pair came to his mind. He remembered the way she had sprung to Cameron's defence, especially since nobody had accused him of anything. The way she had turned to him in tears. "You think, perhaps?" he left the suggestion in the air.

"I have the feeling that she has decided that Mr. Cameron would make a fine husband. In the absence of her mother, I will have little to say about it. It's my impression—hope even—that the young man will live up to her expectations." Sir Anthony leaned back in his chair and rang the bell on his desk. When the servant appeared he said, "You'll join me in a nightcap before you return to your ship, Commodore?"

As he returned to the ship Martin reflected on the events of the evening. The sang-froid of the Governor and his daughter throughout the entire proceedings, made him change his opinion of the nature of some at least of those serving their King in distant parts. Life was not only parties, balls and diplomatic presentations. When a situation like the attempted coup here in the Bahamas occurred, cool heads and attention to detail were an essential part of recovery. And he had been privileged to see them at work here.

Chapter fifteen

Decisions

ANTONIO RAMOS WITH the Sao Paulo was on the other side of New Providence at Andros Island, showing the flag at Andros town, to re-assure the population that the Union flag still flew over the islands. Martin had more or less guessed that the ships under Roger Newton on the former frigate Hasty would hear the news of the arrival of his squadron and withdraw.

The detachment of the Portuguese ship on an independent patrol was a matter of practicality that gave Antonio Ramos the chance to shake down the ship and crew at leisure. Though they had all worked together for several months the ship they had formerly occupied had been old and cranky. The frigate they now had was comparatively new and its characteristics were very different from the San Andreas. The Sao Paulo responded swiftly to sail and wheel, and the crew had quickly learned to react faster.

They were exercising the guns when they came across the slave ship. The smell would have given it away if nothing else. With a broken fore-mast the ship was a sorry sight. The crew were involved in clearing the broken timbers from what was once a deckhouse. It appeared that the falling mast had smashed the frame of the deckhouse allowing the seas to cause a certain amount of havoc below deck. With her cargo of slaves, it was surprising that they were not employed to clear the deck and lend a hand with restoring the damage.

Antonio was wary of the men on the ship especially since there seemed to be something wrong with the whole feeling of this encounter.

He hove-to, and made his mind up not to take chances.

"Run out the guns, starboard broadside." Raising his voice he called across to the stranger, "I am going to board you. Tell your men to lay down their arms and assemble on the foredeck."

Lieutenant Da Gama, first Lieutenant of the Sao Paulo, reported. "The guns are run out and ready for action. I believe there are more men than there appears to be in that ship. If she is a slaver, I would lay money that this crew did not bring her from the Gold Coast."

Antonio nodded. "I am inclined to agree. Get together an armed party. Keep them out of sight." He raised his voice and called over to the other ship. "Come over, Captain, and bring your papers with you."

Da Gama returned and reported, "I have 30 men below deck, all armed including the marines."

"Good! I anticipate they may try something pretty quickly, otherwise they will lose the initiative. I suspect that you may be right about the men on board at present. From here we cannot see the other side of the ship there could be boats full of men hiding behind her."

He turned to the master gunner. "Perez, send a shot over the bow of that ship. Let us see if there is any reaction." Turning to the second lieutenant he ordered, "Have the swivel guns mounted to the rails. I think we may need them. The man ran below calling orders. Then men appeared carrying cradles with the swivel guns, three of them. All three were clamped to points on the ships rails. Another party appeared with powder and shot. Sacks of small musket balls for maximum effect against men.

The master gunner lined up his selected gun and standing back fired. The sound was loud in the comparative silence.

All the swivel guns were loaded, muskets were issued and men stationed along the starboard rail waiting.

For a time nothing happened, then the midshipman at the foretop called a warning and pointed to both ends of the damaged slaver. The swivels adjusted their aim, and the gunners on the foremost and aftermost guns of the broadside levered their carriages around to point to each end of the other ship, waiting for something to happen.

Antonio had become aware of a growing murmur coming from the depths of the slaver, there came a sudden roar of noise, and some screaming.

The deck hatches erupted and a stream of humanity burst through onto the deck.

The horde stopped for a few moments, as if holding its breath, then men poured over the far sides of the ship. Shots were fired, and there was screaming. Struggling men fought and at the bow of the ship the water churned into foam as they glimpsed bodies falling into the sea arms and legs snatched down into a frenzy of blood, torn clothes and body parts, as sharks gathered and fed in an orgy of feeding and death. As the sea calmed the noise continued, though the cause was out of sight of the watchers.

The small boat with the captain on board had left the side of the damaged ship, the oarsmen frantically trying to get clear of the carnage behind them. From the deck of the slaver, a shout brought men to the side, they produced muskets, and without ado opened fire on the small boat, one of the rowers was hit and the man steering in the stern also, the boat sheered round and began drifting back toward the slaver, the other rower, grabbing his dead partner's oar, tried to straighten the boat and regain control, but more musket fire came and the surviving oarsman collapsed. The captain still unhit, stood pistol in hand, and watched the gap between boat and ship shrinking. He lifted the pistol placed the barrel in his mouth and fired, the pistol, obviously, hastily reloaded, misfired, the flash in the pan, blasted the skin of his face and eyes. His scream echoed across the water as he tottered in the boat.

Reaching hands caught him and dragged him on board. His screams were short lived, and parts of his body were tossed overboard to the ever hungry sharks that still patrolled the waters around the ship.

Antonio called La Gama, "Stand the men down from the guns. We'll wait!"

As they watched, the small boat was hauled round to the starboard side of the slaver. At the call of the Midshipman aloft, Antonio gestured to let the head of the ship fall off, as they cleared the bow of the slaver the boats came into view, all crowded with slaves, headed for the scatter of small islands lying between North and South Andros Islands.

***

The working party sent on board the slaver wore cloths wrapped around their faces, as they collected the dead found throughout the ship, men, women and children. Slaves and their captors, possibly pirates also. All were consigned to the sea. The pumps were manned and salt water scoured the slave decks and the blood-spattered main deck. The log book and other documents in the captain's cabin were found untouched. In the strong-box were documents and a bag of gold coins to be delivered to a man in Georgetown on Great Exuma Island to the south of the archipelago.

Da Gama and a prize crew, with the help of the carpenter re-rigged the foremast and sailed for Nassau, while Antonio continued to the south to visit the consignee for the gold, in Grand Exuma Island.

***

News of the sighting of the three ships, under the command of the erstwhile Captain of the Royal Navy, came as an unpleasant reminder that the former Captain Newton was of a different opinion to Martin.

The approach of the three ships was signalled by Hera, patrolling the strait between Governor's Island and New Providence. At the news Martin set sail with Lively, Spartan, and Vixen, meeting with Hera off Hog Island. The enemy sails were all in sight and Martin took a course to give the best advantage with the wind. It was unfortunate that it was at the time of year when the wind was inclined to be fluky, shifting and fitful, ranging at times from a light breeze to almost a gale.

Spartan took first blood, the experienced Lieutenant Marlow having been already nearest to the schooner to windward. Her shots punched holes in the canvas of the schooner's mainsail. The name, Abigail, was picked out in gold on the stern of the schooner, which demonstrated her sailing qualities by adroitly coming about and letting the Spartan feel the benefit of her stern chasers which managed to inflict damage to Spartan's fife rail, causing the sails on the mainmast to fly free as the cleats to which the sheets were secured were smashed.

The first blood went to Abigail but Martin was realistic about the skirmish, for that was what it was. As the two frigates closed the range, matters began to look a little more serious

The two ships were fairly evenly matched, Vixen with her forty guns and the Hasty a 32 gun frigate with the four extra 18 pounder guns on the after deck. She may not have had as many guns but in weight her guns more than outweighed the broadside of Vixen. The former Hasty had been re-named Huron, and was still commanded by Captain Roger Newton.

The bow chasers on Vixen fired at the extreme range, as the bow rose on the waves. One ball splashed into the sea on the port side, the other hit the starboard anchor bowsed at the bow of the Huron. The released anchor dropped into the sea, the trailing chain and rope causing the bow to drag round to starboard. Martin called the helmsman. "Steer to port, east by north. Starboard guns, stand-bye."

Brooks' voice was heard, calming the gun crews eager to get into action. As the bow came round to the new course his voice could be heard, "Run out your guns. Captains, on the uproll as you bear, there came a rapid succession of explosions, as the guns came into line with the target.

Immediately the discharged guns were reloaded. Answering fire was coming from the other ship.

Hera meanwhile was chasing the Abigail whose captain was jockeying for position to support the Huron.

Lively closed up, joining the action, catching the second schooner Martin Horner 22 guns, with a withering broadside that took the schooner's mainmast and turned the wheel and helmsman into bloody splinters. The Martin Horner came sharply up to the wind with guns still manned and firing, HMS Lively was caught unprepared and her mizzen toppled. While the crews of both ships chopped and hacked to clear the raffle of gear, the guns of both ships continued to fire causing damage and casualties to both ships. HMS Spartan joined the fray. The guns of the Martin Horner gradually ceased their efforts. The American flag appeared and was dropped to indicate their surrender. HMS Vixen's the battle with Huron was ongoing,

Captain Newton, realising that the attempted coup had failed, found the determined opposition more than he expected, decided to extricate himself with as many of his people as could. Martin Horner was already lost, but Abigail was still active. He signalled her to break off the action and headed for the rendezvous point at Key West, off the Florida Coast.

The suspended anchor had been chopped away and the Huron was now under proper control. The guns of both ships had been in action for what seemed like hours but was in fact thirty five minutes only. The guns of the Huron were doing damage, and Martin welcomed the assistance of HMS Spartan. She created a diversion, taking pressure off Vixen.

It seemed to Martin that the battle was going to result in both ships being reduced to matchwood, beyond repair. So-far the damage was not critical, but that could change in an instant. He could hear the pumps working down below. The doctor was rushed off his feet with casualties, though the bill could have been worse.

Martin soon realised that the man he was up against was a wily opponent, his experience was clearly demonstrated by the skill he showed handling his ship, despite being attacked from more than one direction.

The Huron took her chance, as the battle raged back and forth the ships changed position until the Huron was sailing in the opposite direction to Vixen. The schooner, Abigail, had eluded Hera and was running north. Huron drew clear and took her chance, taking after Abigail on a northerly course, abandoning from the scene of battle.

Brooks, with his blood up, was bewailing the fact that they had lost ground and the chase would be a long one.

Holding up his hand Martin stopped him, ordering the ships to return to Nassau harbour. To Brooks he said, "There will be another time at another place. This is not over, just temporarily deferred. Now is the time to return and re-fit."

***

Captain Roger Newton was unhappy. His own assessment of the capabilities of his opponent, Captain Sir Martin Forest-Bowers RN, had fallen rather short of real life. Underestimating his enemy had been something that he had not been guilty of in the past. He was at first inclined to dismiss his near defeat as bad luck.

The sneaking feeling that he might be fooling himself was suppressed. He would have to set his mind to other ways of influencing the politics of the Caribbean. The ease with which he had suborned Sir Adrian Maxwell demonstrated clearly that while national spirit existed, money was still the great equaliser. As long as the British continued to charge heavy taxes on trade to and from the islands, there would always be people who could be persuaded.

At the Key West base used by Newton and his partner they discussed the result of the Bahamas sally.

"British got wind of things and had ships there waiting for me." Newton said bitterly.

"What about 'what's his name,' Maxwell? What happened with him?" Absolom asked.

"He'll hang, I guess. He made the mistake of acting too soon, blinded by his lust for the Governor's daughter. He could have bought any number of wenches, but he had to have her and it's cost him everything."

***

Absolom Warner had been a partner of Roger Newton since the pair had met up for a second time in the Mediterranean four years before. Their first meeting had been five years earlier. Absolom had been involved in piracy working from the Barbary Coast. His ship had been captured by the ship on which Roger Newton was first lieutenant. The extent of Roger's debt was not by his current status, large. At the time however, it had seemed enormous.

The private deal agreed between the pirate prisoner and the naval officer was struck one dark night off the coast of Algeria. Both kept their side of the agreement. The pirate got his freedom and therefore kept breathing. The officer paid his debts with enough over to keep him in some comfort for the next few years, by which time he had reached the exalted rank of Post Captain. The return to the status of debtor was almost inevitable and the plans for his departure from the navy began with bare-backed departure, desertion in other words, with whatever he could carry. Then, when the raid on the Sicilian village occurred, he took a chance and made his men aware that they could have the women, provided the men were eliminated. One thing led to another. It was apparent they could leave no witnesses, so the women had to join their men-folk. He had to admit many were already dying, having been used to an extent not normally endured by women. Allowing the witness to escape had been a stroke of genius. He had made sure that the crew realised that they would all get the rope if they were caught. Thus, when he proposed that they tried their luck as pirates, the majority of the men joined him in stealing the ship. With the aid of his friend, Absolom, the wreck was staged. The bodies were provided by the dissenters in the crew, who had been summarily executed to add veracity to the story, to convince the navy that his ship had been lost with all hands.

The journey from Sicily, having carried out a few cosmetic alterations, had been a hair-raising one. Provisioned by a series of savage attacks on passing ships the renegades had reached the harbour used by Absolom. The partnership had been agreed and the decision taken to create a new base in the Americas. Their choice of the Florida Keys was based on the location and the undeveloped state of the islands. The settlement on Key West had been visited during Newton's service as a Midshipman before its acquisition by the new American Nation. Since they had been established on the island it had prospered. The Islanders sensibly accepted the situation they had no way of changing.

***

Absolom spoke after the pair had considered matters for a while, over their brandy and cigars. "I can say that, despite the Bahamas business, our accounts are showing a considerable profit from the other work we have undertaken over the past few years. Perhaps we should hold back a little over the next few months." He held his hand up to stop the comment his partner was about to make. "The Americans are involved with their acquisition of the Louisiana Purchase at this time but they are getting more and more upset with the British. My sources are confident that, when they have completed reinforcing their fleet with the new frigates, they will be challenging the way the British stop and search of their merchant ships. It will offer us an unprecedented opportunity to collect all sorts of ships while the two nations squabble. Their conflict will cover many sins. Each will blame the other and we will make a killing."

"I do agree, Absolom. But my worry is that this British Captain is a terrier. He has the force to make things difficult if he remains in the area."

"He is really that good?"

"One of my men was with him as a Midshipman. You know him. His name is Hayes. He currently stands as Lieutenant in my ship. I do not think much of him as a seaman, but he is useful in boarding parties, and had no conscience that I have ever detected. However his comments about Forest-Bowers are envious and obviously he hates him. My guess is that he is everything that Hayes is not. That makes me think he deserves respect. The fact that he was made Post Captain in his twenties means that he is an exceptional man. According to the Gazette he has gone from strength to strength."

Absolom looked at his partner steadily, his brown eyes steady, the golden brown of his face showing no sign of concern. The question that hung between the two men demanded an answer. As far as Absolom was concerned it was an answer for Roger Newton to give. Whatever Newton said, Absolom would accept. Over the term of their partnership, it had been ever thus.

The decision was made and announced in an even tone, without any particular emphasis. "We let the matter rest, unless or until we discover if the Bahamas ships remain there. In the event they do, and interfere with our current business we will rethink the matter. My guess is that they will return to home waters. We will then only have the American navy to worry about."

***

In Nassau the decision was made in dealing with Maxwell. Rather than languishing in prison awaiting the noose, he would survive at least, working on one of the plantations that he had once owned, on Jamaica.

In the Governor's House the meeting between the captains of Martin's squadron had been joined by two frigate captains of the West Indies command, who had arrived that same day to check up on rumours of revolution. Captain Brown, HMS Tiger 38, and Captain Mainwaring HMS Phoebe 40, were both known to Martin and their presence was a re-assurance that the islands would be secure when the squadron departed in three days' time.

The Governor, Sir Anthony Warren, was preparing for the handover to his successor who was unpacking in Government House as the group met.

The presence of the Governor at the meeting was a tribute to his popularity with the naval contingent.

After thanking the Captains assembled, he explained briefly his disposition of the revolutionaries. "It appears that the pirate elements supporting the uprising have returned to Florida area, Thanks to the presence of the Navy, I would not expect their return without considerable reinforcement. My successor will control matters from today. Thank you, gentlemen, officially and personally."

Later, when he and Martin were alone, he mentioned his plans.

"I am returning to England with my daughter, as you know, Martin. I understand we are to travel in company with your ships. I hope we will not lose contact in future."

Martin smiled. I understand you will be taking a seat in Parliament which will require your presence in London. My home in London is always open to friends." He smiled. "I also believe your connection with the Navy is going to be of a permanent nature?"

"It certainly seems so, and I cannot say how relieved I am that this decision of my daughter comes at this time. It has been a matter troubling me ever since she attained her, er… growth." He hesitated for a moment. "It is times like these that remind me how much I miss her mother. She always knew what was best for Catherine."

"If you'll permit me, sir, I think recent events have shown clearly that your daughter has benefited from your efforts over the past years. You must be proud of the way she has reacted to the trials of these past days."

"Oh, I am. But I will be relieved the day I lead her down the aisle and pass the responsibility over to someone more in tune with her requirements? Does that make me a bad parent?"

Martin laughed. "I think the reverse. In fact, I myself will undoubtedly be as relieved when my own daughter elects to marry. I am of the opinion that the young, having been brought up as best we can, should be released to live their chosen lives, and create their own families. I ask you, sir, the same question. Does that make me a bad parent?"

The arrival of the Sao Paulo in Nassau was the signal for the convoy to Britain to gather in some sort of order to prepare to sail.

One week later the convoy sailed.

Chapter sixteen

Transition

1810

THERE WAS A busy air about the Admiralty as Martin entered the main door. He went directly to the Office of Admiral Bowers where he found a group of others involved in an active discussion with two civilians who were looking appalled at something suggested by one of the officers present.

At Martin's appearance the Admiral called the others to order. "For those of you who do not know him, this officer is Captain Sir Martin Forest-Bowers, and yes, he is my son. The important factor is that he is probably the best qualified person here to discuss the problem concerning you two gentlemen."

Turning to Martin he said, "These two gentlemen have been ordered to discuss our situation in Sweden with the appointment of Count Bernadotte as heir-presumptive to the Swedish crown. There are embassies in Sweden and Norway which may well become redundant since Bernadotte is French. It is presumed that his sympathies will lie with France, rather than in the non-partisan area of neutrality. The position of Russia in the mix is also creating the thought that we will be occupied with matters which, up to now, we have been able to side-line.

Martin looked around the assembly of naval officers and civilians. Then turning to his adoptive father he said quietly, "Can we have a private word?"

Admiral Bowers looked at him searchingly. Martin was very much the son he had acquired by default, but nevertheless a much appreciated and loved member of his family.

"Gentlemen, there is a small matter I must clarify with the Captain. Please carry on with your deliberations. We will rejoin you shortly."

Ignoring the surprised looks and the odd frown at this comment, he led Martin through the door to his private office.

Closing the door he turned to Martin, eyebrow raised in enquiry.

Martin looked him directly in the eye. "Why is this discussion taking place without the Comtesse present?"

The Admiral started to reply, then shook his head. "It did cross my mind to invite her. Then I ran through the other people involved and realised that there would be no point. These people here would crucify her rather than listen to anything she might say. It also occurred to me that, while the Generals at Army Headquarters at Horse Guards might hear what she says, as a woman in male company, any response she proposes would be discarded until all other avenues had been explored. By which time that response would probably be meaningless, this would be pointed out as confirmation of their opinions that her contribution was useless."

Martin considered this and nodded slowly. "I should never have doubted, father. While I knew you resented my participation in secret dealings, I should have remembered that you never failed to act on the information provided. I will consult with Alouette and report back to you."

The Admiral nodded with a small smile. "It will take time but I will make sure the credit goes where it belongs. But the secret will be kept from all but those who should know."

***

Taking tea with Alouette later that day, Martin related the events of the meeting. "I would have been happier if you had been present, but I understand now that it would have been pointless, with a group such as that."

Alouette chuckled. "Martin, you put things so nicely. What you mean is I would have been ignored completely, though politely. Whilst the men discussed important matters among themselves."

She was thinking at the same time. "I am not sure that they understand the situation regarding Bernadotte. The invitation to join the Swedish line of succession came from Sweden. Napoleon had nothing to do with it. In fact I would almost suggest Napoleon will be happy to see the back of the Marshal. While he will expect Sweden will continue to follow Russia, my guess is that it will not.

"Bernadotte is an interesting man who has had conflicts with Napoleon in the past. If he has accepted the mantle of Sweden's leadership, I would expect him to place Sweden first in all things."

Martin looked at her. "Alouette, you never cease to amaze me. Please prepare a paper of your opinion as you have explained it to me. I will see it gets placed where it will do the most good."

"As you wish, Martin. Now let us talk about America!"

***

In the house that evening, Martin gave the paper to the Admiral as they stood waiting for the ladies before going in to dinner.

He watched as Charles Bowers read the document, then read it again. He looked up at Martin. "This is convincing. I have the impression that whoever wrote this knows Bernadotte personally?"

Martin smiled. "She does!"

The second letter Martin passed over was on the subject of America. "This, I'm afraid. Is not such happy news. We have an explosion about to occur, and our people are walking about the magazine lighting matches."

"We do not need another war at present," the Admiral mused.

"A section of our government has still not accepted that America is no longer a colony waiting to pop back under Britain's wing saying sorry. The aggressive attitude of our ships to American merchantmen is causing more and more resentment among the Americans, and their frigates are clearly going to be a handful for our ships to deal with."

The Admiral looked up in surprise, "You really think so?"

"44 guns 24pounders, a hull built like a '74' crewed by ex-British seamen. Yes, I really think so!"

They went into dinner, the Admiral deep in thought.

The party at the weekend was attended by Antonio Ramos and his ward, and Sir Anthony Warren and his daughter, Catherine. The tactful invitation to the officers of HMS Vixen currently lying in the Thames at St Katherine's dock ensured that both of the young ladies were monopolised within minutes of their arrival.

Jennifer giggled at the immediate annexation of the two pretty girls, while Martin nudged her gently, pointing out that it was just a few years since she herself had been the similar focus of attention. Martin gazed around the room, now filled with a swirling crowd of people. The orchestra in the conservatory struggling manfully to compete with the chatter of the throng. He saw the Admiral speaking with the Comtesse; Alouette smiling and nodding at something Charles said. Then Antonio joined his wife, his tall figure resplendent in his dress uniform. Their recent wedding had been attended by the families, plus Sir Anthony Watts, who had given the bride away in the absence of her father. Martin had stood as best man. The wedding had been held at the church in Eynsham, and the couple had spent their honeymoon at Walton Hall, Martin's family home, loaned for the occasion.

The reason for the quiet wedding was a combination of the delicacy of Alouette's position and the lack of time available. Since neither had an extensive family to satisfy, it was a matter for their friends to rally around and arrange, and this was what had happened. In addition to the families of Bowers, and Forest-Bowers, Lieutenant Santos, from Sao Paulo. Sir Anthony Warren and Catherine, his daughter, attended as did Lieutenant Cameron, who escorted them and Lieutenant Harman who escorted Maria Diaz, Antonio's ward.

The entire staff of the estate prepared the wedding feast which was arranged under the trees on the lawn at the Hall. The centrepiece of the repast was the roast ox, and there were barrels of ale, and tables groaning with food. Musicians from the Oxford theatre attended to play for the dancing.

***

Two weeks later the orders came. Commodore Forest-Bowers and Commodore Antonio Ramos paired once more for a voyage to Canada and a cruise from Canada to the Caribbean.

There would be a group of staff travelling in convoy with the naval force, and it was anticipated that a diplomat would accompany the cruise.

It is true that Martin wondered about the point of taking a diplomat travelling with the warships but, since no explanation was forthcoming, he did not pursue the matter. It was only after a discussion with Alouette on the subject that the situation was clarified somewhat.

Her position at the head of the mysterious department set up by Sir Anthony Watts, known for some time as, plain Mr. Smith, had been reinforced by her report on Count Bernadotte. The subsequent assessments of his place in the political firmament reinforced the suggestions and conclusions reached in the report. Due credence was given to the expertise that had gone into gathering and correlating of the information it contained and the conclusions reached.

Martin's conversation with her on the subject of the Canadian voyage had been both revealing and disquieting. Seated at the desk in the anonymous house which was the headquarters of the organisation, Alouette passed on her understanding of the situation.

"America is still in process of becoming a country in its own right. Canada has, to a large extent, settled for the place she now occupies within the Empire. While there is still trouble from the French, we believe it is containable.

"The Americans are more of a worry because we cannot divert too much attention from our current enemies in Napoleon's Europe.

"I would be much happier if I could guarantee that British warships would not harass American shipping. As things are, we are on a knife's edge, between going to war and keeping the peace. You will agree that it is a delicate balance to maintain and thus a diplomat with your squadron should be an advantage.

"Between us, if you can remove the odious renegade, Captain Newton, both American and British authorities would be most grateful. His activities are gaining him a name for ferocity and invulnerability. The location of his base is known to be on the Florida Keys, though which one is still undiscovered. Apparently the local population is very protective of the base and, judging from the lengths they go to in keeping it secret, benefit from keeping it so."

Martin considered her comment. "In the circumstances, is there no way the cessation of the systematic harassment of American merchant ships cannot be turned into orders for the ships of the fleet?" Martin asked. "I know my father agrees with you and would support that action."

"Well you might ask. As you will be aware it has been asked in the highest circles. Unfortunately, there is still an element in the government who regard the return of the Americas to British rule as an achievable situation. They are insistent on continuing the harassment on the basis that it will induce the Americans to give up their independence and return to the British fold."

She looked at Martin, shrugged, and said wickedly, "Do you not miss the past? We had things much easier then. We could just tumble into bed and forget our worries for a while. How about it? Shall we?"

Martin stood up smiling. Alouette was more beautiful now than ever. "If I thought you really meant that I would be tempted. But we both have others to think of, so I must regretfully decline your generous offer." A little wistfully, he stepped over to her and kissed her warmly on the lips, quelling the urge to take advantage of the moment. As he left her it was clear to him, that there would always be part of him that belonged to the Alouette who had risked her life and shared danger with him, over the past years.

***

The following days were busy. Making arrangements for the lengthy voyage and extended visit to the Americas was not the easiest of tasks, especially leaving Jennifer after her lengthy illness and dramatic recovery. Parting once more would be a painful process.

The preparations for the voyage were well advanced and the name of the diplomat announced to a small circle of people. While the entire arrangement had been kept very much to a select few, the matter did become public knowledge.

The man himself was no help in the matter. Rather than keep matters discreet, he seemed to go out of his way to publicise the matter. The Honourable Dominic Gordon, son of an Sussex landowner, he seemed to be well provided with money, and willing to spend it. Martin was invited to meet the man at an evening soiree in the house of Lady Pamela Brown-Oliver.

Though he had never attended one of her parties, he was aware of them by reputation.. The lady herself was a 'sixty-year-old harridan,' in the words of Alouette, who, of necessity, had to deal with the lady on occasion. The combination of getting to know the Honourable Dominic Gordon, and supporting Alouette and Antonio who were required to attend, persuaded Martin and Jennifer to accept the invitation sent at the request of the diplomat.

The party arrived at the venue together to be greeted by the lady herself, a forbidding-looking woman, nearly six feet tall. Her face resembled a mask created by the make-up she was wearing. Rather than concealing the wrinkles it somehow emphasised their existence. The grimace that accompanied the handshake at the introductions nearly caused Jennifer to laugh aloud. Luckily she managed to contain herself until she reached the cloakroom. There she spluttered and coughed, still unwilling to reveal her amusement and disgust at the macabre image portrayed by her hostess.

Alouette showed her concern at the obvious discomfort of her young friend and accompanied her, insisting on being told the cause of her discomfort, suspecting and dreading the recurrence of her illness. When she discovered the cause of the problem, she laughed out loud, to the astonishment of the trio of ladies who entered the room during the interlude.

Eventually after composing themselves once more, they returned to their concerned escorts to find they had now been joined by Lieutenant Harmon with Maria Diaz, aglow with the excitement of her first grown-up soiree with her own chosen escort.

As Martin looked around at the party, he had a moment of déjà-vu. A moment of recall to that first encounter with the family of which he was now a part. His eyes fell on Jennifer, the wife he could not have anticipated. He thought of the way she had looked at him in her direct manner, when she told him that she would marry him one day. He smiled and realised that they were all looking at him.

Jennifer said, "Ah, you've come back to us You seemed lost there for a few moments."

"I was remembering it has been 18 years to the day, since I joined the family."

Jennifer took his hand. "Oh, Martin. I did not think."

He put his finger to her lips. "Hush, my darling. I was grateful for the encounter that led to our meeting, and you may be assured that I always will be. I suppose seeing us all here like this, I miss Jane and the Admiral."

"I really think they would have been rather uncomfortable. The company here is not the sort they would normally mix with. In truth, nor is it the sort we would normally mix with." Jennifer smiled and tapped her nose with her fan.

At this point the Honourable Dominic arrived and introduced himself. "Judging by your attire I presume that you must be the people accompanying me to the

Americas." This was said with an air of lordly condescension.

Martin looked at the man curiously. Slender, willowy almost, he had a pale face and was dressed in expensive clothing, but he looked very tired, almost ill in Martin's opinion. "I am expecting a passenger on my next voyage. Would you be the Honourable Dominic Gordon?"

"Just so." The man answered. "At your service." He made a bow and turned to Jennifer, lifting her hand to his lips he muttered quietly, "and especially at yours, Madam."

"My husband mentioned you. sir. Are you aware of your departure date yet?"

The man stood up surprised. "Why no, madam. I have not yet been informed?"

She turned to Martin. "I am surprised, with such a short time remaining to your departure, I would have expected the entire expedition to be informed by now."

"I confess I would have presumed so." He turned to the uncomfortable man and said, "It will probably be because there will be last minute instructions to be passed on."

The diplomat drew himself up to his full height, "When are we talking about?"

Jennifer said, "I believe it to be next week-end, four days hence."

The face of the young man was a picture, "I have not... I cannot.... There is no time to do anything in just a few days. Excuse me." He dashed off in a hurry.

Antonio, having been engaged in conversation with Maria and her partner, looked at Martin eyebrow raised?

Martin shrugged. "I think he has the impression that we will actually leave at the weeks' end."

Antonio said, "Aren't we?"

Martin grinned, "We sail from London then but we do not leave Portsmouth until the end of the month. Three weeks hence."

Antonio thought for a moment. The smile spread over his face. "I think I might enjoy this evening after all."

Alouette arrived back from a private conversation with Sir Anthony Watts, also a guest at the ball and her former mentor. "What is so amusing? Have I missed something?"

Both men laughed and Antonio told her about Dominic. She joined them laughing, then took Antonio off to dance, leaving Martin and Jennifer to themselves for the moment.

The party lasted into the night in a fairly orderly manner. After midnight an element of wildness began to appear so Martin, Antonio and Lieutenant Harmon left with their partners, having done their duty on this occasion, merely by being there.

***

In the aftermath of the evening event there followed a formal visit by Dominic Gordon, who managed to appear at the Admiralty during the afternoon of the following day. He looked pale and wan and was considerably put out by the failure of the naval men to explain fully the difference between sailing from Dartford for Portsmouth, and sailing from Portsmouth to the Americas.

Admiral Bowers was not sympathetic. His opinion of the Honourable Dominic was that his presence for the task in hand was inspired by his father Sir Ranalph Gordon, MP, who was embarrassed by his presence in London. The embarrassment was the result of the public antics of the company he kept, rather than his personal participation in them. The concern was for his son's well-being.

As the group seated themselves for the briefing and discussion, Martin took pity on the young man and made an effort to accommodate his inexperience where it was evident. The result was a comparatively smooth transition to the point where Dominic, despite his diplomatic status, was informed that the Commodore would be the final arbiter of any agreements reached.

For the first time since he had taken his place at the meeting Dominic spoke up. "Surely, gentlemen, in my position as special envoy, my decisions must be deciding in all matters of negotiation with the American authorities?"

Admiral Bowers nodded to Sir Anthony Watts who was seated at the table but had taken no part in the discussion so far.

Clearing his throat, Sir Anthony spoke. "Mr. Gordon, you are a member of the Diplomatic service. You therefore appear on the Diplomatic list. You have no experience of actual diplomatic negotiation whatsoever, nor have you shown any inclination to actually justify your position in the Foreign Office. He looked the man in the eye and added, "Do I have that right? Have I misread your career up to date?"

Dominic Gordon met Sir Anthony's gaze for a few moments then dropped his eyes, a flush spreading across his cheeks, as he reluctantly nodded his head.

Sir Anthony continued, "Because Commodore Forest-Bowers has, over the past years, gained considerable experience in diplomatic negotiation, he will be in charge, and you will act upon his instruction. Is that quite clear to everyone here?" His gaze moved around the group, all of whom nodded in agreement to the instruction.

Sir Anthony rose to his feet. "I am leaving this meeting now as my successor is better qualified to explain fully the background to this mission. I suggest you all take heed of the instructions you are given. In these circumstances, your survival can depend on understanding what your task really is." He looked around the group. "Gentlemen, good luck!"

The door of the room closed behind him only to be opened almost immediately to admit Alouette.

Chapter seventeen

A Capital affair

ANTONIO LOOKED AT Martin as they travelled to Dartford to join their ships. "I cannot forget the look on Gordon's face after 'plain Mr. Smith' dressed him down." Sir Anthony Watts had always been referred to as 'plain Mr. Smith' during his tenure as spymaster for the British Government.

Martin smiled, "That was nothing to the look on his face when Alouette walked through the door and briefed the meeting." Both men laughed aloud at the memory. Dominic Gordon had questioned her presence immediately.

Alouette had proceeded calmly to point out that her presence at the meeting was secret on pain of imprisonment, she should at all times be referred to as 'plain Mr. Jones', and under no circumstances was any reference to be made to her gender outside the room.

Her briefing had been specific. The American government was preparing for war. That was evident from reports from loyal Americans and her own spies. The purpose of the voyage was to re-assure British interests in Canada and the Caribbean and give warning to the Americans that the British still controlled the seas.

"I am aware of the increasing threat posed by the frigates currently building on the east coast. I am also aware that they are not yet ready. Diplomacy rather than open warfare is the intention. I leave you with this thought." She impaled Gordon with her stare. "You can come out of this excursion with either a career ahead of you, or your future behind you." She lifted her head and smiled at the group. "Good luck, gentlemen. I look forward to your successful return." She had swept out of the room leaving a memory of her perfume and the impact of her words."

Martin thought about Alouette's words as HMS Vixen made her way down the Thames. The brief was vague enough but at least the actual orders had been dictated by the Admiralty. Though there was plenty of room for things to go wrong, there was also some acceptance of the fact that the project was official. Too often in the past ships had been sent on missions which were so obscure that blind luck, had on occasion, been the only way that they could be carried out with any degree of success.

His thoughts turned to Dominic Gordon, His first impression had been that the man was a complete waster. But after the briefing by Alouette he was beginning to think there was more to the man than he had, in the first place, guessed.

The voyage round to Portsmouth was uneventful, and it was with some relief that Martin looked forward to a period, however short, at the house in Eastney.

Jane met him at the quay accompanied by Maria Diaz. She was staying with Jane until the squadron sailed. Her excuse was that her guardian, Antonio Ramos, who was sailing with Martin, would be here. The fact that Neil Harmon was a member of Martin's crew had apparently also been at least a contributory reason for her Hampshire visit.

The preparations for the voyage were completed except for the details of personal farewells. For Martin's ship, HMS Vixen, with a crew that, by now, were almost exclusively volunteers, the farewells were signalled by the size of the crowd on the quay to wave them farewell. Despite the distance from the quay to the anchored ship, as she weighed anchor, the faint sound from the shore carried on the wind to remind the departing crew, that they would not be forgotten.

***

Bishop's Rock was clear astern as Martin came on deck, he was greeted by the Master, Jared Watson. "The last we'll see of Britain for a while." Watson commented.

Martin nodded his head. "There are a few miles to travel before we see land again."

"We are taking the direct route to Halifax, Nova Scotia. Our ships are sound enough, and providing the weather is not too unkind we should manage the voyage fairly quickly."

He nodded at the other ships of the squadron, its numbers swollen by the addition of two schooners and a packet ship. The schooners, Marianne and Driffield, both former blockade runners. Apart from carrying a sensible quantity of cargo both had a turn of speed and could out-sail the other ships in the flotilla, with two exceptions. The mail packet, Jenna, built for her normal task, carrying mails, and HMS Hera. Jenna accommodated the Honourable Dominic Gordon. The two schooners' carried trade goods in their holds. HMS

Hera, Lively, and Spartan, were scattered to north, south and directly ahead. Sao Paulo was sailing abreast of Vixen to leeward.

Martin paced the quarter-deck deep in thought. The sojourn at Eastney had been a happy time though far too short for its naval participants and their ladies. It appeared the relationship between Maria Diaz, Antonio Ramos's ward, and young Harmon was continuing. Martin decided that in view of the time they had spent in each other's company, despite the absences that duty entailed, there was a fair chance that the relationship would survive. He smiled, wondering if Maria realised what it meant to be married to a serving officer in the Royal Navy. Shrugging mentally, he returned to his memory of the run-up to the departure of his command. Alouette had joined the party at Eastney for a final briefing on the task at hand and had remained until Antonio set sail with the squadron.

HMS Vixen had been alongside for most of the period, the carronades mounted aft were replaced by new 24 pound models with improved aiming and swivel arrangements. It did mean that the crew were able to be given time ashore prior to the voyage.

Martin's attention was diverted by the call from the masthead. "Hera is signalling, sir!" Lieutenant Cameron, who had the watch, sent up the duty Middy, Percy Gibbs. He sprang to the shrouds and started to climb rapidly, telescope strapped over his shoulder. From the foretop he was able to make out the signal flying from Hera's halyard.

He called down to Cameron, "Enemy in sight,' sir!" He called. He slid down to the deck and went to the flag locker, where he extracted the single acknowledgement flag. He ran that up the halyard, the junior middy took the telescope and climbed the mast. From the foretop he called down, "New signal! Single ship, two decks."

"Acknowledge!" Martin ordered. "Mr. Watson, let us increase sail and we will alter northward. Mr. Cameron have Gibbs signal to all ships to alter course and close on Vixen, steer west-north-west. We will try and avoid contact. We have our task to perform, and I would rather we were not delayed by an engagement at this time."

After a moment's reflection, Martin turned to Cameron. "What news of the intrepid Miss Warren?"

Cameron blushed. "We agreed to wait until the end of this voyage. We will discuss our future at that time."

The sky was darkening. Stars were beginning to show up here and there against the heavens'

As night fell there was no sign of the ship seen by Hera, so Martin resumed their mean course for Halifax under cruising conditions.

***

The Squadron encountered four merchantmen sailing from Canada in convoy, and Spartan encountered an American merchant ship being attacked by pirates. By the time HMS Lively joined her, both pirate cutters were reduced to kindling.

The grateful American passed over a barrel of rum in thanks, and proceeded on her way, apparently to Bristol.

Then three nights of stormy weather scattered the ships causing a delay they did not anticipate, a delay that allowed them to elude an ambush set for them 50 miles off the coast of Newfoundland.

Hera found scattered debris and survivors clinging to the rigging of the foremast of their wrecked ship. The captain had survived but was delirious. A young boy and two men, ordinary seamen, who survived, were looked after and treated for exposure. The captain was obviously dying.

He was transferred to Vixen to be attended by Doctor Mills. His ramblings in delirium made it quite clear that the word of their passage and their purpose had been sent ahead of them. An unofficial ambush had been put together with the temporary assistance of two of the completed American, 'big' frigates. They had been waiting for over a week until well past the expected time of arrival, when the storm hit. The other ships returned to port leaving the Betty, the wrecked ship, as lookout. It had been a rogue wave. It pooped the schooner and the captain, who was beside the wheel at the time, had been thrown against the fife rail round the mainmast. It had in the words of the doctor, scrambled his insides.

Before he died the plan had been more or less explained except for the source of the information. The doctor would allow no pressure to be put on the dying man.

It was the boy who inadvertently gave the clue. He described a posh fellow who had appeared in Baltimore from a French ship. After meeting with the American Captain of the frigate in the harbour, he moved into the hotel. The Middy, Athol Gibbs chatted with him and discovered that the posh fellow was registered as Sir Bertrand MacIlroy, Bart.

The ships arrived at Halifax and Martin made contact with the authorities. His other contact, arranged through Alouette, was Logan Stuart. He was a business man with interests both sides of the border. His erect figure reflected his former occupation, of soldier in the years prior to becoming a businessman. It was only when he stepped forward that Martin realised that Stuart's right leg ended in a stump. Upon being informed about the abortive ambush, he shrugged, his comment was succinct. "We have so-called patriots here, who are as radical as the people who persuade British Naval Captains to harass American shipping." He then went on to other matters. He was particularly interested in Sir Bertrand who, up to now, was unknown to him. He suggested that Martin keep in touch as long as possible. Whatever he found would be passed to Alouette. He was also able to give Martin contact names in several of the ports down the coastline between Halifax and the Florida Keys. All were, he assured Martin, in regular touch through coastal traders. They parted with the promise of further investigation into the presence and activities of Sir Bertrand MacIlroy, with the network keeping as close an eye on his activities in the America's as they could.

The party was received by the Governor with the ceremony expected for a diplomatic mission. Dominic Gordon, having been presented, watched proceedings with interest. For Martin, the change he observed in Dominic was re-assuring. The pale, willowy young man was now tanned by the weather, and his body was filling out. His sober dress was in keeping with his diplomatic status. The tousled blond hair was retained sensibly in keeping with his dress and demeanour.

In conversation with the captain of the packet which had carried Dominic, Martin discovered that the young man had accepted a challenge from the captain, to tail onto the ropes when they were changing sails. It seemed that from that time Dominic had divided his time between reading, and his self-imposed deck duties. The captain had been impressed and had paid up the wager, a case of wine, with good heart.

The discussion with the agent in Halifax, had been revealing to Martin, It was made quite clear that the activities of the renegade, Newton, was having an adverse effect on diplomatic relations. His depredations on American ships were all carried out under British colours; on others, American. This confused matters, especially since the number of incidents between Royal Naval ships, and American, was increasing. Pressure from sources in England was continuing, from people determined to return the Americans to their former status as a colony. The stubborn maintenance of the belief, that it will only require such harassment to tip the scales for a return to the Empire, appeared to be held by a group of people, who had no understanding of the personalities involved.

Before resuming their journey down the east coast of America, Martin sat down with Dominic and discussed the information they had been given, and Dominic's part in the next stage of the voyage.

At his own suggestion Dominic undertook to carry out the formal duties of diplomat, suggesting that he trawled the official side of their tour, leaving Martin free to contact the agents' en-route.

He suggested, "I would prefer that we spoke regularly on my role, and on the attitudes I encounter. I am aware of my inexperience in these matters, but I have been trying to get as well informed as possible in anticipation of taking an active part in our mission."

Martin listened to the man sitting before him, impressed by his manner, and the obvious thought behind the suggestions made. "I agree. I will be happy to discuss, and advise, if necessary. It will make it easier to carry out the undercover aspects of our mission, though I fear Sir Bertrand MacIlroy has already given the game away."

"We are calling at Boston, I believe?" Dominic ventured.

"We are. It is an important port and diplomatically important as a former capital and major base for the American Navy. We have a very good agent there who will be in danger, according to Mr. Stuart. I do not know the name of the agent, though I am told he will contact me if it is safe. Curiously, Stuart made a point on the subject. It may be where our roles are reversed. You may, in fact, be the point of contact through your diplomatic negotiations. For that reason. I must divulge the identification sequence for an open meeting in public."

Dominic looked puzzled for a moment, then smiled. "I understand. Of course it makes sense to make contact in a social meeting. How will I know?"

"Mr. Stuart indicated that you will be asked if you were able to see the performance of Catherine Steel in the play, 'The Pioneer', while you were in Halifax. The answer would be, 'no', the lady is currently playing 'Juliet'. The identity of the person should not be remarked in any but a natural way. Contact, subsequently, will be as he or she designates."

"She?" Dominic questioned with raised eyebrow.

"It is possible. Consider Alouette! She spent several years after the death of her husband, as an agent for the service she now runs."

"Of course. I did not even think of that." Dominic said thoughtfully.

***

In the Boston headquarters of the Savage Trading Company Julia Savage sat checking off items of inventory. The company, started by her grandfather, was involved in the trade with Native American tribes. The profitability of the trade had been increasing on a regular basis since the trading began 45 years ago.

In the period since the country had become independent there had been increasing problems with the relationships, long held, with the Iroquois Nations. The formerly friendly relationships were being eroded by the advancing tide of settlers entering the hunting grounds held by the nations from past times. The tribes were being pushed back. More and more villages had moved north over the border into the Canadian lands still part of their nation.

Thomas Savage, Julia's grandfather, would have moved over the border himself but he had fallen ill. His son and daughter, Julia's parents, had been killed in an attack by Hurons six years ago, when they were visiting friends near Albany.

Julia sighed and sat back from her work. For the last months she had been liquidating the assets of the company, so that, with her grandfather, she could cross the border prepared for a new life. Most of the company assets were already lodged in Montreal. The transfer of the last ships was already arranged.

There was trouble on the horizon. She was sure of it, now the assets of the company had been transferred to Montreal. The company ship, Sweetwater, at present in harbour, would be leaving with her grandfather this evening. She would follow next week in their other ship, Sagamore after her meeting with the Englishman.

Porter Williams came into the office and spoke. "Miss Julia, the British are entering the harbour." The bang of the saluting guns could be heard in the background. "There they go. Haven't heard British guns since Bunker Hill."

Porter Williams, fifty five years of age, had been with the company for nearly thirty-one years. He had inherited this local office and the current American business from the Savage family for services rendered over those years.

They had made no announcement and Porter had not even told his wife. Julia put her books in the drawer and turned the key. She passed the key to Porter and accompanied him to the door. They left the building and walked together down the sidewalk to the nearby harbour.

The reception committee stood on the dockside. Julia took her place alongside Hiram Goss, the Mayor of Boston. As council convenor for the town she was part of the reception committee sent to greet the diplomatic visitor.

The barge dashed up to the quay with a flash of the oars as the boat came alongside the pontoon especially provided for ease of landing. As the visitors came ashore Julia found herself looking at the young man with the slightly tousled blond hair. He was dressed in the high necked tunic of the diplomatic corps.

Dominic took her extended hand as she nodded her head in greeting. The words spoken were almost lost as she remembered to ask if he had seen the play 'Pioneer' while in Halifax.

His reply took her very much by surprise when he completed the code referring to 'Juliet'. Her shock was reciprocated when Dominic caught the comment about the 'Pioneer', regardless of the comment by Martin earlier. He had not really expected the agent to be female, and such a female!

Martin and the group were handed into the carriages for the trip to the town hall where the banquet would be held. The council chamber had been set up for the official talks to take place during the afternoon.

The proceedings were brisk. After a short speech by the mayor the two parties discussed the worsening situation and the interference with trade by the pirates. Martin promised he would do all in his power to remove the threat, but was unable to prevent the individual intervention of naval ships with the American trading craft. There was mutual agreement that the practice should be stopped with hopes, privately, that the looming war could be averted.

At the banquet Julia found herself sitting next to the Commodore. She noticed that his eyes twinkled when he mentioned Juliet in his conversation.

"So, Julia," he corrected himself. "I have the feeling there are things you would like to say to me that should not be for other ears."

"Why, Commodore. I believe you are flirting with me." Julia said with a small smile.

"Miss, there is nothing I would rather be doing at this moment. But I confess, in this company, flirting would be definitely suspect. However a private word would be useful. Perhaps you could be induced to take a stroll with my colleague, Dominic Gordon? "

"Would this be an attempt to play cupid, sir? In your position too?"

"Do I presume an assignation with Dominic would not be acceptable?"

She looked at him seriously. "You really mean that, don't you?"

"It's him or me, I'm afraid." The eyes were twinkling again.

"How could I refuse an invitation like that?" She said demurely. "Commodore, I have the feeling that my invitation to take tea with me would be acceptable?"

"Your servant, Madam."

"It's Miss, actually, sir. And why not bring Dominic with you? The shop is just up the street and I can supply provisions for trade with the Iroquois nations."

***

Later, when the official luncheon was concluded, the party walked through the immediate area of Boston and called in for tea at the Trading Company. It was there that the opportunity came for Julia to pass over the report she had prepared for onward transmission to Canada. At the same time she reported her plans to transfer her operations to Montreal.

Chapter eighteen

Ending and Beginning

AS SHE WATCHED her grandfather depart in the company ship for Halifax, she was joined on the quay by Porter Williams. "Hey, Julia. I am sad to see the old man go. You don't need to go, you know. I would gladly hand the business back to you if you decided to stay."

She looked up at him, towering over her, a big solid man, dependable and reassuring.

"I must go. Grandfather needs me and he cannot stay here. He has too many enemies."

"Hell, they are just windbags, got nothing better to do than pick on people. The revolution has been over 30 years or more. It don't mean a thing now."

"You know that's not true, Porter Williams. It's yesterday to the Harpers and the Mitchells." She named two of the most powerful families in Boston at the time.

A boat approached the quay, the faces of the occupants difficult to distinguish in the twilight. Julia called out, 'Sagamore?'

One of the rowers called back."Aye, Miss!"

At the quay the man rose from his seat and helped Julia down into the boat.

***

On board the Vixen Lieutenant Brooks knocked on the Captain's door and, being called, to enter he went in.

Martin and Dominic were talking over a glass of wine.

As Martin looked up, Brooks said, "Bo'sun Peters thinks a ship has dropped her hook just offshore of Spectacle Island. They were very quiet. A boat has pulled to shore.

Martin and Dominic both rose to their feet. Martin took his sword and a pistol from the table top, as Dominic rose he looked around, he was unarmed, Martin took the sword, given him by Charles Bowers when he became a lieutenant, from its place on the bulkhead and tossed it to the younger man. "Let us see what we can see," he said lightly, and led the way on deck. The dinghy was returning, making a wide sweep around the moored frigate.

Martin called down to the bo'sun's mate and the jolly boat crew at the foot of the accommodation ladder, "Quietly, lads. Let's take a look at that dinghy passing ahead of us.

Martin and Dominic descended the ladder and boarded the jollyboat.

They pulled away with a will and rounded the bow of Vixen, they were within a few yards of the dinghy when the men noticed the jolly boat approaching.

"Bear off, mates. We're passing through." The Dorset burr almost put Martin off for a moment. Then they were alongside the dinghy, and the fact that there was a bundle in the bilge, jerking and grunting, came into the conversation.

"Just taking a pig back to the ship for provisions, the Dorset-man said.

The bo'sun's mate chuckled. "Sounds as if that pig is not too willing." He leaned across and ripped back the cloth covering the supposed pig. The cloth was a boat cloak and the pig was an angry Julia Savage, gagged with the skirt of her dress pulled up for the purpose. It incidentally revealed her considerable length of leg to the interested onlookers. Dominic removed the wedge of dress from her mouth and pulled her skirt down to cover her exposed legs. He released her hands. As he untied her ankles she lashed out and punched the oarsman in the mouth. Then stood and treated the other man to the same medicine with her other fist. "Bastard pirates!" You'll be over by Spectacle Island, I guess."

Neither man said a word. Julia swung round to Martin. "Thank you, sir. That would not have been a comfortable passage for me as you may guess. I thought they were from my ship, the Sagamore moored opposite the quay.

Martin turned to the two men and pulled out the dirk attached to the scabbard of his sword. He tested the blade then turned to the two men. "Now, which one of you two would like to tell me what ship you come from and what you are doing here? As he spoke he fingered the knife and started to draw diagrams on the wooden thwart. The men looked at the dirk apprehensively. One said "She is the Mohawk out of New York."

Julia looked at the two men hard. "Did Captain Hanson send you for me?"

The man hung his head. "Not for you particular, Miss. Just to find a filly for the voyage like. You were there on the quay askin' if we was from a ship. We thought you were booked like. So we took the chance and grabbed you."

Julia lifted his chin and looked him in the eye. "You are a lying bastard. I would have been used by the crew and passed on to Captain Newton's bunch of pirates when you got to Florida, if not over the side in shark waters. The dirk was snatched from Martin's hand and plunged into the man's stomach. The man doubled over in agony. Dominic grabbed Julia. To his surprise she was in tears.

"What? Why?" He asked at a complete loss.

"He is wearing my grandfather's watch." She said, tearfully. "Sweetwater sailed today for Halifax. My grandfather was aboard. It was one of my ships taking him to our new home in Montreal. They must have taken her today."

Martin looked at the bo'sun's mate. "Back to the ship, rouse the men and get the longboat in the water. Quietly now."

"Aye, Aye, sir. "Pull with a will, lads. We're hunting tonight!"

***

At the ship the men gathered. The dinghy crossed to the Spartan, and passed the news and orders on. By the time the boats left the Vixen there were boats from Spartan, Lively and Hera. Antonio Ramos arrived in time to join the party as the boats passed around Thompson Island to approach the ship lying between Spectacle Island and Thompson Island. A shadow without lights, the boats stopped rowing up-tide. They drifted with the tide down on the silent ship. As they closed the ship it was possible to see the outline of two men at the stern rail, watching for the dinghy toiling the last few yards against the tide. The men jeered the rowers, and then flung a line to them. At the stem, Martin and his men mounted quietly over the bows of the ship. Four of the men ghosted down the deck. The two men at the rail died. They were laid out on deck beside the rail as the remainder of the boarders scattered around the deck waiting for the signal.

When Martin was sure they were all in place he cocked his pistol and fired.

The men smashed hatches and plunged into the interior of the ship. There was no quarter offered, and none given. Pirates received the same treatment they handed out.

***

Captain Hanson survived, battered and bloody, but he survived. Dragged up on deck he was defiant and loudly abusive at what he saw was a raid by British sailors on an American ship. When he saw Julia Savage he was not so sure. When Julia held up her grandfather's watch in front of him, he looked blank.

"This," said Julia, "was my grandfather's watch. It was being carried by one of your men. He was abducting me at the time. Thanks to the efforts of the Commodore and this gentleman," she indicated Dominic. "I have been rescued, and I have recovered my grandfather's watch. Now I would like to know where my grandfather is."

"I know nothing of this. I do not know your grandfather."

"Think Sweetwater, brig registered in Boston, en-route to Halifax with a cargo of trade goods." She snapped her fingers. "Just like the goods you have in your hold, you know, the goods consigned to Hudson's Bay Company, Montreal."

The light faded from Hanson's eyes. He knew there was now no answer he could give to convince her that he was innocent, his shoulders slumped in defeat. After all he wasn't innocent. He had joined forces with a private schooner, Pelican. She had been engaged against the Sweetwater when he had come upon them, His men had boarded the brig and that must have been when that fool had taken the old man's watch.

***

The raiding party had lost two men killed and several wounded. The pirates had suffered badly. There were fourteen dead and twenty-six wounded. Several had gone over the side and were unaccounted for, plus six unwounded prisoners.

The entire party was taken into the Harbour, the boats towing the ship to where it could be secured properly.

Hiram Goss was at a loss. On the one hand there was the matter of a pirate ship taken by British seamen in Boston harbour. Good, that a pirate had been captured, a known man, long overdue for the rope. Bad, a British ship had been involved.

Julia walked in at this point. "Hiram, two things; first, they are handing the Mohawk to me to replace the Sweetwater. Second, they are suggesting they use her to get into the pirate base in Florida, to destroy it."

Hiram thought for a few seconds, working it out. "Can you trust them?"

"I'll be with them. I will captain the Mohawk myself."

"Are you sure? She is a bigger ship than Sagamore and Sweetwater."

"As you well know, I have been sailing the East Coast since I was thirteen years old and skippering ships since I was seventeen. I recall you were bo'sun at the time on Sagamore, the time we fought off that French cutter in '06?"

Hiram smiled as he remembered the fight they had, eventually smashing the bowsprit of the Frenchman, allowing them to force her to run aground. "I get the message. Just look after yourself, girl. If you come back here, make sure you know who is calling the shots before you step into a mess of trouble. There are folks in the town who still think of the Savage family as traitors, King's men. Therefore enemies of America."

"Thanks, Hiram. I'll miss you, and the place. But there are folks I'll not be sorry to leave behind."

Hiram rose to his feet and escorted her to the door. She kissed his cheek, and there was a tear in her eye when she left his office for the last time.

Hiram pulled out his handkerchief and blew his nose noisily. Then turned and went back to his desk.

***

The carpenters were busy on Mohawk, replacing the broken hatches and furniture. Several men came forward, looking for work to crew the ship.

Julia conducted the interviews personally. Several of her key personnel came from within the squadron, but there were still positions among the crew. For Julia it was important that they realised that there could be danger from the attack on the Florida base of the pirates.

She was not concerned about their politics, only that they would be loyal to the ship in the first instance.

Because of the spy system operating along the coast Martin decided that the attack should be conducted immediately rather than at the end of the diplomatic tour down the coast. Dominic suggested that the diplomacy could benefit from reports of the defeat of the pirates in their Florida base. So there seemed little to lose and much to gain from reversing the schedule at this point. The chances were that the news of the capture of the Mohawk would not reach Florida before the squadron arrived.

The decision made, they sailed immediately while repairs were still in progress.

***

The weather was fine and the ships made a fine sight as they sailed south. The crews took advantage of the weather to air clothes and bedding with the help of wind funnels created with the sails brought out to air in their turn. There was an almost festive feeling among the crews. Those men wounded in the raid on the pirate ship were brought up to enjoy the sunshine and fresh air on deck.

For Julia the settling down of the crew in their new quarters, and training with the guns, occupied the first part of the voyage. Sail handling was second nature to most, as all had been selected from among trained seamen. Jackson Hobbs was first mate, presumed to take over as skipper when this particular voyage was over. Thirty-five years old, he was well used to the life of merchant seaman in the current turbulent times. With 18 guns the Mohawk was a formidable opponent for any merchantman, and capable of causing trouble for a naval sloop, which she resembled with her two-masted brigantine rig. Her 130 ft length made her well suited to her fighting role and, though with a smaller crew, equally well suited to her merchant status. The weight of the guns dictated her current fighting role.

The guns were exercised every day on instruction from the Commodore. Martin had made that clear after his experience in the last encounter with Captain Newman, especially since there were rumours of other pirate ships using the Keys.

There would be no concessions given to the people of the Key. They had to be aware of the nature of the ships that using their waters. They needed to be shown that the legal users of the trade routes would not tolerate pirates, or their supporters.

In the days that followed, the various captains met and planned their part in the attack. The rendezvous point, taking into account the possible pursuit of fleeing ships, would be Savannah, in Georgia. The command would devolve to Commodore Ramos in the event Martin was lost for any reason. The final briefing was conducted off Key Largo, as they approached the island of Key West, where the pirate base was reported to be.

Antonio Ramos's task was to sail for two days southwards, round the string of islands and attack from the south. Accompanied by HMS Spartan and HMS Lively the ships should be in position to attack in four days. He would send a small boat forward to spy the anchorage and take soundings from the south. It looked as if the attack might need to be with small craft. The only charts they had were those taken from the Mohawk. Though they were reasonably detailed their pencilled-in amendments suggested a rather casual approach to navigation, which was not re-assuring to the naval element of the raiding party. In addition they only indicated entry to the anchorage from the south for the bigger ships. There was a channel from the Gulf of Mexico but, depending on tides and the movement of the sandbanks in the shallow waters, it could be a slow painstaking business.

Martin finally decided to dispatch the Sao Paulo with the two sloops immediately on their agreed patrol to cover the possibility of returning craft coming in to block off the entry channel and trapping Martin's ships inside Key West Harbour.

Chapter nineteen

The raid

HAVING AGREED TO the plans, Martin, with HMS Vixen and Hera, would follow Mohawk into the anchorage between Tank Island and Key West itself, at the western end. First they would lie off and allow time for the Sao Paulo and the sloops to get into position. On entering the harbour the plan was to capture or destroy any ships they found there.

Martin hoped to catch Newton at the location as they closed. He dispatched the jollyboat, with sail rigged, under the command of Midshipman Gibbs, to scout the pirate base and negotiate with local fishermen to find as much information as possible before making a rendezvous at Boca Chico Key, getting someone with local knowledge of the waters around Key West preferably.

As planned the Mohawk led the two naval ships on the last stages of the voyage to Key West. Sailing under all sail she gave a good impression of a ship fleeing from pursuit.

At Boca Chico Key the jollyboat shot out from the shore to run alongside HMS Vixen. A lowered sling brought Athol Gibbs aboard, and he had plenty to say.

"Sir, there is a passage as shown on the charts but it is defended. There is a sort of fort at the entry to the channel, It has guns sited but there is no garrison there and my informant says the men supposed to be there spend most of their time in the township. They depend on a lookout post giving warning. They reckon to have plenty of time to man the guns, if they are needed.

"The Huron, Captain Newton's ship is expected back at any time now but there are two other ships, Blackhawk and Paragon in harbour at present. Blackhawk was once the French naval corvette Chantel, very similar to Vixen, sir. I have the feeling she is a deserter from the French Navy. Paragon has 20 guns. No one knows her origin. Abigail is with Huron. She is also expected back from the Mexican coast at any time now."

"Are the crews on board the moored ships? Martin asked.

"From what I could see, certainly enough men to man the guns. The rest are ashore and judging from the noise enjoying themselves in the taverns."

Martin turned to Lieutenant Bristow, the Captain of Marines. Prepare your men for the assault on the tavern. Take the marines from Hera. Lieutenant Brooks take the longboat and board the Paragon." He turned to Julia standing with Jackson Hobbs waiting for orders.

"I think the chances are that Blackhawk's crew are also mostly ashore. I would like you to lay Mohawk alongside her and take her. Mr. Gordon has offered his services. If that is acceptable he can return with you. I do stress that the men who crew these pirate ships give no quarter. They treat women as slaves and kill without compunction." He looked at Jackson Hobbs. "They are as much enemies of America as they are of any other honest seafarer."

Hobbs smiled grimly. "There'll not be silliness from the Mohawk, Commodore. The men are all ready and willing."

Dominic appeared with Martin's sword at his side and pistols in his belt.

Martin noted wryly the way Julia reacted, as did Jackson.

"Best get in place then." Jackson suggested, and the trio left the cabin to return to their ship.

Martin looked at Brooks. "How soon can you be ready?"

"The men are preparing now, sir. We will be ready to go when you give the order."

"I want the longboat prepared to drop when we reach the harbour. Get the jollyboat unrigged and hauled up to deck level. Send in Harris. He should be here by now."

Brooks departed and Lieutenant Harris, Captain of the Hera entered.

Martin gave his orders. "Take all the marines on board and enter the harbour at Key West. As soon as the action begins, land the marines and haul off to prevent any reinforcement of the anchored ships. Back up the marines with gunfire if necessary. When the shore is secured you may join whatever action is occurring offshore. Is that clear?"

"Yes, sir." Harris turned and left the cabin almost at a run. Martin looked after him. Of all his officers he knew Harris least. He shrugged. So far he had done well. He decided he would make a point of getting to know him better when time allowed.

The rowers approached the anchored ships quietly, the oars moving silently in the cloth-bound crutches.

The bulk of the Mohawk, under topsail and jib only, crept slowly toward the outer ship, Blackhawk, as the group of rowing boats converged on the Paragon.

Patrick Brooks looked at the shoreline, lit by a scatter of lights from the buildings there. The sound of music and the growl of voices came from the open windows of the establishments catering for the seamen ashore on this warm evening.

As he watched the schooner Hera came into view casting her shadow over the water and plunging the small flotilla of raiders into darkness.

A swift look around, then Lieutenant Brooks started to do what he was paid for. Happy to be given the chance, he raised his voice as the longboat slid alongside their target, just above a whisper, he said, "Boarders away!"

The first of his men climbed the side of the Blackhawk, no great task for a top-man, while the others waited until his head appeared,

"What are yew men waitin' fur, a bloody invitation?" He tossed a knotted rope over the side, then followed it with a second. As the men boarded silently more ropes appeared.

On deck, Brooks crouched listening to Lieutenant Keats, one of the first aboard, who was reporting on the current situation. "Two watchmen, both dead, the captain or perhaps not, on his bunk with a woman who did not like him."

Brooks looked round sharply, ready to query the comment.

Keats grinned. "She was just completing the task of cutting off his... how do call them? ...Cojones? Genitals? Is that right?"

Brooks grinned. "I get the message. Did she say anything?"

Keats shrugged. "She turned and saw the bo'sun at the door and threw the knife at him. It missed. The bo'sun didn't!"

Martin boarded the ship from a boat, having come ashore with the marines.

"Where is everyone?" He asked. "They surely did not leave the ship this deserted?"

Midshipman Gibbs appeared dragging a boy, unwounded, but with a bruise on his face. "Sir, Mr. Brooks sent me. He said you would want to speak to this boy. From what this boy has to say, I think Captain Newton has stripped the ships of crew and loaded them all aboard the Huron and Abigail. It seems there was a hell of a row between the man, Absalom, who ran Key West and Captain Newton. Tell the Commodore, boy." Gibbs shook the lad.

Martin looked at the miserable lad. *About eleven,* he thought. Addressing him directly, he asked, "Tell me who you are?"

"I'm James Woods, sir." The boy stood as straight as he could, still in the grasp of Athol Gibbs.

Martin looked at Gibbs and nodded. "Well found, Mr. Gibbs. Leave the lad with me and return to your duties."

With a swift, "Aye, Aye. Sir" Gibbs was gone

Martin turned to James Woods, who was still standing where he had been put. "So, Mr. Woods, where did you come from? Where is your home, lad?"

"I was taken from the merchant ship Compass mostly a year ago. My dad was killed with a sword in his hand, and they took Ma." There was no need to elaborate. Undoubtedly, the boy had seen and heard what that meant in the company of pirates. Though Martin noticed a slight quiver of the lips the boy still stood defiantly, refusing to give way.

"You were saying about Captain Newton? Where was he bound with all the men and but two ships? What about boats?"

"I served in the house of Absolom, the Captain's partner. It was easy work most of the time and I heard lots of things while I was there. The Captain always wanted to go to Campeche in Mexico. He said he had been told that the place was rich with booty and gold and silver from the mines inland. Absolom did not agree with him and has always put him off since I've been there." He paused then, "The Captain has become ill. He gets angry and, when that happens, nobody is safe. Last week he lost himself completely and he struck Absolom a terrible blow. We all thought he had killed him. The Captain was sorry, I think. But he then started giving orders,

"The captains of the Blackhawk and Providence had no chance, he left them an anchor watch only. All their men were taken on board Huron and Abigail and they sailed last week for Campeche. Absolom has recovered a little but the people think he will die anyway."

In the background the sound of odd shots and cries had ceased. The waterfront was quiet except for the tramp of the marching Marines along the quay toward the Hera where she lay alongside.

Martin stepped back to the gangway. "I think we will go ashore and, with your help, James, we will see Absolom and find out what is going on with Captain

Newton. Mr. Harmon, a boat, if you please, and ask the doctor to join me. I believe he may be needed ashore."

As Lieutenant Harmon disappeared on his errand, Martin turned to the boy. "Well, James. What would you like to do now?"

Looking puzzled the boy shrugged. "I don't know what you mean, sir?"

"You have lost your father and your mother, so your future is up to you. What do you want to do with it? Stay here? Come with us and take your chances in America as your father intended? Or perhaps join the ship and become a member of the Royal Navy?"

Martin smiled and continued, "You don't need to answer straight away. Think about it. I think there would be a place here for you if you wanted it. From what I have seen of America, you could become a pioneer, I believe."

Lieutenant Harmon returned at that point and the Commodore and the boy left the cabin with the question unanswered.

"You have the ship," Martin said to Neil Harmon. Please do not damage it." He said with a smile.

"Of course, sir, I... I... would not dream of it, sir." He stumbled flushing, pleased to be in command for however short a time.

***

The boat was challenged at the quay, and the watchful marine supervised the landing of the Commodore. He called over to the sergeant, seated at a table next to the nearest building. "Commodore on deck, Sergeant."

The sergeant leapt to his feet, calling to his men. Six marines lifted their muskets and trotted over to form a rank. The sergeant turned and saluted. "At your orders, sir!"

Martin smiled, impressed despite himself. "We are going to a house in town. This young man will guide us."

"Very good, sir." The Sergeant saluted, turned and detailed two men to accompany the boy, while the other four followed the party.

Organised, the small column moved off with James Woods proudly in the lead.

***

The house of Absolom was a big quiet place, a little above the town. The gates were open. As James was quick to point out, they always were.

Inside the house there were servants moving about and by the time they reached the front door there was a tall, slender woman waiting. She was calm and the lights glinted off her dark skin. "What can I do for you, gentlemen? The master is indisposed."

"This man is a highly skilled doctor. He would like to see your master to perhaps help in his treatment. I also would like to see your master for another reason.

The woman turned and waved them in, calling orders to those inside. As they walked she said "I am Naomi and I run the house." The words were simply said, but they made it clear that she was in charge."

The doctor was taken to a room to the rear of the house. Naomi steered Martin and the boy, James, into a room off to the right which was obviously a reception room for visitors.

She clapped her hands and a servant appeared, "Can I offer you tea, gentlemen?"

As Martin accepted he began to realise that the smooth formality of his reception, and the attitude of the staff was a reflection of the normal running of affairs in this house, and due to Naomi, he presumed.

He turned to Peters, the Bo'sun, who had been just behind him all the way, "Send a message to Mr. Harris on Hera. Ask him to patrol to the south-west. Look out for the return of the Huron and the Abigail possibly with some prizes.

They were seated having tea, the marines at the gate to stop any interference. Martin was wondering at the strange situation when Doctor Mills returned. "Sir, I think you should come and see Absolom now!"

Martin rose to his feet. Naomi also rose and led Martin through to a bedroom at the rear.

There was a big bed with four posts supporting fine muslin curtains, presumably to keep off the mosquitoes clustered around the wall lamps. The man propped up on the pillows was dark-skinned from his North African background, but there was a pallor like a shadow, under the gleam of sweat on his skin.

"Commodore, I am sorry to meet you under these circumstances. But then, I suppose in others there would be bullets or blades to interfere."

He stirred, and Naomi was there beside him with a cloth, wiping his brow. "Thank you, my dear, though I am not really worth the trouble." He looked at Martin once more. "I fear my former friend, Roger Newton, has finally succumbed to the effects of untreated syphilis. His rage as he left here was…" He hesitated, thinking. "Unbridled is the word. Had he simmered down before leaping into action, I would not be lying here facing my last moments. Instead I now realise I would be standing, sword in hand, back to back, fighting for my life. The expedition to Campeche has long been an ambition for Roger. He struck me in passing and ruptured my spleen, according to your excellent doctor. Sadly he arrived too late to do something about it. For me perhaps, happily. I really hated the thought of the noose." He stopped again, took a sip from a glass and continued. "Roger Newton was a good friend to me, I was aware of course of his faults, overextending his debts and killing too many innocent people as a result. To me, until recently, he was my best friend. If he finds out that I have died because of the way he left this house, he will be devastated."

Martin asked Doctor Mills, "Is there anything that can be done?"

Roger Mills shook his head. "If there was a way to pour blood into him to replace the blood he has lost, perhaps. I know of none."

Absolom smiled grimly. "As I said, Commodore. If nothing else, I have eluded the noose."

As the visitors turned to go Absolom beckoned Martin to his side. "A private word, if you please, sir."

Martin waved the others away. "Well?"

"There is a hoard of treasure in this house, six chests and sealed keg. I believe you to be a gentleman, sir. Naomi is here against her will. She was sold to me in Africa. She had been my housekeeper ever since. Neither Roger nor I have ever touched her, though, god knows, I have been tempted. Please take the treasure and, if you will, give the keg to Naomi. I believe some of the contents were hers anyway."

Martin was aware of the effort Absolom was making to pass on this request. He found himself nodding in agreement, "She will be cared for just as this boy will be. I will see the keg is kept for her."

Absolom fumbled at the head of the bed and produced a key, a thin-toothed blade. "The library, Troilus and Cressida." He gasped and fell back.

Martin closed Absolom's eyes, and stood back.

Outside the door the others were waiting. Martin shook his head at the unspoken question and put his hand on Naomi's arm. "He is gone and we must go." He swung round to Peters, "We will need a cart." Turning back to Naomi, "Pack anything you need to take, and for the boy if there is anything." He checked her as she turned to go. "The library?"

She pointed at another door in the hallway and went through to the back of the house. The doctor and Peter followed him into the library and he searched the shelves.

The collection of Shakespeare was on a central shelf. He removed the copy of Troilus and Cressida and sighed when he saw the slim slot in the woodwork at the back of the shelf.

The key slid in and the section of the book case moved back and swung to one side. The room held small a stack of chests were in the centre. The keg stood to one side on its own.

Between them they dragged the heavy chests through into the library. The keg needed both men to carry it.

Martin closed the secret door. They straightened the carpet and waited for Peters to return. Naomi appeared with a young woman who helped her carry her bags.

"Sadie is my maid. She will accompany me. James, help with the bags, please."

The Bo'sun appeared., "I have a cart, sir. Is this the cargo?"

"Yes, keep the keg separate. Place it in my cabin on the ship. It belongs to the lady."

Naomi looked at him in surprise. She opened her mouth to say something, but Martin shook his head. She closed it and shrugged. One of the Marines from the gate appeared. "Lieutenant Keats and his party are at the gate, sir."

"Good. Tell him to send his party back to the ship, leaving six men here with me."

The marine disappeared and Keats arrived with his six men.

The entire party with the loaded cart followed the carriage back to the quay. Julia Savage was supervising the prize crew for the Paragon. The Blackhawk was still at her moorings but the rumble of the guns being moved made it clear that she was being prepared for action.

Martin spoke to Julia, and Naomi and her maid were sent out to the Mohawk to travel with Julia, north.

Before she entered the boat Martin spoke briefly to Naomi. "I have your keg in my cabin. I will deliver it when you have decided where you wish to stay. If you would rather, I will pass it over to Mohawk. But I think it will be safer with me just now."

Naomi smiled. "Until you produced it I knew nothing of it. I will trust you, sir." And she turned and stepped down into the boat.

Martin caught sight of Vixen at anchor in the channel. Brooks was back on board by now.

He called the other boat alongside. "Take me out to the Vixen." He ordered the bo'sun's mate in charge.

Once aboard, he called Brooks to his cabin.

"Take the ship out to the shoals offshore and return at dawn to collect me. There will be battle tomorrow I am convinced. I will be spending the night ashore. I have things to do and people to speak with.

He returned to the shore leaving a delighted Lieutenant Brooks in command, already calling for sails to be spread while Martin looked forward to a depressing round of the buildings in town and an eventual confrontation with the Mayor.

***

The Mayor of Key West was not a prepossessing sight, but, as Martin conceded, his position had not been an easy one to maintain. He had arrived from the Everglades in Louisiana, and found the people of Key West agreeable and welcoming. His past had included teaching mathematics to unwilling schoolchildren, and he had settled here, welcomed as a teacher in the locality. His wife was a local from the mainland. The school had been started by the Episcopalian church and she had been the first teacher. Their marriage had been anticipated and his influence in the community was accepted leading to his election as Mayor. The arrival of Absolom, followed by his partner Roger Newton, had changed things considerably.

With Absolom it had been possible to treat, with Newton it was impossible. Honore Verlain was not a happy man, and now he had another man to deal with,

British, though he had Americans with him. But then Newton was British.

Chapter twenty

Tigers and tails

ROGER NEWTON WAS not happy. This was putting it mildly. He was enraged. His beautiful ship was battered, the men working to replace shattered timbers from the fire of the guns at the fort in Campeche. The gunners had been very good, and obviously prepared for action. He could only conclude that the incipient rebellion in Mexico against their French masters had caused the increase in efficiency and the repairs to the previously-crumbling fort.

When Abigail had reported no ships in the harbour, he had assumed the door was open.

It was open, but despite the French colours he had displayed, the fort had opened fire. His swift action to reverse course had been the only thing that had saved him. As he had retreated hastily, a strange flag had been raised over the fort. It seemed that the incipient revolution had reached farther than he had realised.

Looking around the ravaged bulwarks on the port side of Huron, he reflected it was a far cry from his days as a Naval Captain, when a quick visit to the nearest dockyard would have been taken care of. On more than one occasion he had wondered what his career would have been had he not gambled away more than he could possibly pay. He had reassured himself that the crew had

had something to do with his final decision, but underneath it all he was not fooling anyone but himself. He was here, today, because he had elected to run. As a result he had wealth, comfort, as many women as he desired, and one friend. He wondered if Absolom would forgive his outburst of temper. He shrugged. The way things had gone this past few weeks he could have lost his only friend as well. He smashed his hand against the mizzen mast. Wincing and shaking his mutilated hand, he strode forward across the quarterdeck and shouted at his First Lieutenant. "Any sign of Abigail?" She had been sent ahead to see the way was clear while Huron repaired herself as well as she could.

"Mr. Watson, please tell me we will be ready for action once more, today!"

Lieutenant Watson looked warily at Newton, "Should be completed by mid-watch, sir." His Cornish burr still there in spite of being away from home since he was nine years old. To his surprise the captain did not fly into a rage.

Nodding, he said, "Well done. We took a beating." He waved the lieutenant away, saying quietly to himself, "There will be a battle." He did not know why he was convinced of this. He was just aware that there was a threat in the air and he resumed his walk along the quarterdeck.

As promised, the essential repairs were finished by mid-watch, but it was close to evening before the Abigail hove into view.

As the schooner closed, Roger Newton strode back and forth, containing his impatience, realising that it would not be until after dark that the other ship would be close enough to make contact. Even though he was aware of it, he still felt impatient. Eventually he went below to eat at the request of his steward.

Captain Matt Hooper joined Newton in his cabin at ten on the clock. A tall elegant, stylishly dressed young man, his dark curly hair hung over his collar. His boat cloak was draped around his shoulders. The night was dark outside and the schooner rode off a cable-length to starboard.

The young American shook his boat-cloak and draped it over the back of the other chair in the cabin. Seated on the bunk he accepted the glass of wine from the steward and sank most of it in one. "Whee! that was fun!" He said with a chuckle. "I guess the ownership of Campeche is changing hands a little more often these days. Once the buccaneers thought of it as the local family bank and restaurant. Now the damn place keeps fillin' up with soldiers. Did you see the flag? What the hell was that? Morelos? Weren't Government, that's fur shore?"

Roger Newton looked at his companion with disgust. "Why can't you speak English, man? Your language has been getting worse ever since you took up with that quadroon woman Emma."

Completely un-fazed, Matt Harper just laughed. "Man, that woman is a tiger in bed. She lights my fire just by lookin'."

"Well, Mathew. Was there any sign of problems at Key West?" Newton spoke casually but he listened keenly for the answer.

Mathew smiled. "Like you said, I kept out of sight. Didn't go in or nothin'. Noticed the Mohawk had arrived. Otherwise it was a mite quiet. I thought about goin' in. Then remembered what you said and steered clear, Paragon was alongside still, I guess that lazy bastard, Wilkes, will be set down in the Inn with his ladies. They are sure a pox-ridden bunch of excuses for women. I don't understand how he is still alive. I guess he just sells them. He don't fuck em."

His comments were not giving Newton any encouragement. His last encounter had been with one of Wilkes's women.

"We'll set course for the Keys in the morning. I guess I'll be seeing Naomi tomorrow. I'm still not feeling right." Newton rose to his feet.

"Hey, Roger!" I did not realise you were not feeling so good. Sure I'll send over my man from Abigail if you like. He's pretty good."

"Thanks, Mathew. I agree he's pretty good, but I'll wait for Naomi if you don't mind. We'll set course in the morning."

Mathew left, still a little troubled. Roger Newton was the reason he was still alive, and rich. Then he thought that Emma was waiting in his own ship. With a wave and the word "Tomorrow," he was over the side into the boat still waiting alongside to take him back to his pretty schooner.

***

In Key West, Mathew Harper's visit was not without witness. John Harris, commanding HMS Hera spotted the flick of the sail as he was returning to Key West. Martin had sent him to cruise the area south of the archipelago, keeping a low profile while watching out for the returning pirates.

He got lucky, by changing course at the last moment. As the head of the schooner came round to the new course the lookout called the sight of the sail halfway round. His arm and hand stuck out like a signal pointing in the direction of the sail. Harris immediately came to a course in the new direction and it was not long before they had the contact outlined against the sunset sky to the west, their own ship concealed by the darkening sky from the east. Harris identified the Abigail, a ship he had seen before and encountered during the Bahamas episode. There was no immediate sign of the Huron.

Hera returned to Key West and Harris reported to Martin at the big house, once used by Absolom. He found Antonio Ramos seated with Martin and Julia Savage. Absolom had been taken to the graveyard where a grave had been prepared. Naomi, who had run the house was now lodged in Mohawk. Martin decided to use the place as a meeting place for his people while he was ashore. HMS Vixen, currently under the command of Lieutenant Brooks, lay off in deep water beyond the fort at the entrance to the deep-water channel.

There was a relaxed attitude about the room. The big windows were open to the sea-breeze and the quiet buzz of conversation made it seem less a conference, more a social occasion. He was given a glass of wine by Peters, Martin's bo'sun, and invited to sit and join the group.

Startled, he did so, finding a place next to the smiling Julia, who raised her glass to him as he joined the party.

Martin leaned forward and tapped his glass to get attention. He then leaned back to give them their instructions for the following day. In measured tones he made the point that Captain Newton was no normal pirate. He was a highly trained professional seaman. His ship and crew were naval, both trained and skilled at what they do.

"Despite our greater strength, this will be no easy task. Commodore, please return to your ship tonight and sail south then give chase from astern, to cut off any retreat in that direction . You, Harris, take Hera out before midnight tonight. I want you out to the west to give chase from that direction, pushing Huron into confrontation. I intend to tackle Huron in deep water, so I will have Vixen at sea by the time the enemy arrives. Julia, I want Mohawk out to tackle Abigail. It may seem that I am overreacting, but since my base is 3000 miles away, I cannot afford to get caught out and possibly seriously damaged with only part of my mission carried out."

He looked at the others before him. "The other ships, HMS Spartan, and Lively have already been detailed to by-pass the returning ships to cut off any chance of escape.

"As most of you are aware my task here was to bring my diplomatic friend," he nodded to Dominic, who had been seated in the corner in the room while the tactics for the forthcoming engagement were discussed, "to tour down the east coast of America, mending relations disturbed by the attitude of the Royal Navy over the past few years. This is a case of first things first."

He rose to his feet. The others rose also. Lifting his glass, he said, "Lady and gentlemen. To 'tomorrow' first!"

They all raised their glasses and repeated 'Tomorrow'. Then they took their leave. Only Dominic, Julia and Martin remained.

Martin said, "I will be leaving for the Vixen in five minutes. Miss Savage, please join me in the carriage."

Julia checked him for a moment. "I will join you there, Commodore." Martin left her with Dominic and went to collect his charts and instruments, and check that his servant was ready for the return to the ship.

Julia turned to Dominic, finding him standing right behind her. She smiled. "You are a nice young man, and I confess I was flattered when I noticed that you took a shine to me." She lifted her hand and stopped him stepping closer, and reaching for her. "But I confess I was cut out for a different life. I'm not ready to entertain at tea parties, and I'm not cut out for a fling. I like you, Honourable Dominic Gordon, but I don't love you. I will happily be your friend, but I won't be your lover. If we understand each other, nod your head?"

Dominic was stunned. Never had he been spoken to so bluntly by a woman. He nodded his head almost automatically in response to the command.

Julia reached up and kissed him. Then was gone, off, out to the carriage which stood at the outer door waiting for Martin and Peters, Martin's servant. Leaving the forlorn figure of Dominic still trying to understand what had gone wrong.

As the carriage departed Martin asked, "Did you tell him?"

Julia looked at him. "Why are you so interested?"

Martin said, "I have my own reasons."

Julia did not answer immediately. She sat swaying to the motion of the carriage seemingly lost in thought.

Then Martin heard her say quietly, "Of course I told him."

At the quay both stepped down from the carriage and Peters collected Martin's bag.

The cutter lay alongside. Martin handed Julia into the boat and seated them both, as the crew cast off. At the Mohawk Julia swung aboard, and immediately started calling orders to weigh anchor and make sail. As the cutter sailed away Martin saw her hand lift in farewell. He lifted his in return then concentrated on his plans for the forthcoming fight.

He dismissed Dominic from his mind for the present. He had been given the task of arranging the list of places to be visited on the way north after the removal of Roger Newton. The cutter would collect him after Martin had been delivered back to HMS Vixen. Brooks should be waiting at the deep-water channel already.

Martin lifted his eyes. He could just make out the loom of a ship at the entrance of the channel ahead of the cutter.

Martin sighed. There was little else he could do now. The die was cast and there would be blood, and hell to pay in the morning.

It was not easy to sleep. It had been different in the past. Then it had only been himself to worry about, now there were a whole series of people who depended on him, not the least his present crew and the lives and livelihoods of the people ashore and the others of his fleet. Men and women could die, would die, all because of him and his reading of the orders—no, his interpretation of the orders.

***

When he rose in the early hours of the morning his sheets were wet with sweat and his eyes were tired. The breeze revived him somewhat and he allowed it to blow through his tangled hair, drying it and throwing it where it will. The sun was not yet up. On the horizon the feint line of light was just announcing the new day when the voice from aloft called, "Ship in sight, hull up, she lies west-south-west of us and she hasn't seen us. I'll gamble."

"Take that man's name. He's earned himself a guinea." Martin said to Brooks who had just taken over the watch.

"Shall we run out the guns?" Brooks asked.

"Let us see if we can get a little further south of her first. If we're spotted, we'll run out the guns then."

Martin went below and dressed in clean linen and a fresh shirt, then his full uniform. Peters appeared as he always seemed to and attached the sword to the frog from the dress belt. He then dusted off the bicorn hat and presented it to Martin.

"There we are, sir, just the last touch." He produced a box and took out the two pistols. Already loaded and primed for action one thrust each side of the belt ready for use if required.

Martin mounted the stairs to the deck. There was a call from the masthead and the ship heeled round to starboard, pointing directly at the distant swaying mast of the enemy schooner. "Two ships: one frigate, one schooner approaching from due west, mebbie ten miles off sir."

"You may call the gun crews. Both broadsides, can prepare to run-out. Signal all ships, 'Close enemy ships and engage at will'".

The usual clatter of the preparations seemed louder, noisier even, somehow. Martin though the sky had never seemed so blue, everything this morning seemed keener, sharper.

Martin decided it was because he had an empty stomach, he called Acting Lieutenant Gibbs, and had Dominic roused to take breakfast with him. He guessed that Sao Paulo would be chasing the enemy.

***

The sound of a distant gun brought the Commodore back on deck. Brooks reported, "I believe that to be Commodore Ramos sir."

Martin raised his telescope, the two sail were much closer now and showing no signs of turning away. To the East the outline of the Sao Paulo was becoming increasingly clear as she pounded along under full sail, with the wind on her bow. A puff of white smoke, followed by a bang, marked the discharge of her bow-chaser. There was no sign of the fall of the shot. Neither of the targeted ships showed any sign of changing course. The Vixen was closing the distance, and Lieutenant Cameron called from his position on the gun-deck. "Permission to try a bow shot,, sir?"

"Permission granted, Mr. Cameron!" Martin called.

The gunner on the bow chaser, poised and ready, waited for the bow to lift to the next wave, then struck the lock and the gun fired. It seemed the entire ship held their breath except the bow gun crew, who ran back, cleared, rammed a bag of grape shot home and ran the gun up to firing position once more. The first shot, having been willed on by the entire crew of the British ship, struck the spritsail beneath the bowsprit of the

Huron. the small sail set there disintegrated and ball carried on through the hawse hole severing the anchor cable in its path.

For the second time during action between them the starboard anchor of the Huron dropped, though this time it was no longer attached to the anchor chain or rope. Still lashed in place the anchor tipped sideways, the unattached outboard end once more in a position to interfere with the mobility of the ship, especially when the heel of the ship could cause the stock of the anchor to bury itself in a wave and drag the head round too fast.

Abigail split with her consort, turning to meet Mohawk sailing free under American colours. Her gunports were open and crews prepared standing by them. A gun fired between them and action was joined.

While the two other ships were engaged, Vixen and Huron circled each other, each warily trying to get the best advantage from nature and their ship.

Men, working on the fouled anchor, managed to get a line on the ring at the head of the stock, a brave seaman crawling out on the extended stock, a line tied round his waist, while the ship careered though the water. Men from both ships watched as he reached the ring which still had the end of the broken anchor rope attached. Clinging for his life with one hand he tried to push the line he was carrying through the hole. He needed both hands, but he tried, and nearly fell off. Gripping the stock between his legs, he released his other hand and went to work with both hands. He managed to get the rope through and tied it off so the others could pull the anchor upright and lash it in place, out of the way but not embarrassingly lost. He sat up and waved to let the others know that the job was done.

The bow hit a big wave and suddenly he was gone. There was a gasp the rope round his waist snapped tight, and the onlookers turned away. In the bow of the Vixen, a nod from Cameron, and the gun discharged sending a lethal charge of pistol balls into the gathered men on the foc'sle of the Huron. They watched the anchor rise to its normal place, where it was lashed in position.

As the ships closed Martin called, "Port broadside, ready?"

The answering roar indicated it was.

"Starboard broadside, ready?"

Another roar this time, from the starboard gunners.

"Standby port broadside guns, only. As you bear. Fire!"

Martin said calmly to the helmsman, "Ease across the bow, tidy now. Starboard wheel." There was a seemingly continuous roar, the calm voice came to the helmsman through all the din.

"Now hard to port. The frigate spun hard toward the starboard side of the other ship, the swinging bowsprit just clearing the rail of her upper deck. The bowsprit took and snapped the shrouds of the mizzen and jammed on the shrouds of the mainmast. As the mizzen swayed, having lost its support from one side of the ship, three of the topmen armed with axes ran out along the bowsprit. They hacked at the shrouds retaining the bowsprit. On the Huron there was confusion for a moment. Then the burly figure of Hayes appeared, shouting orders and sending men to save the rapidly disappearing shrouds. The swinging action of the Vixen snapped more of the ropes. But Hayes's men managed to get a line to the maintop, and were able to secure the mainmast in position. As the Vixen dropped away from the side of the other ship the guns from both were still in action. There were two guns dismounted on the Vixen and a great hole in the side of the Huron. Four men from the Huron were among the wounded laid out on Vixen's deck.

All three of the men from the bowsprit had survived uninjured.

Martin watched the mizzen on the Huron fall despite the efforts of her crew.

Like two boxers the two ships lay off, both battered, both looking for the best way to renew the contest. He had been shocked to see the familiar face of Hayes on the other ship. He shrugged. There was never going to be a career in the navy for a man like that. Perhaps this would be when Hayes achieved his revenge. Martin was still ignorant of the reason for the hatred he had aroused in the man.

Chapter twenty-two

The long goodbye

NEWTON ALLOWED THE head of the Huron to drop slightly off the wind. Then snapped it back, almost too far, then again it dropped off the wind, and snapped back sharply. It gave the impression of a tired man trying to keep awake, or a wounded man not complaining, just trying to get on with the job regardless.

Martin nearly fell for it. Then he remembered the Mediterranean and Captain Graham, playing on your enemy's weakness, but remembering not to fall for the tricks of the trade.

He had seen that somewhere before and could not really remember where or when. It did not really matter. He should not fall for it, but he should not ignore it either.

"Mr. Brooks, haul taut and take us across her stern. Port broadside, stand by!"

As the Vixen moved off once more, the Huron sprang into life, her sails were also hauled taut, but more carefully, the strain on the cable supporting the main mast, causing it to creak.

On the deck of the Huron the bo'sun cursed, he was working on replacement shrouds for the main mast and, until they were complete once more, his beloved ship would be a cripple. Hayes appeared, armed to the teeth. "Have you not finished that yet?"

The hectoring sarcastic voice was like a goad to the bo'sun, who blamed the brutal lieutenant for the condition of the rigging anyway. "If you think you can work faster or better, step in. Otherwise fuck off."

Hayes stepped back. The flashing eyes and knife in hand were quite compelling. But he was an officer. He must not be addressed like that by a deckhand, bo'sun or otherwise. His hand flashed out almost by instinct and clouted the man round the ear. "Don't you dare talk to me like that. I am an officer and will be addressed as sir!"

The bo'sun looked at Hayes, the contempt in his eyes open and obvious. "Yew are an excuse, a poor one at that, for an officer. So here is what I will do. I will get on with my work as if you never came over here this morning. When this little incident is over we can talk again. Now fuck off. Sir!"

Hayes withdrew hastily leaving the bo'sun to his task.

When Newton was reassured that the shrouds were reattached he started to re- establish the position he was working toward when the mizzen was taken down. The spar was now lashed down on deck and though it impaired the sailing of the ship to some extent there was no serious problem with manoeuvring in these conditions.

***

On Mohawk Julia was in her element. The ship was handy, more agile than her own rather more pedestrian craft which were, after all, armed trading ships rather than warships. Though Mohawk had decent hold capacity she had been designed as a blockade runner. Thus both aspects of her living had been catered for. The skirmish with Abigail was showing just what a handy craft she was. She had been dodging and shooting with surprising agility, as both ships tried to gain advantage. Julia decided the time had come to put a stop to this.

"Mr. Hobbs, Abigail is making another run. when his bowsprit reaches ours bring her head up and all guns fire. That will give her a bellyache if nothing else."

"It surely will, skipper. Here she comes. Pretty little ship, ain't she." Hobbs appreciated the schooner's trim lines.

"She certainly is. Trouble is she has teeth." Julia grinned. "Luckily, so have we."

The head of the Mohawk spun round to parallel the racing schooner. The side and view between the ships disappeared in a cloud of stinking, choking gun-smoke as both ships fired their broadside guns.

Both ships lost way. The breeze took time to clear the smoke. Meantime the gunners on the Mohawk were not waiting for orders, they were still loading and running out, the thunder of the explosions, followed by the squeal of the wheels of the gun carriages on the deck.

The tall mainmast on the schooner swayed, and, shattered at the base, dropped base first through the planking of the upper deck with a horrendous crash. From there, snagged and trapped it leaned drunkenly to one side and was still.

Through the thinning fog it was now possible to see the results of the two broadsides. Julia had been aware that there had been damage done to the Mohawk. One of her broadside guns was lying on the deck at her feet. Elsewhere there were shattered timbers which had left a swathe of splinters on the once-pristine deck. Through the holes in the bulwarks, it was possible to see the sea washing into and out of a large hole in the side of the schooner. She watched fascinated as the ship rolled sluggishly and a body was disgorged from the interior. As it flowed into the open sea, a shark rose lazily half out of the water and selected the arm and shoulder of the body and bit, burying its teeth deep, then with a shake, separating it's selection from the body and disappeared below the water.

She shook herself and stood upright, realising she had leaned back against the deckhouse. She put her hand to her mouth to stop herself being sick at the sight and looked about properly. Two guns had been dis-mounted. All the masts were safe and undamaged. There were plenty of dockyard pennants about, broken ropes to be repaired and replaced. With a shout she got the attention of the crew and life restarted on the Mohawk.

***

Across the water, at the scene of the encounter between Vixen and Huron, the guns were still blazing. Then the ships fell apart, though there was little to be seen through the thick smoke. As the smoke cleared there appeared to be damage enough on both sides, to keep the crews well occupied just keeping the ships afloat. Vixen still had her masts intact, one of the guns which had been dismounted, was now ready to go back in action. The other would require a completely new carriage. It was lashed securely to the base of the mainmast to prevent it being lost or interfering with the crew's actions on deck. There were seven dead, and twelve wounded. Naomi was working with the doctor on the wounded, both were wrapped in sheets bloodied from the need to deal with wounds and shattered limbs.

***

Julia was weary, though the battle had not really lasted that long, so far. Judging from the look of the other ship there was still more to do. A boy ran to her with a big mug of beer that she gratefully drank, the spillage tracking through the dirt that marking her face from the dust and smoke of the battle. The gun captains on the reduced broadside raised their hands to let her know they were ready.

Julie stirred herself and called for the helm to come round to bring the guns to bear. The schooner was down by the head Men were running back and forth on the deck clearing the raffle of gear from the smashed mainmast and lashing the leaning spar to the rigging to stop it overbalancing. Meanwhile the guns were being reloaded and run out. Mohawk got the jump on the Abigail because her superior mobility made it possible.

Above the cloud Julia could make out the top'sls of the Sao Paulo, approaching from the west.

***

The fore mast of the Huron fell to the disciplined gunners of the Vixen. It was evident neither ship would escape unscathed. The guns of the Sao Paulo managed one broadside, before the gunfire stopped.

As the smoke drifted away the full horror of the intense encounter could be seen. Scarcely a gun remained mounted in Huron. The shattered bulwarks left little to the imagination, bodies, dismounted cannon, splinters and broken timbers painted with blood.

Turning to Vixen, it was in better state but not much. More guns still in their carriages, but dead and wounded men everywhere. There were men moving about on the naval vessel, crewmen attending to the dead and wounded.

***

Julia spotted the boat from Sao Paulo coming around the stem of the Huron. Another boat had obviously boarded from the other side of the ship as men appeared on deck.

The approaching boat came alongside the Vixen and the occupants climbed aboard to give aid to the men needing it.

Julia left them to it. There was plenty to do on her own ship, and. from the look of it, for the crew of the Abigail.

The message came across from the flagship. All wounded and dead to the shore use Absolom's house for a hospital. All help gratefully received.

Naomi appeared in time to hear the message. "I go now and prepare. Sadie will help and I know others ashore who will be happy to assist.

Julie nodded immediately. "Mr. Hobbs, a boat for the ladies, direct to the big house, if possible."

"Yes, Skipper." On the shore side of the ship there were several boats moored. He called two of the men, "Get the ladies ashore and help them set up a place for the doctor to use to operate and look after the other patients. Stay and help. Don't run off and leave them. You understand me?"

Both men took one look at the man towering over them and answered fast, "Yes, Sir!"

By the time the boat reached the shore there were three other boats coming from the ships involved in the battle. More were loading up. From Vixen, the Doctor and his boxes were already being loaded. Another of Sao Paulo's boats was coming from the Huron, loaded with wounded from the looks of things.

***

Newton's battle had gone rather the way his life had gone over the past few months, from bad to worse. As he had approached the ship of the English Captain/Commodore he had realised the man was no fool. Their earlier encounter could have gone either way. It worried him that he had somehow allowed the man to get the advantage of numbers on this occasion.

As the ships had approached each other, the ranging ball from the Vixen had cut the anchor cable on that same anchor. Newton could feel the immediate effect on the trim of the ship.

"Get that anchor secured!" He shouted and two of the seamen forward ran to the task.

They were not in time to prevent the terrible impact of the Vixen's first broadside, guns firing in succession rippling down the portside of the attacking ship.

Its effect was shattering. The mizzen mast was shot through and started to fall, until snagged by the tangle of rigging. Through the smoke Newton was able to see the Vixen spinning round, her bowsprit slashing through the shrouds of the mizzen and catching then at the mainmast shrouds on the starboard side of the Huron. Roger Newton could feel the pain as his ship was wounded, He was aware that the guns of his own ship were firing, but the agony....? He looked down at his hand clutching his stomach. There was something wrong. His hand was red, bloody even. There was blood leaking through his clothes, between his clenched fingers. The hand would not move. He tried to see what had caused all the blood and his hand would not move. Something was stopping it.

Lieutenant Hayes appeared, "What are your orders, sir?" Hayes eyes strayed down to Newton's waist. His face paled. "Sir, you are hurt!"

Newton looked at the man and grinned, "Keep firing, Mr. Hayes. Send the doctor and keep firing. Remember we have guns on both sides of the ship, Mr. Hayes."

The laugh that followed this comment was ghoulish to Hayes's ears. "Aye, aye. Sir" He managed and ran off to give orders. The bo'sun, working at the broken shrouds, spat and told his mate, "I'll take my chances in a boat, I reckons. Ain't no hope here, now the captain's gone."

"Captain's still alive, Bose,"

"Just take a look at him and tell me how long?" The sardonic tone said it all.

His mate looked at Roger Newton standing there beside the mainmast, the ramrod from one of the enemy guns had him pinned to the mast, the swab end standing clear by two feet. The remainder driven by the gun's charge through Newton's hand and stomach, leaving him impaled like a specimen upright against the mast, his life draining from him as they watched.

One of the last balls fired from Huron nearly ended Martin's career. A large splinter from the shattered bulwark caught him high in the shoulder, throwing him to the deck beneath the imminent threat of the damaged main-spar, now dangling by its sheets and the remnants of its sail.

Peters was there, carefully dragging his Captain clear of danger and calling for the doctor.

Roger Mills took one look and shouted to Lieutenant Brooks. "She is all yours, Mr. Brooks. I need to get the Commodore ashore."

"Right, Doctor. There is a boat there." He pointed to the shoreward side of the ship and left it to the doctor and Peters to get on with things.

\

**

They carried Martin into the main bedroom of Absolom's former house, and stripped his clothes off. Whilst he was still unconscious, the doctor removed the splinter, taking care to find every scrap of wood within the torn flesh.

Naomi appeared with cobwebs and honey. The doctor started to protest, then realised there was no reason to stop her using them. They had worked for wounds for thousands of years. What he had was no better, though he did understand there were new remedies being discovered. At this time they were as good as any.

**

On Abigail, Mathew Harper looked at the devastation of his once beautiful ship, now just a single gun firing to the last. It fell silent and the ship started to go. The terrible wounds in her side were not going to be sealed in a hurry, and there was no time anyway.

It's odd, Mathew thought. *"There is a beautiful woman looking at me across the red and angry water littered with bits and pieces of the ships and men that had been involved in the skirmish."*

He tried to lift his hand and wave, but it was too heavy for him to lift for some reason. He looked at his hand, there was a pistol gripped firmly there, the hammer was back and he could see down the barrel.

The ship lurched and stared to slide under, Mathew's hand jolted against the pedestal of the steering mountings, his finger tightened and the pistol fired.

When the sharks came for Mathew he was dead already, so he was unaware of the way his body was ripped apart.

The Abigail died with him. Of the forty-one survivors, nobody had a bad word for Mathew Harper.

Chapter Twenty-three

Gunboat diplomacy

THE SMALL BOAT was not remarked as it approached the shore of the island. The small community of Key West was enjoying the relief at the removal of the pressure from entertaining the local pirate base for several years. Despite the income generated by the pirate presence, the strain of maintaining the place in accordance with the demands of the pirates had been telling on the small population, many of whom were of a religious bent and were uncomfortable with the louche regime maintained by their benefactors.

The boat ran aground and three men stepped ashore, each with his own weighty baggage.

Bo'sun John Cody, formerly of the frigate Huron turned to his two companions. "Well, gents. This is where we parts company. From here on, I don't know you and you don't know me. Got it?"

"We got it, John, and good luck to us all, though I reckon it would do no harm to keep company as far as the town."

John looked at the others. "If yew likes mates, but no further!"

Taking up their bags the three walked off into the night. Hayes encountered them before they reached town. With a pistol in his belt and sword at his side, he was the better for half a bottle of Roger Newton's best brandy. Like the other three men, he had rowed ashore before the Huron finally sank, taking less in the way of loot than he had hoped for. Others had prepared better for their departure.

He was pretty certain that Bo'sun Cody would have been well prepared, which was why he was pleased to encounter him in this way.

Placing his hand on his pistol, he stood in their way. "Just drop those loads into the cart I have here. It will save all that dragging about for you men. It was a hard day for us all, so better to relax a bit now."

"Why, that is a kind thought, Mr. Hayes. I would not have guessed that you would be so concerned for our welfare. Come on, lads, let's put our bags in here with Mr. Hayes own bag, t'will save a lot of heaving and shoving for us on the way to town."

The three men loaded their bags into the cart. As they turned around, Hayes drew his pistol and pointed it at Bo'sun Cody.

He squeezed the trigger, and looked perplexed when the pistol failed to fire. His semi-drunken state did not help.

He shook the pistol then threw it aside and drew his sword. Cody watched this happen and picked up the pistol. He opened the pan and tapped a little powder into it from the powder horn he carried at his belt. He then cocked the pistol pointed it at Hayes and fired.

The bullet knocked Hayes flat on his back. He lay there spread-eagled in the middle of the road. Cody walked over to him and made sure he was dead. He turned to the others, "Three way split?"

"Bastard would have stolen our own wealth."

"Now we'll steal his." Cody said with a crooked grin. He unbuckled the sword belt and scabbard, and collected the blade from the dead hand of Hayes. "Waste not, want not!" He said with a smile, Grab the cart, the pair of you. Let's be going then!"

The three disappeared down the road toward town, and the area was left to the land crabs and the body of their former Lieutenant.

***

The operation on Martin had taken a lot out of him and he woke with fever under the close attention of his female attendants.

The continual application of water-soaked cloths was having some effect on his condition but there was more needed to be done.

Doctor Mills was concerned the cobwebs and honey were doing something but there was more wrong with his patient than the wound. Some fever seemed to have taken hold, which made more to be dealt with than he anticipated. The cool cloths were of real use but his condition was such that he found Martin was either shivering or sweating. Naomi and Sadie her maid, both stripped off and joined Martin in bed giving their body heat to keep Martin's in between the high and low levels specified by the Doctor.

For four days Martin hovered between life and death. On the fifth day the doctor decided that the crisis was over. The two women, who had lent themselves to save him, gratefully abandoned their patient to wallow in a bath and recover themselves from what must have been a trying business.

As Doctor Mills admitted, the presence of the two ladies physically may have made no difference. But the will to save the man, freely expressed in the way they proffered themselves, and the comfort of their presence, was a definite fillip to all involved in the treatment. Roger Mills never did discover the source of the fever. Nor could any of the local sources provide any information about it. Other than it was often fatal.

For Martin it turned out to be beneficial. By the time he had recovered his senses his wound was well on the way to healing and his general health improved as his appetite returned.

HMS Hera had remained in Key West to transport Martin to rejoin the diplomatic party in its progress north along the eastern seaboard of the American coast.

***

Julia Savage had been released to sail north to Halifax, to re-establish her business and await the eventual arrival of Naomi and her maid. No plans had been made to cover the process of contacting the eastern states, apart from a simple progression, in the circumstances, northward.

In the absence of Martin on his sickbed, Dominic elected to commence his mission. He had been active in promulgating the message which Martin had been trying to drive home since his arrival in American waters. The defeat of the pirates from Key West had been a real help in this matter.

After more than ten days recovering, Martin insisted on re-joining the expedition along the coast. The remainder of the entourage left Key West with a send-off from the local people, who assured them of a friendly welcome whenever they were in these waters.

As Hera flew north, the sea air had a beneficial effect on Martin, and the group who had nursed him back to health.

There was a reclining bed/chair placed on the quarterdeck in the shadow of the mainsail. From there Martin was able to stand, and walk the deck when he was able, or just relax and watch the activities of the captain and crew of the schooner. As he had promised himself he was getting to know Lieutenant Harris better. What he discovered, he decided he liked. He turned to Naomi, who was seated sketching with charcoal stick and paper in a specially constructed chair, beside the table placed between them. "Madam, I am continually mystified by the knowledge you have at your fingertips. I do not condescend, how could I? I am a mere student at your feet in many of the subjects at which you excel."

Naomi sat and sketched on for a moment. Then she put the pad and charcoal to one side, and turned to face him. "Commodore!" Her almost lazy, drawl sent tingles down Martin's spine at the underlying invitation of that voice. "Martin, you are not aware of my origins. In fact, it is not a subject I make public. You may have noticed that I am very pale skinned. That is a heritage of my Circassian mother. My father was a Boyar who came and went from my mother's life. He did not ask. He took. He departed leaving his treasure behind. I discovered that his return had been anticipated by my mother. When I was three, my father died, attempting to add to our family, with my mother's knife in his heart.

"There were repercussions, but the wealth of my mother was sufficient to have me sent to Alexandria to be educated, a thing unheard of among the poor and illiterate, but known in the secret world of the shapers of the political world. From Alexandria to Padua, Padua to Vienna, private tuition followed by capture.

"Absolom was not specifically a ladies' man, if you take my meaning, but I never met a man more avid for learning. He protected me and prevented the others from using me as they would. One pair at least, who attempted to, were both killed by his hand. He was what he was, a callous pirate, surviving however he could. His relationship with Roger Newton was always friendship. The business was important, but to Absolom, Roger Newton was a friend. I believe Roger felt the same way. When he struck Absolom I am sure he did not intend to do the damage he actually did.

"I enjoy my learning. I understand things I would otherwise have puzzled over. I could navigate this ship, if needs must." She smiled. "Now you see why I am still an unmarried woman at twenty-eight years."

Martin looked at her, and possibly the flash of lust showed as he admired the smooth line of her cheek, and the impossibly blue eyes against the dark hair that crossed her cheek. The impulse to stretch out and brush that stray hair off her cheek was almost unstoppable. He dropped his eyes. "Naomi, I may say that you are possibly.... You are the most beautiful, talented woman I have ever met. I enjoy your company and, were I yet unmarried, I would attempt to take you as my wife. Since I am married and happily so, I can enjoy your company and extend my gratitude and protection to any future activity you may wish to undertake."

"You miss your wife, Martin. Of that I am sure. But you are recovering quickly and soon you will be fully active again. I anticipate travelling to England with you, if that is possible. Between Absolom and you, I have an abundance of wealth, so I can pick and choose. My future is in my own hands. Now I think you should go below and relax in your cabin. Too much of this sea air will be exhausting for you."

Martin looked at her. "You are an exacting taskmaster," he said with a smile. "But I promised to obey orders. So to my cabin I will go, though sleep may be the last thing on my mind."

"That remains to be seen. Be gone to your rest, sir."

Martin went below and, unaided, removed his clothes and lay down in his bed, the single sheet to cover him.

He dozed off and was wakened by the removal of the sheet and the feeling of the half-familiar, smooth body embracing him then engulfing him. He made to move, but was stopped by warm lips and a slight adjustment of the intruder to enabled all their mutual working parts to engage as they were intended. With a mental shrug, Martin submitted, deciding this treatment was perfect for eventual recovery?

***

The journey north was accomplished with maximum speed and minimum fuss. They encountered several ships on the way, one, significantly, a naval ship captained by a post captain. The encounter was fortuitous. The frigate Sufferin had ordered an American merchantman to stop. HMS Hera arrived as the frigate started to lower a boat. On Martin's instructions, the Hera stopped in the path of the jollyboat. The officer in charge of the boat furiously motioned the schooner to move.

Lieutenant Harris took his trumpet, and called "What ship?"

The officer in the boat, also a Lieutenant, angrily called back "Sufferin."

Martin appeared on deck. The commodore's pennant appeared at the masthead. The flag for Sufferin's Captain to repair on board swiftly flew up the halyards. The jollyboat returned to the frigate. The lieutenant was replaced by the captain and the boat was swiftly pulled over to the schooner. Lieutenant Harris called the merchantman and sent him on his way.

Captain Sir Peregrine Horrocks RN was not a happy man. His reception on the schooner was immaculate. He was piped aboard and escorted directly to the stern cabin where Martin waited.

"How do you do, Sir Peregrine," Martin said politely, offering his hand across the desk.

"I'm put out, sir, very put out, I must say." Sir Peregrine was obviously angry.

"Why, sir? Should you be so angry, put out as you express it? Will you take a glass of wine with me, sir?"

"No, I will not. You have interfered with my duties, sir."

Martin stood up. His full height allowed him to stand tall between the crossbeams, without his hat. "Sit down, sir, and hold your tongue. I am senior here and you will respect that or suffer the consequences!"

The frigate captain seemed ready to explode, but common sense intervened. He took his hat off and sat as ordered.

Martin then quietly spoke, "Now, Captain. What orders are you carrying out. I have the impression you were stopping a ship of a neutral nation for some reason?"

"I…I was carrying out the orders I was given." Horrocks stammered.

Martin held his hand out. "Your orders, please." He said without comment..

The package of orders was passed over hesitantly. Martin rang the bell on his desk. When Peters appeared, "Bring wine!"

He returned to reading the orders.

Eventually he stopped. The wine appeared and he poured two glasses. One, he pushed over to his guest.

"Tell me, Captain. Where does it say, 'stop and harass ships under neutral flag'."

"It um doesn't say per-se. sir."

"That is my interpretation. So explain, please. Exactly why you were intent on persecuting the ships of a friendly nation?"

"I had my orders direct from the Admiral, Sir."

"And which admiral was this?"

"I understand Admiral Bowers, sir."

"You know the Admiral personally then?"

"I believe so, sir."

"You believe so? How, sir, is that? You either know the man or not. Which is it?"

"I was briefed in a darkened room in the Admiralty. I was introduced to Admiral Bowers who gave me orders to stop and harass American shipping, as they would soon return to British rule and this would help things progress."

"Can you describe Admiral Bowers?"

"I believe I can. He was a tall man with a thin face. I could not see the colour of his eyes, and he was wearing a wig, but of slender build."

Martin looked at the man quizzically. "Tall, you say. As tall as you, sir?"

"No, taller. By six inches, I would venture."

"Do you know who I am?"

"No, sir, I do not."

"I am Commodore Sir Martin Forest-Bowers RN. Admiral Bowers is my father. I can assure you, sir, that whoever gave you your instructions, it was not Admiral Bowers. Your description of the man is not that of my father, who is of a height with you yourself, and though he will not thank me for saying so, sadly not, as you describe this man, slim."

Horrocks looked appalled. "He was dressed as an Admiral. I had no reason to dispute his identity or his specific instructions."

Martin said, "I accept what you say, Sir Peregrine. But before leaving Portsmouth I was given a copy of the order given to stop all harassment of American shipping by British Naval craft. I am finding it difficult to understand what part of that order you believe should be disobeyed."

"I have no record of such an order. As I have said I was given my orders in person at the Admiralty."

Martin shook his head, "No record of this order? In the circumstances, I can take one of two actions. I can accept your word that you will cease all harassment, or I can arrest you for disobeying admiralty orders and inciting a foreign nation to make war. Which shall it be?"

"Sir, I have been used, sir. I was truly unaware that such an order had been given."

"How did your appointment at the Admiralty come about. Were you summoned in the usual manner?"

"I had already received my usual orders at the Admiralty as normal. I was contacted by Sir Bertrand McIlroy, an old school colleague of mine. He called upon me and advised me that I was summoned to a private meeting at the Admiralty with Admiral Bowers. I cannot understand why he would place me in such an embarrassing position."

Martin sat back. "I also am in an awkward position. I can accept that your school-friend is convinced that, with a little pressure, the Americans will return to the Crown, but that does not excuse this blatant attempt to countermand the orders of the Government in this matter. I have been involved in calling upon the authorities along this coastline for the last few months. My knowledge of these people causes me to believe there is no chance that America would return to the Crown. In addition, I am convinced the unless we stop this harassment of their ships, we will be at war as soon as the construction of their new class of frigates is someway complete. I have seen one of these ships. I command a frigate as do you. I consider that one of those frigates will be more than a match for any of ours. They do not lack good seamen and with a broadside of 22 twenty-four pounder guns, and the frames of a seventy-four, you may work it out for yourself, Captain."

Captain Sir Peregrine Horrocks was looking a little sick. However he drew himself up to his full height, "I am at your service, sir. I have explained my situation and I await your judgement."

"I'll not judge a man who is merely obeying orders. Please send for one of your officers and stay to dine with me tonight. I have some fine vintage brandy and a superior wine."

"You are most kind, sir. I will send for Lieutenant Warren. He is newly promoted from Midshipman and has heard mention of you from the Gazette."

Chapter twenty-four

The French connection

THE SCHOONER CAUGHT up with the other ships of the squadron at Charlestown. They had spent some days at Savannah in Georgia, following a visit to Columbia, the capital of the state. The Honourable Dominic Gordon in HMS Vixen, escorted by Sao Paulo, HMS Spartan, HMS Lively were en-route to North Carolina, specifically Pamlico Sound, with a view to visit the Governor in Raleigh, the new capital of the state. It entailed an overland journey, but Dominic considered it justified in the circumstances.

Martin transferred his flag back to HMS Vixen and the journey was continued.

The matter of the ladies, carried at present by HMS Hera, was of concern to the Commodore, especially since he himself had been the reason for their presence. It was therefore a simple decision, suggested by Dr. Mills, to have them taken on HMS Hera direct to Halifax, where they could re-join Julia Savage, at least until the squadron reached the city. There they would have the opportunity to rest and prepare for the lengthy voyage across the Atlantic to Britain, anticipated during the next three months.

Many of the men had been attended by the ladies when injured in the past few weeks and to the embarrassment of the ladies but the obvious pleasure of the men, the ladies were rowed around the ships of the squadron to say farewell before departing northward.

As HMS Hera sailed north, the remaining ships set sail for Raleigh Bay and Pamlico Sound beyond. They moored at the entrance to the Pamlico River, where the diplomatic party transferred to HMS Lively the smallest of the ships. She towed two long boats as she sailed up the river towards the distant city of Raleigh.

When they reached the limit of sailing, they still had nearly one hundred miles to go to the Capital. At Washington they hired two wagons and a carriage, plus horses for the Marines and others of the escort.

The others consisted of local militia, a body of men dressed in dark blue tunics, with black buttons. The major in charge had a small black star on his cuff. All wore a black stocking cap all wore moccasins and all carried rifles. They had horses, led by three of their number. Only the Major rode with the party. The other twenty-seven scattered through the surrounding woodlands. As far as Martin could see, they ran, easily keeping pace with the column, making little apparent noise.

At camp that night after a fifteen mile stretch, Martin, admittedly still recovering from his wound, was feeling the pace.

The Major, Aaron Jackman, of the North Carolina Militia, having seen the horses secured, dispatched three riders to scout the area, to make sure there were no marauders in the vicinity. Having eaten, the twenty-seven runners split into three parties. One party joined the marines in patrolling the area. The others slept or yarned with each other and the off-watch Marines.

Dominic searched out the Major and invited him to try the brandy he carried in his flask. In conversation, he learned that the country they were passing through was rich and fertile, but it was also periodically raided by bands of the native American tribes. Savages they were, though they could be friendly. Sadly, over the years their lands had been taken over by settlers, which had meant that the tribes were being pushed away into the unknown lands beyond the mountains, hunting grounds of other tribes who rode horses and hunted the wild bison that roamed the plains country.

Dominic studied the face of the man in front of him. "You, Major. Where are you from?"

"The name is Aaron Jackman, your excellency."

"I am not excellent, and my name is Dominic Gordon, sir." He held out his hand. After a moment, Aaron took it and shook.

"Howdy, Dom. Call me Ron." He grinned and Dominic found himself grinning back at him.

"How do, Ron, what in hell do you do in the evenings here?"

Ron thought for a moment. "Well, in town there are things to do, I guess. There are socials, and folk do a little drinking, spooning and reading. That's become more popular, now the schools are working. Out here!" He paused, breathed in and let his eyes drift around the area. "Out here, we either live with the land or we die! Life becomes a little more simple in one way, complicated in another."

Dominic looked at his companion. "Complicated?"

"Take a look around you." Ron swung his arm out, taking in the sky, the trees, the flickering fire, and the sleeping men. "These are things you can see. What you don't see is the man sitting on watch half-way up that tree, two others laying-up in the woods, there and there." His finger stabbed out twice in the direction where his men were on watch. "In the sky you see a million stars, a beautiful sight. Possibly the last sight you will ever have, if you look too hard. What do we do in the woods at night? We try to stay alive!"

A thoughtful Dominic went to his blankets that night. The words of the Major had made a deep impression on him. Any doubts he may have had over whether the Americans wished to remain independent or not were resolved by the short conversation with Aaron Jackman. He slept soundly that night, secure in the knowledge that the party was watched over.

***

Martin was impressed by Major Jackman and his men. Lieutenant Bristow, in command of the Marines, was also. "Sir, had I known there would be an escort like this I would have been less concerned about the security on this journey."

Martin eased his seat on the saddle, "I know what you mean. There is an air of quiet competence about the entire company. They move through the woods like shadows. I understand how it was possible for them to defeat our troops here during the rebellion."

The Marine looked thoughtful. "Would you be bothered if I asked the Major to instruct me in the use of the rifles his men carry?"

Martin smiled. "I would be worried if you did not. The accuracy of their shooting has only been experienced by our soldiers in the field. In action on a ship, such accuracy would be devastating to an enemy. I am impressed by the job the marines do with their muskets. You may take it that I will willingly purchase any rifles needed to reinforce our marine contingent in this way."

***

Over the next four days the column progressed, finally reaching the capital city of North Carolina.

The contingent of militia under Major Jackman melted away as the party reached Raleigh. Martin was assured that they would be in place once more for the journey back to the coast. Security was, meanwhile, undertaken by an honour guard from the state Regiment of Cavalry.

The Marine contingent was reduced to four men on duty throughout the four-day visit. Their commander, Lieutenant Bristow, appeared and disappeared by arrangement over the next four days.

As Martin remarked afterward, "As a diplomatic exercise the visit was pointless, as an exercise in friendly relations it was a triumph."

***

Martin noticed on the return journey that the marines were now in possession of two cases of weapons, in addition to the rifles which had replaced the muskets they had carried on the trip inland.

At every stop the marine contingent practiced loading their rifles. On two occasions they were actually permitted to fire at targets, placed by the Major Jackman's militia.

By the time the party had returned to the waiting boats, the marines were comfortably loading three times in a minute. Major Jackman predicted that they would achieve four, in time.

Before the party moved off down river, the Major had a quiet word with Martin.

"Commodore Forest-Bowers, a word before you depart."

Curious, Martin stepped away from the others with the Major.

"Well, Sir. You have looked after us well, I believe. How can I be of assistance?"

"Sir, I have news that there are dissidents in the area. I have reason to believe they will assault your party before you reach the safety of your waiting ship. I would be happy if I could leave four of my best riflemen with the party on the boats. You may be assured the remainder of my men will be combing the banks until your party are safely back aboard your ship."

"Major, I am disturbed at your news. I appreciate the trouble you have taken to see us this far. I would be happy to accommodate four of your riflemen, and I am most re-assured to know your men will be scouting the banks of the river. While I hope this is a false alarm, I will ensure my own men are aware and prepared to look after themselves. If you decide to leave this great country of yours, my door will always be open to you." He held out his hand, and shook that of Aaron Jackman.

When the party boarded the boats for the downriver journey two extra trunks were loaded and, with the complements of Major Jackman, consigned to Lieutenant Bristow.

So the final stages of their long journey began. The current, assisted by the sails, sent the longboats sliding down the river. The portage at the upper rapids was the scene of the first attack. As they approached the shallows, two of the scouts came out of the woods and reported an ambush ahead.

The marines filed ashore and took off their red coats. From the trunks sent by Major Jackman, they took buckskin jackets and donned them. The same stocking caps used by the militia covered their hair, and boots were replaced by moccasins. The uniforms went back in the trunk. While the marines disappeared into the woods. The boats were pushed the rest of the way to the portage area. As the two boats were lifted onto the wheeled frames for the short journey around the rapids, a spatter of shots was heard in the woods. There were several war whoops to be heard. The crew members and the four militia-men prepared to repel boarders. About a dozen savages burst out of the woods, screaming and waving war axes. The four militia men coolly shot the first four men. Martin shot the nearest man with one of his prize pistols. Peters swept his cutlass across the face of his attacker, taking his raised arm off at the wrist. The hand and the axe it held fell to the ground. The four rifles spoke once more.

Out of the woods came the marines three dropped to their knee and took aim and the last of the savages dropped.

Curious, Martin examined the nearest dead man. He was big man, golden brown, well-muscled.

"A fine looking man." He muttered.

"Unnoticed, the Major was by his side. "Indeed he is, sir. I am sad to see him here in this state."

"Why, Major? What brought him to attack us?"

"Unscrupulous men, sir, as you will find everywhere. Men who see a profit in murder, or political advantage. There are always such people to be found. Obviously somebody thinks there would be an advantage in removing you from the coast. It's difficult enough to sink a ship, but not so hard to mount an ambush on land in these circumstances, especially when you have the means to hire savages to do the job for you.

"All the blame therefore lies with the savages, and all it can cost is a few axe heads knives and the odd handful of gee-gaws for the squaw. By the way, Commodore, there may be a clue in the fact that currently there are two French ships lying in Raleigh bay, more or less covering your way north from Pamlico Sound. I guess they do not realise that the channel at Oregon Island will be deep and wide enough for your ships to go through. They will learn, of course, though, I suggest, not until too late to give them advantage. One of the French ships has two decks of guns, her name is Lorient. The other is smaller but 40 guns, called L'Empereur.

"Major Jackman, my thanks for the hospitality. Presuming we are not yet at war, I hope we meet again. If we are at war in the future, you will understand why I would prefer not."

"A pleasure, sir. My men will leave at the river mouth. With a salute and a wry smile the Major disappeared into the woods.

***

Re-joining HMS Lively was a relief for the landing party. The remainder of the journey was accomplished in more comfortable circumstances.

Lieutenant Keats, in command, had news of the French ships, including a frustrated raid attempt by the

French using their boats to sail through the island chain between Raleigh Bay and the Pamlico anchorage. Commodore Ramos had arranged for watch boats to be stationed for just such an event. The surprise hoped for by the French was not achieved. In the event the boats were repulsed with heavy losses.

The two boats attacking HMS Vixen were surprised as they came alongside, carronade balls were rolled into the boats smashing them before they had managed to hook-on and the swivel guns wrought terrible havoc among the survivors struggling to climb aboard.

The French officer in charge was wounded and captured along with seven survivors from that party. Spartan and Sao Paulo both moved as soon as it was dark and in effect ambushed the other two boats. One, only, survived to return to the anchored French ships.

Martin conferred with Antonio Ramos and Lieutenants Keith and Marlow.

That night, as darkness fell, the anchor lights were transferred to hastily constructed rafts, to act as a decoy, while the four ships sailed north to the Oregon passage through the island chain and out into the Atlantic. Having elected to make a final call on Washington, they turned west into Chesapeake Bay and anchored at the entrance to the Potomac River. There the diplomatic party took to the longboats and sailed up river to the Nation's Capital.

Their visit was politely received but, with a heavy heart, Martin realised that the feeling in Washington was not interested in promises, broken in the past and likely to be broken in the future.

The departure from Chesapeake Bay was un-resisted but did not auger well for the future. The sight of two of the new frigates was hardly re-assuring.

In Halifax, their arrival was greeted with a celebration. The ships were taken into dock for attention and additional repairs following their battle damage from the action against the pirates. As the year end approached, Martin realised the news was of growing unrest with reports of further harassment of American shipping. The impressment of American sailors and the imposition of trade embargos were exacerbated by attempts to raise the Native tribes against the forces of the young nation.

***

The business affairs of Julia Savage were progressing favourably. Dominic Gordon had grown up throughout the expedition, and was now being head-hunted by the Governor, to join his staff in a senior capacity.

Martin approved of his refusal of the opportunity in favour of the chance of preferment back in London. There would be chances enough for a young man of his talent during the years ahead.

Naomi and her maid were accompanying the Squadron upon its return to Britain. Since Julia had refitted the Mohawk, she was taking the opportunity to accompany the convoy with a cargo of Canadian native goods, in charter to the newly-reconstituted Hudson's Bay Company. She undertook to carry the ladies and would captain the ship herself. Jackson Hobbs was now firmly ensconced in the trading office of the company, and had already organized travellers to collect and distribute trade goods throughout Manitoba and Labrador.

The convoy, now including two more merchantmen, Henry James and Bangor, was ready and departed Halifax on January 30th 1812.

***

The French ships Lorient and L'Empereur had left American waters on the 15th January 1812, with the intention of making landfall at Brest, weather permitting.

The captain of Lorient approached the Admiral with a certain amount of trepidation. August Treville was one of the reduced numbers of professional seamen in command of a line of battle ship in the Navy of France. His Admiral had been captain in the ferry running from Marseilles to Ajaccio in Corsica. A friend of the Little General, Admiral Jean-Luc Pasteur was without doubt the smallest, meanest, little pipsqueak of a man known to Treville. His so-called and often quoted expertise in seamanship was less than inspiring to the professional sailors aboard. It was now apparent to Treville that the Captaincy of the Marseilles ferry was one of those jobs passed on to favoured members of the clan, or whatever secret society prevailed on the island more renowned for vendetta than talent.

He knocked at the cabin door and a slurred voice bade him enter.

"Sir, you sent for me?"

The Admiral sat in his chair behind the desk. The bottle of Cognac and two glasses stood more or less steadily in the calm waters of the Gulf Stream.

"If we are heading for Brest, why does my compass indicate North-East? Captain, I am as you are aware a navigator. I can read a chart. Explain why we are heading this way?"

"As a navigator, sir, you will appreciate that since the world is round the best course is a great circle, taking advantage of the push of the Gulf Stream we will make better progress in this way. As it pushes us north and east It helps us make distance across the ocean."

The bemused face looked up at the impassive face before him. "Of course. I was just making sure that we were both aware of these things landsmen fin' so mysteri..sss." The slurred speech made it quite clear to Treville that the man was incapable, and should not be given command of a garbage scow let alone a pair of warships.

"I recall that damn frigate we met at Raleigh Bay. Cheeky bastard killed my flag Lieutenant. I suppose we may get the chance to meet him on this course?"

"It's possible." Treville shrugged. "But the ocean is wide. Who knows?"

He was thinking, *God help us if we do. That English Commodore Forest-Bowers is a professional.*

Pasteur took a drink and mumbled, "Keep your eyes open, man. That 'Rostbiff' needs a roasting." He burst out laughing, pounding the desk.

Treville saluted, "I will keep my eyes open, sir."

He left the cabin while the admiral laughed at his clever humour.

"Perhaps," He murmured. "It would be good to meet this Englishman. A stray bullet could rid me of this idiot admiral."

He spoke aloud, albeit quietly. Nobody heard what he said, but there were several on the ship who would agree with his thoughts.

Chapter Twenty-five

45 degrees N

THE WEATHER IN the Atlantic played its usual games, two days of sunshine, cold and clear, and then the rising waves presaged an approaching storm. The squadron responded by making preparation for the weather expected. With extra battening of hatches, and the replacement of sails with storm canvas, the ships closed the doors to the coming weather. When the time came, the arriving storm flirted with the ships, tossing them on rising seas. The ships rode the waves with discomfort for the crews and passengers, but no real problems. The storm was concentrated to the south of the area, allowing the squadron to skirt the northern edge and continue to make progress on their homeward voyage.

***

The two French ships were not so lucky. Some way to the south they were caught in the heart of the storm and suffered damage accordingly. By the time it had passed, both ships were suffering from leaks which meant keeping the pumps at work through all the watches. Whilst there were crew members to spare on both ships, there were also many sick from the motion, as well as from injuries gained from being thrown about by the violent movement of the ships.

Admiral Jean-Luc Pasteur had not been seen for three days. Captain Treville had been grateful for the break. According to the Admiral's servant, his master had spent most of the time in his berth hugging a bottle of brandy, and praying for mercy from the Almighty.

This news had given Treville a certain amount of amusement. After all, his Admiral was a seaman, a navigator no less and, while the stormy weather had been fairly boisterous, it was not unusually so for the Atlantic.

The weather had caused damage. When the crew of a ship such as this was composed of men who had recently obtained their release from the burden of an autocratic regime, it was necessary to remind them that their very survival depended on doing the routine jobs of maintenance needed to keep the ship afloat.

Captain Treville found the need to keep a restrained attitude to his crew very frustrating. Too often he had to explain why orders were given. It has to be said that, though he supported the revolution in general terms, there were times when he was tempted to use a rope-end on some of the more recalcitrant members of his crew.

Replacing worn and frayed ropes on sail and rigging was vital before the ship was faced with another period of bad weather. He looked across to the L'Empereur, noting that she also needed replacement rigging. Judging from the noise carrying over the calming sea, her hull was leaking rather more than the Lorient. The sound of the pumps from L'Empereur seemed to be continuous. As he watched, Treville saw the crew of the other ship working to lower a patch over the side of the ship. He winced as a man was struck by the massive patch. The man fell into the still rough sea. The scarlet slash of colour from the blood of the unfortunate man's ragged wound dissipated rapidly in the welter of foam around the damaged hull. He turned back to the activity on his own ship. There was nothing to be done for the man in the water. Neither ship could stop to try to pick him up. Perhaps on a calm summer day he might have survived. As it was, the sea was still too rough and the man was probably unconscious or dead when he hit the water.

He looked aloft at the masthead. There was a figure there hopefully keeping an eye out for signs of sail. He shook his head. He did not have much faith in the qualities of his crew. He just hoped that their own sense of self-preservation would inspire them to make some effort, beyond the minimum which seemed to be the best he could expect up to now.

Despite his comments to the Admiral when last they spoke, Treville was worried that they might encounter British ships en-route to and from Canada and the Americas.

He had no illusions about the effectiveness of the two French ships. Even without the damage, his experience of the efficiency of his own crew was not re-assuring.

***

Conditions for the British squadron were not ideal, and there was still some damage to be put right after the period of bad weather. Mohawk had suffered less than the two other merchant ships in company, both of which had suffered problems with their rigging only now, finally repaired after two days of lessening seas and improving weather.

For Martin the delay, though inevitable, was still irritating. Now he had completed the mission he had been sent to perform, he was anxious to get home to pass on his impression of the attitude and conditions in America. Most importantly, his view on the war which he was now certain was inevitable.

He carried dispatches from the Government officials in Halifax who held the same view. The program of harassment some of the Captains of Royal Naval ships had employed against American shipping, and the attempts to raise the native tribes against the new state, had been enough. The building of the heavy frigates, now well advanced, was probably the deciding factor in the approaching hostilities. The Royal Navy was involved in keeping the French at bay. Having America in opposition as well would not improve matters.

Once more Martin had reason to condemn the idiots who could not see that, once the rebels committed themselves and defeated the troops sent against them, there was no way back, short of peaceful negotiation. And that option had been lost when the harassment began.

The two Commodores sat enjoying a glass of wine together. Antonio Ramos had joined Martin after visiting the damaged ships to see the state of repairs.

"They are now ready to proceed," he said taking another sip. "This wine is travelling well."

Martin smiled. "As you well know, this is part of the batch you gave me from your own vineyard in Portugal."

"Why, so it is. As I commented, it is travelling well."

The squadron had resumed its mean course. Martin remarked to his Portuguese colleague, "Now, perhaps, we can make progress once more. I think we will need as much time as we can get to prepare for battle on two fronts in future."

Antonio Ramos smiled grimly. "Please, convince me, friend Martin. Assure me that someone will take notice of our reports."

Martin shrugged. "All I can do is submit my findings. Some politician will be called upon to direct the response."

Antonio sighed. "That is what I believe. I am sure that the same politician will expect the Royal Navy to stop the Americans in their tracks, disregarding any suggestion we may make."

They were both seated in the great cabin on HMS Vixen, the stern windows open to allow the afternoon sun to combine with the breeze and dry out the dank atmosphere which had made the interior of the ship uncomfortable during the storms of the past three days.

Antonio said, "I was going to invite some of the other captains to join me on the Sao Paulo, but I have a feeling that we are not alone, despite the size of this Atlantic Ocean. However silly it may sound, my palm is itching. I expect trouble from somewhere soon. So I believe I will hold off my party to a time when there is less chance of interruption."

The two men sipped their wine in companionable silence for a few minutes. Then Antonio rose to his feet. "I must get back to my ship. I will not be really comfortable until I see the coast up ahead. Thank you for your company and the wine my friend." He turned and Martin escorted him to the deck, where he was piped into the boat lying alongside. The Sao Paulo was following astern of Vixen, allowing the boat's crew an easy return passage.

Martin watched the boat carrying his friend slide alongside, the men ready to attach the falls so that the boat could be raised, complete with crew and their Commodore, and swung into its place on the deck of the frigate.

As he returned to his cabin, Martin reflected on the hunch that Antonio mentioned. He agreed that it would be foolish to think that they would have an easy voyage home with no other problems. Perhaps there was a French presence closing on them even now?

***

For two days the weather eased and the squadron progressed, making good time on their homeward passage. The third day the wind dropped and there was a haze over the sea. Jared Watson, Master, was looking at the growing haze. He lifted his head and studied the sky, sniffing the air.

Martin came on deck. Feeling the change in the air, he turned to the Master and said, "This does not feel good to me. What say you, Master?"

"Fog is what I say, sir. Here, this far from land, it will linger until the wind rises once more. My advice would be to light the lanterns and keep distance between the ships." He pursed his lips into what could almost be a smile. "Perhaps pray?"

Martin looked at him. After a moment he called Brooks, the first Lieutenant, who had just returned to the quarter-deck. "Mr. Brooks, while the company is still in sight, signal them to light lamps and keep their distance whilst the fog lasts."

Brooks looked at the present conditions. "Fog, sir?"

Martin smiled. "If we wait for this mist to thicken, no signal will be seen?"

"I beg your pardon, sir. I did not mean..." Brooks' voice trailed off, as the raised hand of Martin stopped him.

"It seems we are in for a foggy spell, so we are better to be prepared, I think."

Lieutenant Brooks smiled at the comment. "Of course, sir," He turned to the Midshipman on duty, "Mr. Gibbs, general signal. 'Light lamps and keep your distance.'"

Gibbs responded, "Aye, aye. Sir." He dashed over to the signal locker to arrange the signal.

The mist turned to fog as Jared Watson had predicted. It lingered all day. Apart from one near miss, the ships managed to avoid contact and damage.

As night fell the fog showed no sign of dissipating and the extra lookouts on all the ships spent a nervous night, straining their eyes as the ships made small progress in the almost non-existent wind.

***

On Lorient Captain Trouville was concerned. The same fog troubling the British ships was all around the two French men-of-war. As he peered into the fog he could just make out the vague line of the foremast on L'Empereur. As he watched he realised that the frigate was turning toward the Lorient. Trouville gaped in astonishment wondering what his fellow Captain was doing. Only then, as the frigate turned once more to run parallel to Lorient, did he notice that the gun-ports of the frigate were open and that it was not L'Empereur, but, from the flag lifting idly from her mizzen, she was British. He opened his mouth to cry a warning just as the broadside erupted from the guns of the enemy ship, creating havoc on the main deck of the French 74.

Trouville, unhurt, screamed orders to clear for action and man the guns. To the helm he called for the helmsman to turn toward the enemy ship. The panic stricken man at the wheel steered away, presenting the stern of the ship toward the frigate.

***

Martin stood watching the line-of-battle ship swing away, presenting her vulnerable stern to the frigate's guns.

The calm voice of Lieutenant Cameron sounded from the main deck. "As you bear. 'Fire'."

One by one the guns of the starboard broadside fired into the stern of the French ship. The solid shot ripping and tearing the length of the deck creating mayhem in the stern cabin and shattering the partitions, before careering along through the officer's quarters flinging their possessions all over the place and causing fire to break out in several places. As the carronades fired last, the already open wounds in the stern offered little protection against the 24 pound shot. This smashed the already shattered timbers tumbling the two 18lbs stern chase guns into the waters of the Atlantic. The deck planking on which they stood, was split, no longer able to bear the weight of the heavy guns.

Martin made no attempt to follow the French ship as she disappeared into the fog. He was only too aware that the weight of the broadside from the Frenchman would smash his frigate into matchsticks if it got in one well-aimed opportunity. Also with the fog they would be groping about blindly not knowing friend from foe. "Secure the guns!" he ordered quietly, "Keep a good watch."

Brooks joined him on the quarter-deck. He smiled, "That was lucky!" He commented.

"Not for the Frenchman." Martin answered grimly.

Chapter Twenty-six

Return Match

CAPTAIN TROUVILLE received the news of the death of his Admiral, Jean-Luc Pasteur, with a grave face. The remains had been more or less collected from the wreckage of his cabin and there would be a formal ceremony later when he, and all the other dead, would be committed to the deep. Meanwhile the repairs to the ship were paramount. The damage to the stern was serious and it seems that the brush with the British ship had made a deep impression on the men. The work was undertaken with an enthusiasm that Trouville had not seen since the ship sailed from Brest.

The fog persisted through the day. Though the sound of other ships in the vicinity was heard, the scant wind made close manoeuvring difficult. In the circumstances Trouville had no way of knowing whether the sounds came from L'Empereur or the frigate which had fired on him. He had the lower deck guns loaded and the ports opened, with the gun crews standing by. The swell was subdued so there was little likelihood of the lower deck being swamped through the opened ports. Thus prepared he encouraged the men carrying out repairs to work as fast as possible and damn the noise. He had two guns mounted in what was once the

Admiral's cabin in the stern of the ship, while the repairs went on around them.

By evening the worst was over and he decided the time had come to commit the dead to the sea.

All work stopped and the eighteen dead were lined up on deck. The crew assembled and Trouville read the service for the dead, thinking to himself, for all their proclaimed lack of religion, these men who had rebelled against King and church, still expected a proper service if they died at sea.

Preceded by the Admiral, one by one the bodies were committed to the deep. When the final body, splashed into the water, the bo'sun called the men to their duties. They went without the usual muttering and murmur of discontent.

***

During the night the fog started to lift. Martin was on deck as the sky cleared and the stars started to appear here and there, through gaps in the scattered clouds. The wind rose tugging at the idly-moving sails, filling them and causing the ship to heel slightly as the ship gained way.

The lookout called softly from the masthead, to the chain of men stationed in the rigging to pass messages quietly in the fog. "Six sail in sight."

Martin looked up sharply. There was a stranger in their midst. All the squadron ships were still carrying lanterns. The lookout pointed to the extra ship which was showing several lights.

By her shadowy shape, highlighted by the lights she was showing, she was similar in size to the Vixen. After the encounter with the Lorient, the French 74, Martin concluded that it was probably the frigate L'Empereur, supposed to be sailing in company with her.

As they watched the angle of the lights changed. The stranger had caught a vagrant wind and steered away from the British ships, her displayed lights disappearing as she melted into the fog once more. The lantern on the HMS Hera, the ship closest to the stranger, disappeared also as she turned to shadow the departing Frenchman as best she could.

The weather improved as the night passed. By morning the final vestiges of the mist had gone and a fine sunny day lifted the spirits of the British Squadron. There was no sign of the French, though the topsails of HMS Hera could be seen by the lookout, on the southern horizon. Stationing the merchant ships, including the Mohawk, to the north side of his armed ships, Martin sent Sao Paulo and Spartan to close on the distant Hera just in case she needed assistance.

In fact, as the distance narrowed, signals from Hera proved she was in touch with the two French ships. She also reported that they were now appeared to be changing to a course to intercept the British convoy.

Martin recalled Sao Paulo. When she closed the Vixen, he signalled for Antonio to join him to discuss a plan of action.

Settled in the comfortable chair anchored opposite the desk, Antonio sipped the hot coffee with evident enjoyment. "So, my friend," he said, putting the cup back on the tray. "We are faced with the problem to stay and fight, or to run with the convoy, hoping the French will not catch us?"

Martin nodded slowly. "More or less, though I think it is not really a choice. If we were in a different place where the merchantmen and Mohawk could be assured of shelter, I might advocate running. As it is, we are too far from a safe haven for their safety to be assured. We caught the Lorient by surprise once. I do not envisage that happening again. She is a formidable opponent for two frigates. In addition, L'Empereur will be a problem. She is certainly carrying the same sort of armament as both of our ships. While HMS Lively and Spartan are both well handled, it is asking a lot of them to take on a 40 gun frigate."

Antonio thought about the matter while he finished his coffee, then, "We do not really have an option. Do we?" He smiled and poured himself more of the coffee. "It is just really a question of how we go about it."

Martin smiled back at his friend. "As usual you have gone to the heart of the matter. I have been considering our last encounter with the Lorient."

"In the fog!"

"Exactly! When we opened fire they were caught completely unprepared. We inflicted a lot of damage to her stern. Both chasers were dismounted, and fell into the sea. The stern integrity of the ship would have needed plenty of work to fix. I do not believe there has been time or that they would have had the resources to do more than a temporary repair. I expect they would have replaced the two guns, possibly on the lower deck astern. Especially as the upper deck was pretty much shattered, if I remember correctly." He paused and drank his own coffee while Antonio waited.

"Since we agree that the stern of the Lorient is probably the most vulnerable part of her hull. It would make sense for you to keep things active at the bow, whilst I concentrate on her stern. If we manage to take out her steering if nothing else, we would be in a position to run. Though I have to admit, given the choice, in those circumstances, I would probably want to finish the job."

Antonio smiled grimly. "It's asking a lot of the sloops against the frigate?"

"While we tackle the French, I intend to send Lively with Mohawk and the merchantmen on to Falmouth. Whatever we do in our encounter with the French, I would expect them to be far enough ahead to be beyond the danger of capture from this threat at least."

As Antonio rose to leave, Martin added, "We need to leave the frigate to Hera and Spartan, though as you know, whatever we plan will probably end up with the usual debacle of opportunism and luck."

Antonio walked to the cabin door, saying "It will be approaching dark when the French reach us. I think it would be worth approaching them on a closing course, to retain the windward advantage. It should mean more time before nightfall also."

"I agree." Martin nodded slowly. "We both have work to do before this encounter. The Captain of the Lorient still thinks his big guns will be enough to handle two frigates. Let's prove him wrong!"

As his friend left, Martin could not help wondering if they would survive to meet again. After all, a 74 gun ship was no pushover, at any time.

***

It was almost a foregone conclusion that Hera would find the French.

The topsails of the schooner, visible on the horizon, altered their angle. During the next hour the ships closed to a point, where the signal Hera flew was identified by the nearest member of the squadron. HMS Spartan, cruising almost one mile downwind of Vixen, repeated the signal, 'enemy in sight, two ships.'

It was not quite noon when the signal was received. Martin, having acknowledged the signal, had a decision to make. If he turned and ran downwind to intercept now there would, either be an encounter in the dark or they would possibly miss the enemy completely during the night hours, with the chance that they could complete their crossing without being brought to battle. On the other hand they could run into the French and be seriously damaged, or even sunk, from one broadside from the 24 and 36 pounder guns of the French 74.

There were other options of course, ranging from: Sinking the French 74 (unlikely). Capturing the frigate? Capturing both ships? Plus all the combinations of damage to his ships, loss of one or all, injuries to many, or all, including himself.

He considered all the options available and decided that the ideas, he had discussed with Antonio Ramos, were still the best option.

With a slight alteration of course, the two frigates and HMS Spartan left to rendezvous with HMS Hera, leaving HMS Lively, to escort Mohawk, and the other two merchantmen Henry James and Bangor, on their continuing voyage to Falmouth.

***

Before the ships separated, Julia Savage had herself rowed across to speak with Martin, arriving on deck dressed in breeches and armed with pistols and sword.

In the great cabin she stood, angry at being left out of what was obviously going to be a difficult encounter with the enemy. "Commodore Forest-Bowers!" she said angrily. I have a ship of twenty guns, capable of defending myself and also of mounting an attack. I appreciate that you feel it necessary to escort me and the two cargo tubs through dangerous waters. I also understand your need to take on the Frenchmen just over the horizon. What I do not understand is why you feel we need further escort between here and Falmouth. HMS Lively is hardly better armed than Mohawk. It is obvious to me that she would be better used with your force, leaving Mohawk to escort the other two merchantmen.

Dominic Gordon had accompanied Martin on Vixen thus far. He joined Martin in the great cabin. His arrival delayed Martin's reply to Julia.

When he spoke, he was careful to make sure there would be no misunderstanding. "Captain Savage, Julia, your arrival here is fortuitous. Your offer is appreciated. But I must inform you that when the Royal Navy undertakes to escort a convoy, while there is a naval ship afloat. it remains the responsibility of that naval ship to protect the convoy. HMS Lively will escort the convoy to Falmouth, and onwards as required.

"However it would be appreciated if you could offer passage to Mr. Gordon. I would be happy to transfer him to Lively. But I am assured he would rather enjoy the company of friends, if there is space for him to join you and your passengers?"

Julia shrugged. "What can I say? I have made my offer. You have explained why you cannot accept. Of course we would be delighted to accommodate Dominic.

The others are fed up with my company, I am sure. Please inform Lieutenant Keats that Mohawk is at his disposal, if needed. Bon voyage, Martin. I'll await you in Falmouth."

As she departed with Dominic in tow, Martin stood smiling. Typical of Julia to make such an offer. He sighed. She would have made a great frigate captain were she a man.

***

The three ships gradually closed on the shadowing schooner. The afternoon became evening and then darkness fell.

On the schooner they showed a small light to the three British ships. Lieutenant Harris had drawn closer, meanwhile, to the two French ships, both of whom were showing lights so that they could maintain contact without the danger of colliding. They had also reduced sail for the overnight period, a practice regularly followed by merchant ships, though not always by naval ships. As dawn approached the enemies converged.

Martin, happy to keep the weather gauge, depended on the Hera to keep himself in position for an early morning attack on the French ships.

With his ships positioned against the dark sky to the west, the Frenchmen were silhouetted against the lightening sky to the east.

The first signs of recognition by the French came, when the stern chasers of Lorient opened fire on HMS Vixen. The guns mounted on the lower deck, created havoc on the main deck of Vixen, dismounting two of her guns and killing and wounding eighteen men.

Having the speed and weather gauge, Martin was able to overtake the slower Frenchman. For his audacity, he received the benefit of further strikes from the heavy guns of the ship-of-the-line.

With Vixen's guns double-shotted and run out, Martin got his chance when Lorient put up her helm to allow her broadside to come bear on the frigate. Martin immediately altered course. He steered his ship directly across the stern of the Lorient. With Vixen's broadside guns firing in turn, the double weight of shot, smashed into the already battered stern of the two-decker. The two stern chaser guns, on the French ship, caught unprepared, suffered accordingly, one still reloading. Both guns were dismounted and the ready-use powder bags caught fire and to add to the chaos. The loaded gun had fired before it was hit and created hell in the tangle of Vixen's foremast sail and rigging, luckily no fire started. But Martin was struck by flying debris and thrown senseless to the deck. As the Vixen cleared the stern of the Lorient she encountered the French frigate L'Empereur fully committed to the conflict with Sao Paulo. Both ships were surrounded by clouds of smoke from their guns. The French frigate must have had their port guns loaded and run-out. When Vixen appeared she received the benefit of this preparedness by the French captain. The British ship's already weakened foremast snapped at the foretop, and the upper section toppled with sails and sheets in a mess of timber canvas and rope. Her head fell off to starboard and the port guns now reloaded gave their contribution to the French frigate, in return.

Lorient was in trouble. The second assault on her stern had damaged her rudder and she was having difficulty keeping a course.

Captain Trouville was worried that the further damage to the stern had weakened the construction. Planks springing, with increasing water levels in the ship, meant that the pumps were not able to cope with the renewed damage Lorient had suffered.

Vixen's crew had cleared most of the clutter from her foredeck and with all guns clear, was reloaded and ready, albeit not as spry as she had been, with her reduced complement of masts.

Clawing back upwind, she approached the Lorient once more. Her crew were vainly trying to get her rudder working. Approaching from astern the French ship had no guns bearing from that angle. HMS Spartan appeared sailing across the bow of the French ship. The French ship's two bow guns fired. Lorient was down by the stern, both guns were fired hastily and both shots landed, unhappily for the Spartan. Her mainmast fell, cut through by the 24lb shot and it fell into the mess created by the other strike. Lieutenant Marlow, the helmsman and the sailing master were killed. The splinters from the shattered deck-boards caused a further six casualties.

She dropped out of the conflict at that point. Vixen stopped off the stern, port quarter of the Lorient and fired her aimed guns at the already battered stern. On Lorient the rearmost gun on the upper deck was swivelled round sufficiently to bear on the Vixen. The heavy shot removed the remaining stump of the foremast and killed a further seven men, wounding several others.

In the orlop, Doctor Mills was bloody to the shoulders as he worked on the wounded brought below. The tub with the discarded limbs thrown into it was half full.

He stood back and took a gulp of water from the bucket hung for the purpose from the deckhead. The sound of the guns was almost continuous on the deck above. Plus the rumble of the gun-carriages, as they were pulled to and fro for loading and firing. The supressed thuds of the guns on Sao Paulo and L'Empereur could be heard in addition to the sharper sounds from directly above.

Martin woke with a headache and a start. Young Gibb was anxiously trying to raise him from the deck where he lay, with little success. Martin groaned and hauled himself erect leaning in the shoulder of the diminutive Midshipman. He swayed and peered through the smoke to get his bearings. "Where are we then?"

"We are still hammering the French 74 sir." The boy's voice was hoarse from the powder smoke. Martin sent him below to get a report from the doctor.

On the Lorient, Trouville was anxious. The rib to the rear of the main and gun deck was broken in two places. The ship's carpenter was engaged in trying to clear the problem with the rudder, while another party was trying to reinforce the rib, without much success. The worsening leak was allowing far too much water into the hull. The attempts to stem the flood so far had been a dismal failure.

On Vixen Lieutenant Brooks reported to Martin. "We have cleared the wreckage of the foremast. We still have steering and can make way, though obviously we are not as nimble as we should be. The carpenter believes the Lorient will not stay afloat. He is sure the stern rib on the port side is broken through in more than one place, he has seen the planking springing from the rib and he questions whether they would carry a shaped timber suitable to reinforce the broken rib. In our case we have no problems with the hull. All our damage has been at deck level and above.

Midshipman Gibbs returned from below and stood, waiting to report.

"Sir, the Doctor has reported that we have forty-two wounded. Thirty-six will recover. Six may not survive. Eight will not return to duty. Gibbs gave the report clearly, but was pale-faced and looked queasy.

Martin said, "We will need you on deck with the flag locker. I will discuss matters with the doctor myself."

Martin found a rail to lean against. His head ached and his ears rang. Try as he might, he had no recollection of being flung to the deck. As he rested trying to concentrate on what was happening, his servant appeared at his elbow. "You missed out on your coffee, sir. I gave it a warm-up. It's better hot than cold."

Martin looked at him astonished. All around, the guns were firing and men screaming in pain and anger. Smoke rolled back from the guns. And Peters had bothered to make the coffee hot in the heat of battle. "I brought a chair up, thought you might enjoy it more sitting down like. It's been a long morning, sir." He dragged the chair from behind him and guided Martin to it.

"Now, sir, That's better, I'm sure." Peters took his place behind the chair.

The relieved Gibbs made his way to the flag locker where he joined Acting Lieutenant Harmon. "Better up here in the open air, eh, Mr. Gibbs?"

"Indeed, sir. Much better!"

Martin drank his coffee gratefully. He had not realised how thirsty he had become. From his seat at the rail he could see the wounded Lorient, her shattered stern sagging and the ship heeling at an odd angle. Her guns had fallen silent on her port side, Not really able to train on much apart from the debris cluttered sea.

The sound of the guns of Sao Paulo and L'Emporeur had ceased. The guns of Vixen loaded and run out, were also silent. The ship withdrew to a position out of range of the stricken French 74. The sounds now were of the hammering and clink of metal on metal.

Off to port, the Spartan's crew were raising their stricken mast, suitably trimmed, into place, under the orders of Lieutenant Acton, only recently promoted, but obviously coping with the loss of his captain.

While Brooks concentrated on jury rigging a foremast, Martin watched as L'Empereur drifted into view, she had struck her colours. He had not, at the time, realised that Vixen's chance broadside had killed the captain and that direction and control had been lost.

With a last glance at the Lorient now down by the stern. He went below to speak with the doctor.

Chapter twenty-seven

Waiting

THE THREE BRITISH ships, plus the prize L'Empereur, stood by while the Lorient struggled to survive.

Martin had considered pounding the ship until it sank, but humanity won over pragmatism. He signalled the stricken ship offering to take off the crew, as prisoners, of course. Martin's problem was that, unless he sank the Lorient, he would be seriously in trouble when he returned home.

In his own mind he was certain that the ship could not be saved. If he approached the guns were a serious menace.

He waited and watched as the main deck guns were abandoned, swung over the side into the sea. The lower deck guns were still there though the lower gun-ports were getting perilously close to the water level.

As Martin suspected the lightening of the ship did not make enough of a difference and the stern sank lower until the lower gun-deck gun ports had to be closed.

At Martin's signal, Sao Paulo approached the Lorient from the starboard side, standing off as Vixen approached from port-side. Both frigates stood off waiting, until the French tricolour was finally hauled down. Then both British ships came alongside the stricken Frenchman. Martin accepted Captain Trouville's sword and promptly returned it to him. The surviving crew members from the 74 boarded the two waiting British frigates.

With the survivors on board, the British ships drew back and waited as the doomed ship slipped finally beneath the waves.

Only then did the four ships set sail for Falmouth. With jury-rigged masts and the other damage all four ships had suffered, progress to Falmouth was slower than anticipated.

* * *

The merchantmen, Mohawk and HMS Spartan had been waiting for just over one day when the battered ships arrived. After the formal greetings, the reformed squadron proceeded onward up channel to enter Portsmouth, before evening two days later. Their arrival at Falmouth had been reported and Jennifer and Jane accompanied by Alouette were waiting to meet the ships when they arrived. There was a message from Admiral Bowers to make their report to the Admiralty the following day.

Dominic Gordon was met by a discreet, anonymous gentleman in a carriage. He bid Martin a private farewell, thanking him for everything. He promised he would contact him in London. Then the carriage departed, with a cavalry escort which had appeared from the barracks in time to escort it to London. The prisoners were offloaded and Captain Trouville passed his sword to Martin. "I will not be allowed to keep it, I know. It was the Admiral's sword, stolen from an aristocrat.

Keep it in memory of my unfortunate ship. I will always be grateful for your forbearance, while my ship was dying."

Trouville walked off, flanked by two troopers to join the other captured officers.

***

The Admirals sat listening to Martin's report of the cruise down the coast of America. No one interrupted him. The reports, completed on the cruise back from the meeting with the French, lay on the desk in front of him. They would be studied in detail by the Admirals later. This meeting was to hear his report from his own lips.

When he finished speaking there was silence for what seemed like ages before Admiral Seymour spoke.

"Regarding this so-called instruction to harass American seamen, are you are sure it came from the Admiralty?"

"Captain Horrocks had been assured that the man who gave the orders was Admiral Bowers. When I described the Admiral, he realised that it was certainly not Admiral Bowers. His instructions came from a taller man than me. He was in uniform, with an educated voice. In my presence the Captain apologised for detaining the American ship, and sent the captain on his way. But, gentlemen, in my opinion there will be war. I guess this year or next year at the latest. There is no doubt in my mind that all the harassment has created distrust. It has, if anything, entrenched their independence even deeper."

Admiral Bowers asked, "How did Dominic Gordon perform?"

"Extremely well, in my opinion. He studied reports for the entire voyage to Halifax. By the time we reached Canada he was prepared to negotiate. When left to carry on alone he handled matters as well as they could be. To my surprise, he has developed into a remarkable young man."

Admiral Seymour rose to his feet. "Thank you, Sir Martin. We will have more to discuss, I am sure. But, meanwhile, we will allow you to spend time with your family for the next few days while the reports are studied thoroughly."

Thus dismissed, Martin made his way to the discrete house where he found Alouette waiting to discuss his personal findings on the situation in America.

"I have information on the so-called Admiral Bowers, who has been pressurising the naval captains. He is a man called Walker, Baron Robert Walker, an associate of Sir Peter Mayberry."

Martin looked at her in confusion. "Who are these people? I have never heard of them?"

"They are members of a society dedicated to keeping the Empire intact. They think that the British Empire is the only serious stabilising influence in the world. If the society confined its activities to the newspapers and public meetings, there would be no point in my concern. They have unfortunately been responsible for violence and probably murder, so I am very much involved. I have also found they are associated with a French society with similar interests, though, of course, involved in the French empire rather than ours. The disquieting thing about that is the empire, which they are defending, was created by Napoleon."

Martin stood and walked around the room. "Are you saying that this Sir Peter Mayberry is conspiring with supporters of Napoleon? Surely, that is treason?"

"Exactly. All I have to do is prove it. Then I can act and dispose of this irritating man with his secret signs, and agents who give our secrets to our country's enemies. I have come across these people in the past when I have been in France. I have no doubts they are dangerous. I will deal with them without restraint when the time comes.

"How is marriage?" Martin asked.

Alouette looked at him with sparkling eyes, "It goes well. Antonio is anxious to get as many as his family together as possible, Although he has written to his relatives in Portugal he has not yet had a reply. Maria has adopted us I am happy to say." Alouette looked sad for a few moments. Martin realised That not only had she lost her husband but her child as well.

Alouette continued. "We are still getting to know each other, and Maria has made herself part of our family already. I did point out that with you and Jennifer we were surrounded by family. I know he believes and understands that. But I can see if any of his own blood are still out there, he would want them to know and be in contact. If you are right and the Americans do declare war on us, he will be off back to sea before we can have a second honeymoon.

"I believe Maria and Lieutenant Hammond are discussing an announcement in the first week of May, but do not mention this to anyone until I can confirm it." She tapped Martin's arm with the sheathed dagger she used as a pointer when explaining something on a chart or map.

"My lips are sealed." Martin said with a smile, "Can I ask if there is anything special she would like, in the form of an engagement gift?"

Alouette smiled, "As her favourite uncle, you are in a privileged position. Anything you could think of would be acceptable, I am certain. But I know she enjoys riding, and there are stables attached to our house."

Martin shrugged, "I had in mind perhaps, something a little more personal as an engagement gift."

***

In Knightsbridge at the house Martin entered the drawing room to find Jennifer playing with their daughter Jane.

Jane ran over to her father, and was swept up into his arms high in the air before being cuddled close in his arms. Jennifer crossed the room at a more sedate pace, to find herself gathered into Martin's arms along with her daughter.

"Now I am home." Martin murmured.

"Where you belong," whispered Jennifer.

Also by David O'Neil

Action/Adventure/Thriller series
Counterstroke # 1

Exciting, Isn't It?

O'Neil's initial entry into the world of action adventure romance thriller is filled with mystery and suspense, thrills and chills as *Counterstroke* finds it seeds of Genesis, and springs full blown onto the scene with action, adventure and romance galore.

John Murray, ex-Police, ex-MI6, ex management consultant, 49 and widowed, is ready to make a new start. Having sold off everything, he sets out on a lazy journey by barge through the waterways of France to collect his yacht at a yard in Grasse. En route he will decide what to do with the rest of his life

He picks up a female hitch-hiker Gabrielle, a frustrated author running from Paris after a confrontation with a lascivious would-be publisher Mathieu. She had unknowingly picked up some of Mathieu's secret documents with her manuscript. Although not looking for action, adventure or romance, still a connection is made.

An encounter with Pierre, an unpleasant former acquaintance from Paris who is chasing Gabrielle, is followed by a series of events that make John call on all his old skills of survival to keep them both alive over the next few days. Mystery and suspense shroud the secret documents that disclose the real background of the so called publisher who is in fact a high level international crook.

To survive, the pair become convinced they must take the fight to the enemy but they have no illusions; their chances of survival are slim. But with the help of some of John's old contacts, things start to become... exciting.

Counterstroke # 2....

Market Forces

Market Forces, Volume Two of the Counterstroke action adventure romance thriller series by David O'Neil introduces Katherine (Katt) Percival, tasked with the assassination of Mark Parnell in a hurried, last-minute attempt to stop his interference with the success of the Organization in Europe. As a skilled terminator for the CIA, Katt is accustomed to proper briefing. On this occasion she disobeys her orders, convinced it's a mistake. She joins forces with Mark to foil an attempt on his life.

Parnell works for John Murray, who created Secure Inc that caused the collapse of an International US criminal organisation's operation in Europe, forcing the disbanding of the US Company COMCO. Set up as a cover for money-laundering and other operations designed to control from within the political and financial administration, they had already been partially successful. Especially within the administrative sectors of the EU.

Katt goes on the run, she has been targeted and her Director sidelined by rogue interests in the CIA. She finds proof of conspiracy. She passes it on to Secure Inc who can use it to attack the Organization. She joins forces with Mark Parnell and Secure Inc. Mark and Katt and their colleagues risk their lives as they set out to foil the Organization once again.

Counterstroke # 3....

When Needs Must...

The latest action adventure thriller in the Counterstroke series opens with a new character Major Teddy Robertson–Steel fighting for survival in Africa. Mark Parnell and Katt Percival now working together for Secure Inc. are joined by Captain Libby 'Carter' Barr, now in plain clothes, well mostly, and her new partner James Wallace. They are tasked with locating and thwarting the efforts of three separate menaces from the European scene that threaten the separation of the United Kingdom from the political clutches of Brussels, by using terrorism to create wealth by a group of billionaires, and the continuing presence of the Mob, bankrolled from USA. An action adventure thriller filled with romance, mystery and suspense. With the appearance of a much needed new team, Dan and Reba, and the welcome return of Peter Maddox, Dublo Bond and Tiny Lewis, there is action and adventure throughout. Change will happen, it just takes the right people, at the right time, in the right place.

**Young adult action/adventure/ romance
thriller series
Donny Weston & Abby Marshall # 1**

Fatal Meeting

A captivating new series of young adult action, romance, adventure and mystery.

For two young teens, Donny and Abby, who have just found each other, sailing the 40 ft ketch across the English

Channel to Cherbourg is supposed to be a light-hearted adventure.

The third member of the crew turns out to be a smuggler, and he attempts to kill them both before they reach France. The romance adventure. now filled with action, mystery and suspense, suddenly becomes deadly serious when the man's employers try to recover smuggled items from the boat. The action gets more and more hectic as the motive becomes personal

Donny and Abby are plunged into a series of events that force them to protect themselves. Donny's parents become involved so with the help of a friend of the family, Jonathon Glynn, they take the offensive against the gang who are trying to kill them.

The action adventure thriller ranges from the Mediterranean to Paris and the final scene is played out in the shadow of the Eiffel Tower in the city of romance and lights; Paris France..

Donny Weston & Abby Marshall # 2

Lethal Complications

Eighteen year olds Donny and Abby take a year out from their studies to clear up problems that had escalated over the past three years. They succeed in closing the book on the past during the first months of the year, now they are looking forward to nine months relaxation, romance and fun, when old friend of the family, mystery man Jonathon Glynn, drops in to visit as they moor at Boulogne, bringing action and adventure into their lives once again.

Jonathon was followed and an attempt to kill them happens immediately after his visit. They leave their boat and pick up the RV they have left in France, hoping to avoid further conflict. They are attacked in the Camargue, but fast and accurate shooting keeps them alive. They find themselves mixed up in a treacherous scheme by a rogue Chinese gang to defame a Chinese moderate, in an attempt to stall the Democratic process in China.

The two young lovers, becoming addicted to action and adventure, link up with Isobel, a person of mystery who has acquired a reputation without earning it. Between them they manage to keep the Chinese target and his girlfriend out of the rogue Chinese group's hands.

Tired of reacting to attack, and now looking for action and adventure, they set up an ambush of their own, effectively checkmating the rogue Chinese plans. The leader of the rogues, having lost face and position in the Chinese hierarchy, plans a personal coup using former Spetsnaz mercenaries. With the help of a former SBS man Adam, who had worked with and against Spetsnaz forces, the friends survive and Lin Hang the Chinese leader suffers defeat.

Donny Weson & Abby Marshall # 3....

A Thrill A Minute

They are back! Fresh from their drama-filled action adventure excursion to the United States, Abby Marshall and Donny Weston look forward to once again taking up their studies at the University. Each of them is looking forward to the calm life of a University student without the threat of being murdered. Ah, the serene life.... that is the thing. But that doesn't last long. It is only a few weeks before our adventuresome young lovers find that the calm, quiet routine of University life is boring beyond belief and both are filled with yearning for the fast-paced action adventure of their prior experiences. It isn't long before trouble finds the couple and they welcome it with open arms, but perhaps this time they have underestimated the opposition. Feeling excitement once again, the two youths arm themselves and leapt into the fray. The fight was on and no holds barred!

Once again O'Neil takes us into the action filled world of mystery and suspense, action and adventure, romance and peril.

Donny Weston & Abby Marshall # 4....

It's Just One Thing After Another

Fresh from their victory over the European Mafia, our two young adults in love, Abby Marshall and Donny Weston, are rewarded with an all-expense-paid trip to the United States. But, as our young couple discover, there is no free lunch and the price they will have to pay for their "free" tour may be more than they can afford to pay, in this action adventure thriller. Even so, with the help of a few friends and some former enemies, the valiant young duo face danger once again with firm resolve and iron spirit, but will that be sufficient in face of the odds that are stacked against them?

And is their friend and benefactor actually a friend or is he on the other side? The two young adults look at this man of mystery and suspense with a bit of caution. Action, adventure and romance abound in this, the latest escapades of Britain's dynamic young couple.

Donny Weston & Abby Marshall # 5

What Goes Around...

Just when it seems that our two young heroes, Donny Weston and Abby Marshall are able to return to the University to complete their studies, fate decides to play another turn as once again the two young lovers come under attack, this time from a most unsuspected source. It appears that not even the majestic powers of the British Intelligence Service will be enough to rescue the beleaguered duo and they will have to survive through their own skills. In the continuing action adventure thriller, two young adults must solve the mystery that faces them to determine who is trying to kill them. The suspense is chilling, the action and adventure stimulating. Finding togetherness even among the onslaughts, Donny and Abby also find remarkable friends who offer their assistance; but will even that be enough to overcome the determined enemy?

Donny Weston & Abby Marshall # 6

Without Prejudice

Donny Weston and Abby Marshall, on their way to park their beloved boat *Swallow* in Malta to be ready for the summer, encounter the schooner *Speedwell* at La Rochelle, where problems arise for Commander Will and his wife Mary Pleasance. Tom Hardy and Lotte Compton, both from the *Speedwell* join forces with Donny and Abby to oppose the threats to the Commander. From Valetta the four follow up the threat, only to find themselves faced with a plot to use a famous mercenary in an assassination that will rock the foundations of the Euro community, and the western world.

Backed by Russia and with the tacit approval of the head of MI6, a rogue CIA operative has set things up for a public shooting at a Euro summit.

The four foil the plot and the assassination fails, but ironically the CIA agent, is credited with foiling the coup and promoted. He wants revenge, and comes after the four with blood in his eye and his guns loaded. The outcome is decided in a action-packed shoot-out in high speed boats in the cold waters of the Thames estuary.

Sea Adventures

Better The Day

From the W.E.B. Griffin of the United Kingdom, David O'Neil, a exciting saga of romance, action, adventure, mystery and suspense as Peter Murray and his brother officers in Coastal Forces face overwhelming odds fighting German E-boats, the German Navy and the Luftwaffe in action in the Channel, the Mediterranean, Norway and the Baltic – where there is conflict with the Soviet Allies. This action-packed story of daring and adventure finally follows Peter Murray to the Pacific where he faces Kamikaze action with the U.S. Fleet.

Distant Gunfire

"Boarders Away!" Serving as an officer on a British frigate at the time of the French Emperor Napoleon is not the safest occupation, but could be a most profitable one. Robert Graham, rising from the ranks to become the Captain

of a British battleship by virtue of his dauntless leadership, displayed under enemy fire, finds himself a wealthy man as the capture of enemy ships resulted in rich rewards. Action and adventure is the word of the day, as battle after battle rages across the turbulent waters and seas as the valiant British Royal Navy fights to stem the onslaught of the mighty French Army and Navy. Mystery and suspense abound as inserting and collecting spy agent after spy agent is executed. The threat of imminent death makes romance and romantic interludes all the sweeter, and the suspense of waiting for a love one to return even more traumatic. Captain Graham, with his loyal following of sailors and marines, takes prize ship after prize ship, thwart plot after diabolical plot, and finds romance when he least expects it. To his amazement and joy, he finds himself being knighted by the King of England. The good life is his, now all he has to do is to live long enough to enjoy it. A rollicking good tale of sea action and swashbuckling adventures.

Sailing Orders

For those awaiting another naval story of the 18/19th century, then this is it. Following the life of an abandoned 13 year old who by chance is instrumental in saving a family from robbery and worse. Taken in by the naval Captain Bowers he is placed as a midshipman in his benefactor's ship. From that time onward with the increasing demands of the conflict with France, Martin Forrest grows up fast. The relationship with his benefactors family is formalised when he is adopted by them and has a home once more. Romance with Jennifer the Captains ward links him ever closer to the family.

Meanwhile he serves in the West Indies where good fortune results in his gaining considerable wealth personally. With promotion and command he is able to marry and reclaim his birth-right, stolen from him by his step-mother and her lover.

The mysterious (call me merely Mr Smith) involves Martin in more activity in the shadowy world of the secret agents. Mainly a question of lifting and placing of people, his involvement becomes more complex as time goes on. A cruise to India consolidates his position and rank with the successful capture of prizes when returning convoying East-Indiamen. His rise to Post rank is followed by a series of events, that sadly culminate in family tragedy.

While still young Martin Forrest-Bowers faces and empty future, though merely Mr Smith has requested his services????

Adventure thrillers

Minding the Store

O'Neil scores again! Often favorably compared to America's W.E.B. Griffin and to U.K.'s Ian Fleming, and fresh from his best-selling action adventure, "Distant Gunfire," O'Neil finds excitement and action in the New York garment district. The department store industry becomes the target of take-over by organized crime in their quest for money-laundering outlets. It would seem that no department store executive is a match for vicious criminals, however, David Freemantle, heir to the Freemantle fortune and Managing Director of America's most prestigious department store is no ordinary department store executive and the team of ex-military specialists he has assembled contains no ordinary store security personnel. Armed invasions are met with swift retaliation; kidnapping and rape attempts are met with fatal consequences as the Mafia and their foreign cohorts learn that not all ordinary citizens are helpless, and that evil force can be met with superior force in O'Neil's latest thriller of adventure and action, romance and suspense, mystery and mayhem that willl have the reader on the edge of his seat until the last breath-taking word.

The Hunted

David O'Neal, UK's answer to W.E.B. Griffin and Dean Koontz strikes again with his newest suspense thriller filled with action, adventure, romance and danger. When the Russian Mafia joins forces with other European and Asian gangsters to take over a noted world-wide charity organization to smuggle guns and drugs into unsuspecting nations and begins to kill innocent people, one man – Tarquin Gilmore – Quin to his friends – declares war on the Mafia. To achieve his goal of total destruction of the criminal gangs, he surrounds himself with a few dangerous men and beautiful women. But don't be fooled by their beauty, the girls are easily as deadly as any man. On the other hand, there are a lot more gangsters than Quin and his friends and it's a battle to the finish. A stirring tale of crime and murder, mystery and suspense, passion and romance, guns and drugs... but that is war!

The Mercy Run

O'Neil's thrilling action adventure saga of Africa: the story of Tom Merrick, Charlie Hammond and Brenda Cox; a man and two women who fight and risk their lives to keep supplies rolling into the U.N. refugee camps in Ethiopia. Their adversaries: the scorching heat, the dirt roads and the ever present hazards of bandit gangs and corrupt government officials. Despite tragedy and treachery, mystery and suspense while combating the efforts of Colonel Gonbera, who hopes to turn the province into his personal domain, Merrick and his friends manage to block the diabolical Colonel at every turn.

Frustrated by Merrick's success against him, there seems to be no depths to which the Colonel would not descend to achieve his aim. The prospect of a lucrative diamond strike comes into the game, and so do the Russians and Chinese. But, as Merrick knows, there will be no peace while the Colonel remains the greatest threat to success and peace.

*****

New Dynamic Series with Jonathan Penroc

The Raptors
Book One, Sarah Paige Chronicles

A New World Order?
A one government world?
The United States with a weak president and a divided government. The world in chaos and turmoil. Happenstance or a diabolical scheme? Emerging from the dark shadows are "The Raptors," human birds of prey seeking to establish a new one-world government under their iron rule. For more than a century, no one has been able to stop this mysterious force from altering entire governments, forcing resignations and where necessary, assassinations. No one is safe, not the

President of the United States, not the Shah of Iran, not the Russian Premier. No one has even been able to slow down the onslaught that is gradually, nation by nation, acquiring control of the entire world. Resistance is met with overpowering force and nothing has stemmed their advance as they annihilate one obstacle after another. Then they made a mistake. They killed the wrong person and now they are faced with an infuriated woman out to revenge the killing of her one true love. Having finally found romance only to have it rift away by terrorist fanatics under the control of "The Raptors," Sarah has only one goal: vengeance or death. Can one distraught and determined female take on a clandestine world power? There is a saying, "Hell has no fury...."

~*~

Available from:

WEB Publishers Inc
www.a-argusbooks.com

Made in the USA
Lexington, KY
29 October 2015